SACRED SITE

KIM FLEET

SACRED SITE

First published in Great Britain in 2009
by Picnic Publishing
PO Box 5222, Hove BN52 9LP

The right of Kim Fleet to be identified as the author of this work has
been asserted by her in accordance with the Copyright, Designs &
Patents Act, 1988.

A catalogue record for this book is available from the British
Library.

ISBN: 9780955861390
Printed and bound in Great Britain by
CPI Antony Rowe, Chippenham and Eastbourne
Designed by SoapBox, www.soapboxcommunications.co.uk.

For Jim Williams

1

Mt Parker Sheep Station, Western Australia, 1891

The sight of the young man brought Bilsom up short. MacKendrick hunched over a miserly campfire, his knees tucked under his chin as if he'd got bellyache. His face was streaked with red dirt and sweat, making him look much older than his twenty-one years. Bilsom's horse clattered over the stones in the dry creek bed, disturbing a flock of grey and pink galahs from the dead branches of a eucalypt. They rose shrieking into the sky. Bilsom swung out of the saddle, feeling the stiffness in his hips after a day on horseback.

MacKendrick turned as Bilsom approached. His eyes were startlingly blue in his grimy face.

'What is it?' asked Bilsom.

'You ready to have your life changed?'

'Been out in the sun too long, mate?'

MacKendrick held out his fist and opened his fingers. A gold nugget nestled in his palm.

'That won't get you back to Perth,' said Bilsom.

'This might.' MacKendrick grabbed the billycan and upended it over his swag. Gold nuggets rattled onto the blankets, clattering against each other into a pile.

'I found all this today, just on the surface. My saddle bags are full.' His face cracked into a grin. 'Seems I was right after all.'

Bilsom knelt on the swag and prodded the nuggets, aware of MacKendrick watching him. His voice, when it came, was cracked. 'You found all this on my land?'

'And there's more. Much more.' MacKendrick's voice was awed.

Bilsom tipped back his hat and scratched his scalp. His hair dripped with sweat. His mind tumbled with bewilderment and disbelief. Riches beyond his imagination were here, in his hands. The past few years of hardship and endurance were about to end. A proper life for his family, not this miserable existence scratched from godforsaken soil, beckoned to him.

'I only came out to bring you some more tucker,' he said, strangled with surging elation. He thumped MacKendrick on the back and laughter burst from him. 'Think we'd better have this instead.'

He fetched a flask from his saddlebag and offered it to MacKendrick, who gulped from it greedily and jumped to his feet, cannoning round in a mad jig like a crazy puppy. Bilsom snatched the flask back and took a deep swig. It burned the back of his throat and down to his stomach. He hadn't eaten since breakfast, hours ago, and the rough grog instantly made him light-headed.

'Here's to riches!' cried MacKendrick, grabbing for the whisky. He tipped his head back and howled for joy.

'Here's to taking Hetty and Caro back to Perth,' said Bilsom, with such a surge of relief that he felt dizzy.

MacKendrick stopped jigging. 'You're going to leave?'

'This is no place for women.' Bilsom waved his hand at the scrub stretching to the horizon. 'And with Hetty pregnant, I want her back in Perth where she'll be safe. Not here.'

'What about the station?'

'No point killing yourself over sheep when there's gold here.' Bilsom grabbed the flask. One in the eye for Hetty's father. This would show the mean old bastard he was wrong. He'd done it, he'd made his fortune. Maybe not in the way he said when he'd promised Hetty's father he'd take care of her, but still – gold was gold. He was going to be rich, maybe one of the richest men in Australia, and soon he'd be accepted in every drawing room in Perth, Hetty smiling on his arm. And her old man could choke on his own words.

Bilsom grinned at the thought of Hetty radiant in the finest silk gowns, her waist back to its tiny span from before the pregnancy, so small his hands could almost meet round it. Together they would sweep into elite drawing rooms, overhearing whispers, 'That's Mr and Mrs Bilsom, you know, such a handsome couple.' The same people who'd denigrated him, her father's friends of course, would suddenly seek his favours. But who knows, maybe they'd find the Bilsoms not at home when they came to call.

'Hey, Bilsom!' MacKendrick thumped down on the swag next to him. 'Dreaming of the horse you're going to buy?'

'Something like that.' Bilsom looked over towards Mt Parker, its knobby peak turning to shadow as the sun set. He wouldn't be sorry to leave this lonely place. The landscape resisted all attempts to tame it.

Bilsom snatched the flask back before MacKendrick could glug the lot. He saluted the boy, and said, grudgingly, 'You did all right.'

They spread their swags beside the fire. The burning gum leaves gave off a scent like camphor, the smell of Bilsom's clothes when he shook them out of the trunk in his bedroom; a clean, cold scent.

The two men talked long into the night, fuelled by whisky and dreams. When the flies started crawling round their nostrils at dawn they rolled up the swags and unhobbled the horses.

'Can't wait to see Hetty's face when I tell her we're going to be rich,' said Bilsom. A swathe of golden everlasting daisies stretched as far as he could see. Hetty's favourites. If MacKendrick hadn't been there he'd have taken some to her, to make the dimples flash in her cheeks when she smiled.

At the next paddock they found six sheep carcasses rotting into the red soil. The bodies were ripped to shreds. Flies buzzed in and out of the gaping holes in the flesh. A lamb, its eyes fallen into its skull, lay with a spear still embedded in its ribs.

Bilsom covered his nose with his palm against the stench and prodded the carcass with his toe. 'Speared. All of them. That makes twenty this month.'

'Who's doing it?' asked MacKendrick, keeping his distance.

'Group of blacks who used to work on the station. They walked off a couple of months ago. They take some of the stock and eat it. I don't mind that so much, but this!' He kicked the closest sheep and sighed. 'Come on. I don't want to leave Hetty and Caro any longer.'

MacKendrick blushed and turned his face away, pretending to adjust his tack. Bilsom smirked. In a few years the young pup would be asking him for Caro's hand. As if he'd be able to tame that wild spirit. He chuckled at the thought of his headstrong fifteen-year-old daughter. She'd lead MacKendrick a merry dance. Serve him right.

The yard was silent when they rode in. No clangs from the cookhouse, no women jabbering in their native tongue, slacking from their work. Even the yard boy – white-haired, creaking old Billy – was gone. The silence was oppressive. Bilsom shouted but no one appeared.

'Where are they?' he growled, anger sparking in his chest. 'Prancing round a fire in the bush, I bet. Wait till I catch them!'

A brown face appeared round the side of the cookhouse. Ruby. He started to call to her. She stared at him, then hared off across the yard. A twinge of guilt tugged at his insides: she wasn't much older than Caro.

'Hetty! Caro! Come here! We're rich!' Where were they? Why didn't they come to meet him? Sudden fear made him race to the homestead.

'Hetty? Caro? Where are you?' He stopped. Hetty's dog sprawled on the veranda, dead. A spear jutted from its skull. Black blood congealed on the wooden floorboards.

'Hetty! Caro!' Panic gripped him and he hurtled into the homestead, MacKendrick close behind him.

The stench was overpowering. Guts heaving, Bilsom tore into the bedroom. The blinds were drawn, casting the room into gloom. Hetty and Caro lay side by side on the bed, their skirts and petticoats slashed into ribbons. Their naked legs jutted over the edge of the mattress, blood smeared down the inside of Caro's thighs. The mattress and coverings were soaked in blood. Blood pooled and thickened on the floor. Hetty's stomach gaped open. Flies blackened the wounds.

Bilsom touched Hetty's hand. Cold. They'd been dead for days; almost from the hour he left them.

MacKendrick flung open the window and was sick. Bilsom listened to him retching, then stamped out of the room. He seized his rifle and filled his pockets with cartridges. A single motivation sliced through his mind: revenge.

'What are you doing?' cried MacKendrick.

'I'm going to get the bastards who did this.'

'How do you know . . . ?'

'I know all right. And I know where to find them.'

Bilsom leaped onto his horse, his rifle slung across the saddle. 'You coming or what?'

MacKendrick glanced back at the homestead. 'Shouldn't we . . .'

'You do what you like.' Bilsom jabbed his heels into the horse's flanks and galloped out of the yard and across the paddock. He slowed when he heard MacKendrick behind him.

'Bilsom, wait up! Where are you going?'

'There's a camp at a waterhole beneath Mt Parker,' said Bilsom, nodding towards the peak. 'They'll be there.'

He started firing even before he'd dismounted. There were a dozen of them: Aborigines resting in their camp before a crack from Bilsom's rifle shattered the peace. The women screamed and clutched the children to them. A baby bawled, then fell silent. The men ran round the camp, slipping at the waterhole's edge, as Bilsom fired, reloaded and fired again. They ran blindly as bullets ricocheted from tree trunks and rocks. They dropped one by one.

'Bilsom! Stop!' MacKendrick grabbed his arm. 'How do you know it was them?'

'They're black, aren't they?' Bilsom shook him off, slotted another cartridge into his rifle, tucked the butt into his shoulder and squeezed the trigger. A child spun backwards with the force of the bullet and crumpled onto the sand, limbs twisted at an unnatural angle.

'But you can't just kill them like this!' MacKendrick screamed.

'You saw what they did to Hetty and Caro. And my unborn . . .' He fired again. A man crashed into the waterhole and the water haloed crimson around him. Suddenly all was quiet. Black bodies twitched on the ground. The sand stained with blood.

A mew came from the spearwood bush on the far side of the waterhole and Bilsom levelled his gun again. Ruby slunk out and faced him. She held his gaze, pleading with her eyes. Her hand moved to her belly, swelling under her grubby calico shift. Why hadn't he noticed before? The front of her dress jerked with her heartbeat. He lowered the rifle and she sprinted away through the scrub.

MacKendrick cowered against a gum tree, whimpering, his head in his hands. Snot and tears slimed his face.

'It's finished,' said Bilsom.

2

'So that's what all the fuss is about,' said Esther, jabbing at the plane window.

The mountain rose up from the flat plain like a stack of giant building bricks. Tufts of green jutted from the rocks: full-grown trees made miniature. Sand dunes rippled in all directions as far she could see. Swathes of yellow wildflowers stretched to the horizon, punctuated with spiky mulga stands. Esther's heart lifted. What a job, travelling to places like this, seeing things most people only dreamed about. As an anthropologist working in Aboriginal land rights, she visited some of the most beautiful and remote areas of Australia.

'It's impressive,' she said.

'Mt Parker,' Frank muttered, his eyes squeezed shut.

'Aboriginal name Moolya.'

'You know more than us blackfellas.'

Esther accepted the grudging compliment. It was the best she was likely to get in this field. She swivelled round in her seat to look at Kent, who had his back turned to stare out of the window. In his early thirties, with thick dark wavy hair, he was tall and broad shouldered, folded into the plane's small seat. He felt her gaze upon him and twisted round and grinned at her, his blue eyes twinkling. She grinned back, thrilled by the familiar sizzling fuse from her stomach to her groin when he blew her a kiss. It alarmed her sometimes, how attractive she found him – and not just physically. He was so easy going, she thought, so unlike Rich, her saturnine husband, who would now be pacing their house, sulking and brooding over last night's row.

She shoved Rich and his moods from her mind. She was away from home, she was with Kent and she was free for a few days. Her spirits danced.

'What do you think, Kent?' she said, nodding at the landscape skimming beneath them.

'Looks like good country. Had a lot of rain.'

The plane swooped close to the protruding tip of Mt Parker, casting its shadow like a cut-out over the side of the mountain.

'Come and see, Frank.'

'I'll look at it with me feet on the ground, ta.'

Esther pulled a bottle of water out of her rucksack and shoved it at Frank. He released his grip on his knees for a second to grasp the bottle. 'She's cold!'

'Put it in the freezer last night. Melting nicely by now,' said Esther. 'It'll help your air sickness.'

Frank unscrewed the top and gulped at the water. He was burly, wearing a check shirt with the sleeves rolled up to reveal thick forearms embroidered with tattoos: a wedge-tailed eagle flexed as he glugged back the water. His hair was thick and curly, turning grey, and silver flecks glinted in the stubble peppering his cheeks. He revived enough to open his eyes and squint out of the window. 'Does look like good country,' he said, squeezing his eyes closed again. 'Though not as good as mine.'

Esther exchanged a wink with Kent. The rivalry over which Aboriginal group enjoyed the best country was an old joke.

'My mum's been tracing our family tree,' said Kent, 'and she reckons one of our old people came from here.'

'Really?' said Esther. 'You'll have to show me.'

'Women!' said Frank. 'They never let you have any secrets. And you white women are the worstest.'

'Is that right? So it's not because I'm an anthropologist, then?'

'Nah. Just nosey I reckon.'

Delving into Aboriginal family trees was an important part of Esther's job, but it brought its own grubby conflicts. She knew she would resent a stranger prodding her family secrets, turning over her shameful inheritance, but it was only by miring herself in the past that she could untangle the threads that could lead to a successful land claim. Ironic that protecting the future so often meant exposing the skeletons of the past. Sometimes she questioned whether the emotional cost was too high, whether the process was crueller than the theft of the land in the first place.

The plane descended over wide dirt roads and square houses with iron roofs. Esther craned her neck at the window to see better. 'Is that Tjulpan community down there?' she asked.

'We'll be on the ground soon,' Kent teased her, 'then you can have a good rubber-neck.'

She stuck her tongue out at him.

The pilot hitched his earphones to the back of his neck and twisted round in his seat to let them know they were approaching the airstrip.

'Better ring the door bell and let them know we're here,' said Esther. The pilot gave her a thumbs up and the plane banked sharply to the left, coming in low over the community. Frank groaned and rested his head on the back of his seat as the plane crept lower, slanting sharply the whole time. After two complete circuits buzzing low over the community the plane headed for the airstrip, coming in to land with a bounce.

'At least there were no camels on the strip this time,' said Esther, smirking as Frank shuddered at the memory.

'Or a bloke mowing the strip,' added Kent, reminding them of the time they flew into a remote community but were unable to land because the airstrip was being mowed by a man wearing heavy duty earphones and unable to hear the plane approaching. After several aborted approaches they had finally hurtled over the top of his head, scaring him witless as the plane's shadow engulfed him. He'd moved off the strip quickly enough after that.

The plane taxied to the side of the strip and the pilot released the door. Frank clambered out first and scuffed round in circles coughing and spitting. His jeans hung low on his wide flat backside and flapped over his boots, dragging in the sand.

Esther poked her head out. 'We'll just bring out all the gear, then.'

'Yeah.' Frank lifted his hand and hyperventilated.

The airstrip was a scar sliced through the scrub. Acacias encroached on each side, reeking of honey and tomcats. A wooden shed at the side housed drums of aviation fuel. The door was splintered around the padlock: someone had been chopping at it, desperate for a fix, not knowing that aviation fuel wouldn't give a buzz.

Esther and Kent lifted out the rucksacks and computer case, then struggled with the eskie down the plane's steps. The cool-box was crammed with meat and was ludicrously heavy. The handle buckled as they lumped it out of the plane, the exercise made more awkward as Kent was a head taller than Esther. Though she was slender, years of heaving equipment around had made her strong: there were no concessions out here because you were a woman, and she'd done her fair share of tyre-changing and loading vehicles.

As they reached the bottom step they saw a streak of red dirt hurtling towards the airstrip.

'At least someone's coming to fetch us,' said Frank.

A green station wagon juddered to a halt beside them and a large Aboriginal woman lumbered out.

'I'm Doreen,' she said. 'Come to fetch yous to the community.'

'Nice to meet you, Doreen,' said Esther, shaking hands. Doreen was in her early forties with long black hair scraped back into a plait. Her eyes seemed very small in her big face. Her gaze darted from Esther to Frank to Kent, sizing them up. Esther introduced the men.

'Hello, Doreen,' said Frank, extending a meaty hand.

'Yous got enough stuff?' said Doreen, eyeing the pile of rucksacks and the eskie.

'Only just got us all in there,' said Esther.

Doreen glanced at the plane and winced. 'Don't know how you can go in one of them things. You wouldn't get me up there, I can tell you. My legs go wobbly if I have to stand on a chair to change the light bulb.'

'I think Frank agrees with you,' said Esther.

The back of Doreen's station wagon was filled with jerry cans, blankets, a ripped sweater and a punctured football. They rummaged and made space for the eskie and the rucksacks, then all piled into the car. Frank snaffled the passenger seat and Esther and Kent squashed into the back. Low slung before they got in, the car scraped along the corrugations as Doreen set off back along the dirt road.

She paused at a crossroads and pointed to the right. 'That's the town, Bilsom's Grudge, that way.'

Esther peered down the straight road, noting how the dirt track reached to the town's sign then morphed into neat tarmac lines.

'This way's Tjulpan, the community.'

Doreen released the clutch and they jolted over the corrugated track to the Aboriginal community. At the entrance was a metal sign declaring 'Welcome to Tjulpan Aboriginal Community. No drugs. No Grog'. The sign was shot through, spelling out 'Fuck of '.

Tjulpan community was built in a sprawling cross with roads of houses leading off from the main arms. The houses were built from concrete blocks and set in large yards ringed with metal fences. Dogs skittered round the yards yapping and shitting, and mangy curs zigzagged across the road in front of the car. Doreen hooted her horn and swore at them to shift.

'Bloody dogs,' she said. 'About time the dog shooter came back, I reckon.'

'When was he last here?' asked Esther, dismayed and angry at the squalid community. Too many Aboriginal communities were like this: nightmares of bureaucracy and despair.

'When everyone was away for the sports carnival at Wiluna. Except some bastard warned them and they shut the dogs up inside so he didn't get many.'

The car pulled up outside the community offices in the centre of Tjulpan. The offices were a collection of prefabricated mobiles and brick buildings. Graffiti scarred all four walls of the women's centre and the roof was littered with rocks. Wire mesh protected the windows of the main office. A gaggle of women glugged cans of Coke outside the store and eyed them with hostility. Half-naked children chased each other, squealing, their shoulder blades jutting like shark fins.

In the middle of the community buildings was a grassed area with a large open bough shelter bearing the sign 'Tjulpan Aboriginal Community' in red, black and yellow lettering next to the Aboriginal flag. Painted upside down, Esther noted.

'We have meetings here,' Doreen explained. 'Good in the summer. Shady. Not too much of a problem today.'

Esther could already feel her skin tingling and was glad of the shade. With red-gold hair and pale English skin, she'd learned the hard way to avoid the sun, whatever the season, in Australia.

Kent lugged the eskie out of the car. 'Where do you want this, Doreen? It's the meat for the barbecue.'

'Here, Gavin!'

A beefy man strutted over. 'Gavin's my son,' Doreen explained.

Esther looked him up and down. About twenty, big-built and already tending to fat. He was wearing a new Fremantle Dockers shirt. Gavin smiled and nodded hello to them all, then took the eskie to where the barbecue was hotting up and women were already flapping flies off stacks of bread.

'Just going to get a drink,' said Esther. She wandered over to the store and flipped through the coloured plastic strips fluttering in the doorway. The store had a bare concrete floor with the stock displayed on racks of free-standing metal shelves. A bank of fridges hummed against the far wall. Esther took two Cokes and a coffee chill and stood in line behind a dozen children buying kangaroo ice pops and meat pies. The store's microwave pinged in the background as they heated up pies and chicken rolls, then squirted them with tomato sauce and juggled the steaming pies as they ate them.

'You Land Council?' asked the white woman at the till.

'Yes.'

'Here for the meeting about the mine?'

'That's right.'

'Won't make no difference.'

The white community workers were always the most hostile. Land Council was the enemy, living in comfort in Perth and flying in for a bit of an exotic thrill. Whites who lived and worked in remote Aboriginal communities considered them fakes. The people who lived in the ragged communities were the real thing, with brawls and screaming and rape threats week after week; not some upstarts from the city, breezing in and just as rapidly out again. Esther wasn't prepared to pander to the woman's insecurities. She scooped up the drinks and said airily, 'We'll see.'

The woman sucked her teeth and went to shoo out a stray dog licking its bollocks beneath the shelves.

Esther flapped back through the plastic strips into the stark sunshine, hand automatically reaching for her sunglasses wedged on the top of her head.

'Here you go, mate,' she said, handing Frank one of the Cokes. He ripped off the ring-pull and downed it in three.

'That hit the spot,' he said, and belched.

Kent waited beneath the bough shelter. Esther pushed the coffee chill into his hand, her fingertips grazing his palm. They perched together on the fence, shoulders not quite touching. It was distracting to be so close to him that she could smell the soap on his skin and feel the warmth of his arm pulsing towards her. She watched him tip the iced coffee to his lips.

'I don't know how you can drink that stuff,' she said.

'It's good. Not all drinks have to be warm, you know.'

'Ha, ha.' For someone who had never visited Britain he was quick to remember the stereotypical warm English beer. 'So what do you make of Tjulpan?'

'Disgusting there's that gold-mine just down the road and the community's in this state. It makes me angry. Look over there.' He pointed towards two dogs scrapping over a soiled nappy outside the store.

'How do you feel about being here?'

'Weird.' He turned to face her, his blue eyes drilling straight into hers. 'This could be my country.'

She recalled what he'd said in the plane. 'Tell me what your mum found.'

'She's been tracing our family tree since Nanna Polly died a couple of years ago. Nanna never wanted to talk much about the family; she liked to say she was a whitefella. It was easier for her when Dad was alive because he never wanted to admit he'd married an Aborigine. Ashamed.'

'How did you deal with it growing up?'

Kent shrugged. 'Same as any family with a dark secret. No pun intended. Just didn't talk about it.'

'But how did you manage?'

'We just acted like whitefellas. Dad and Grandpa were white and we lived a nice middle-class white life.'

'Did it change a lot after your dad died?'

'Mum finally told all of us kids we were Aboriginal. I'll never forget the look on her face. She was afraid of how we'd react.'

Esther squeezed his arm. She'd heard some of his history before as he unpicked the threads and knitted them back up again, but never with this silk of bitterness shot through.

Kent continued. 'I was at uni at the time, just about to graduate. It was a shock that she'd kept it a secret all those years, but a whole load of things suddenly made sense.'

'Like what?'

'Well, I knew I looked a bit different, but I felt different too.'

'Aboriginality in the blood.'

'I reckon. It was a relief to find out what made me think different. But I lost a couple of friends when I told them I was a blackfella.' This part of the story was familiar, the words dropped into her ear as his fingers tightened round hers: the friends who shunned him, acting as if they were the ones who had been deceived; the fiancée who hurled her engagement ring back at him and never spoke to him again, shocked how close she'd come to marrying an Aborigine. 'Then when Nanna died Mum found a box of her papers and started going through them, piecing our family's story together. Regular Sherlock Holmes she's become. She wrote off for Nanna's native welfare records. She wouldn't get them while the old girl was alive.'

'Honouring the elders,' said Esther, lightly.

Kent grinned and his eyes flashed. 'Yeah. For all that whitefella upbringing we were black on the inside.'

'So what do the native welfare records say?'

'I can't remember all of it, but Mum says there's an ancestor called Mantitja who came from round here.'

Esther unbuckled a side pocket of her rucksack. 'Mantitja? I'll check it out.' She caught his smirk. 'What?'

'Frank's right. Never let a woman poke round in your family tree.'

'You going to ask anyone here about her?'

'The elders might recognise the name, even though it's going back over a century.'

'Worth a try.'

Esther scrunched her can and lopped it into the bin as Frank ambled over. 'Hey, what's yous talking about?'

'Kent's Aboriginality.'

'I'm black on the inside.'

'You know, some ignorant blackfellas call me coconut,' said Frank, thumping down on the fence beside them. 'Me! A coconut! They say I'm black on the outside and white on the inside just 'cause I pay to send my kids to school. I say they kids aren't going to grow up like me when I was a kid, always in trouble. They needs a education.'

'You got big plans for your kids, Frank?' asked Esther.

'For sure. My kids are gonna be doctors or lawyers. They got the brains all right.'

'So what am I if you're a coconut?' said Kent.

Frank rasped his nails against his chin. 'A yoghurt raisin.'

They laughed loudly at this proclamation, sobering when an elderly Aboriginal man approached. He was over seventy, Esther guessed, with close-cropped grey hair and wearing a ripe T-shirt stretched over a beer gut. His right foot was encased in a huge bandage and protected from the dirt by a blue surgical sock.

Esther slipped from the fence to stand up straight. Frank squared his shoulders and pumped the old man's hand. 'Mr Possum! How are ya? This is Tommy Possum,' he said, turning to Esther and Kent. Esther offered her hand and got a limp fish handshake from the old man. 'He's the leader of the Tjulpan community.'

'Thank you for letting us visit your country,' said Esther.

'This is Esther King,' said Frank. 'Dr Esther, our anthropologist.'

Tommy Possum looked her over, taking in her canvas bush pants and sturdy boots. Esther waited for him to speak, reminding herself of cultural rules. Don't be clever, don't be shy, don't be loud, wait for the answer even if it takes ten minutes to come.

'You want to know about Mt Parker?' Mr Possum asked, eventually.

'If you're allowed to tell me.'

'I'm allowed, all right. I'm an elder here.'

Esther took the rebuke. 'Would it be all right if I interviewed you after the meeting? What you say about Mt Parker will be really important if we're going to stop the mine.'

Tommy Possum's brown eyes fixed on hers. She stifled a shudder, trying to work out what it was about the old man that repelled her. Not the smell, not the bandage; maybe it was just the hostility of prolonged eye contact.

'After the meeting,' said Tommy, and went to take his seat under the bough shelter.

Doreen touched Esther's elbow and motioned for her to sit apart from the others on the far side of the shelter. 'I can't talk in front of him.' She nodded towards Tommy Possum. 'I'm glad you've come,' she muttered. 'There's something bad going on in this community.'

'What do you mean?'

Doreen shook her head. 'It's driving me wild what they're doing here. It's not right. It's sick. I want to make it official what's going on, see if we can't get some sort of help.'

'I don't understand.'

'No one will listen to me. They say I'm just a crazy black woman but they'll listen to you. You've got to stop them.'

Esther tried hard not to let the exasperation show in her voice. She said slowly, 'What do you want me to do?'

Before Doreen could answer, Esther's attention was drawn to the bough shelter, now filling up with people. Frank jerked his thumb towards the crowd, the signal to be ready to start the meeting. She turned back to Doreen. 'They're waiting. This sounds really serious, and I want to help if I can. I'll talk to you later.' Frustrated she'd had to cut Doreen off, Esther joined the mob under the bough shelter.

Frank opened the meeting. 'Most of yous know me. I'm Frank Bell, Aboriginal Officer with the Land Council. Thank you for letting us come here to Tjulpan community and letting us be on your country. This isn't my country so I'm not going to speak 'cept to let you know these here are Esther King, Dr King, our anthropologist, and Kent Stevens, our archaeologist. They're going to tell you why we're here.'

Frank gave her the nod and Esther rose to her feet. She looked round the group of people sitting cross-legged on the grass, her gaze moving from face to face but avoiding eye contact. She spoke firmly but quietly. 'Thanks, Frank. I'm Esther, and I'd like to say thank you very much for letting me visit your country and come into Tjulpan community.' She paused and smiled at them. Doreen and her son Gavin smiled back. 'I'm an anthropologist from England, but I've been working with Aboriginal people for about ten years now. I've worked with the Arrente near Alice Springs and the Yolngu up in the Top End. I'm really looking forward to working with you.'

A murmur rippled through the group as she mentioned the Arrente. Proper blackfella. People who lived in the desert. People who knew how to point bones and make men sick. Assassins. She'd worked with them, this young white woman from England. There were polite smiles and nods.

Esther smirked inwardly: invoking the Arrente worked very time. An easy first run on the respect scoreboard; now all she had to do was live up to it. 'As you know, the Caroline Mine thinks there's gold under Mt Parker, and they're going to come here and ask you if they can blow that site up.'

People turned to each other and she heard snatches of protest, 'Ours . . . Dreaming story . . . sacred site . . . can't just blow it up.'

She waited for the consternation to ebb before she announced, 'It's all right, the Land Council has already objected.'

'Why d'you do that?' Tommy Possum challenged her.

She was taken aback and, caught off-guard, stammered, 'We do it automatically.'

'You didn't have permission.'

'We object to everything that any mining company wants to do where there's a native title claim. It makes them come to the table and talk to you, and it means you can say how you feel about what they want to do.'

'You should ask us first, not just speak for us.'

'I understand that, but if you don't object in time they think you've got nothing to say about it and they go ahead. The Land Council protests straight away, then nothing can happen until they've talked to you first. However long that takes.'

Tommy Possum grumbled a little longer, and Esther saw Kent rolling his eyes at her. Cantankerous old git. If she waited to get a community meeting before objecting to the new mine, then Mt Parker would be gravel by now. It had taken two months to organise this preliminary meeting.

When Possum subsided she continued. 'We can ask the mining company to pay for a heritage survey. When they see how important Mt Parker is, they'll have to make a really good case to destroy it.'

'They do what they like,' the crowd muttered.

'Not always. And you can tell them what you want out of the deal if the new mine goes ahead.'

'It can't go ahead!' Doreen lurched to her feet. 'Listen up! That there mountain is a sacred site. We all know it's a sacred site.' She glared round the crowd. 'We all been told that story for that mountain since we were kids. They can't just blow it up.'

'That's right, Doreen,' said Esther. 'That's why we're here, to find out how the community feels about Mt Parker and to see what we can do to save it.'

'But it's up to us, not you!' said Tommy Possum. 'Us elders, me, I'm the one who says what happens to that sacred site. Not this woman. Or this whitefella.' He glared at Esther. She stared back, knowing it was rude in Aboriginal culture but determined not to be the first to break eye contact.

'She's here to help!' Doreen screamed. 'You know what happened at Moolya.'

'We don't talk 'bout that,' he hissed.

'What?' asked Esther, scenting danger. Tommy Possum seemed overprotective of his authority, as if he was afraid of what Doreen might blurt out.

Doreen faced her, eyes blazing. 'It's a massacre site, that's why.'

Esther's head snapped up. This was the first she'd heard of a massacre at Mt Parker, but if it were true it would be crucial to the land claim and in opposing the new mine.

'You don't know anything about that!' Tommy Possum was on his feet, pointing at Doreen. 'Leave the meeting. You have no right to speak here!'

Doreen glowered at him and pushed her way through the crowd. They avoided her eyes, hanging their heads and waiting for her to stop making a scene. At the edge of the bough shelter she turned back, tears coursing down her cheeks. 'There was a massacre out there. You know it. I know it. Yous *all* know it. Our old people were killed out there. And we need to protect that site and their ghosts.'

3

Tommy Possum shambled over to his house. It squatted in the centre of a bare rectangle of red earth, surrounded by a chain-link fence. Curtains flapped outside a couple of open windows, dragging over the sills. An iron bed frame stood in the shade by one wall, the blankets ruckled into a heap in the middle and topped by a sleeping dog.

Frank loomed head and shoulders above Tommy, clipping his stride to keep in time with the old man. Esther and Kent trailed behind them, youngster and woman knowing their place.

A new white Toyota four-wheel drive was parked in the yard, a stark contrast to the ramshackle house. Frank whistled. 'This yours, Mr Possum?'

'Yeah.'

'How long you had this? Brand new, isn't it?'

'Not long.'

'How d'you get this, then? Rob a bank? Or d'you win the lotto?'

'Won the money at cards.'

Frank spun round. 'Cards?'

Tommy jerked his thumb to the east. 'Tax money time at Warburton. They got $70,000 in refunds.'

'And they flew it into the community in cash?' exclaimed Esther.

'Yeah. Big card game on for days. I won.'

'Wow.' Privately she thought it was criminally irresponsible to flood a remote community with that amount of cash. People ran up debts and starved their families to get the money just to stay in the game and try for the pot. And then they blew it all on a car, which was smashed up three months later.

'I bought this car. My nephew's been driving it.'

'What about you?'

'Can't drive right now.' Tommy looked ruefully at his right foot. The bandages were seeping. Esther turned away, revolted.

'What did you do?' asked Kent.

'Diabetes. Had another toe off.'

Frank sighed. 'I've got to be careful with that. Got to check me sugar levels. How many toes you got left?'

Tommy thought about it, then held out his fingers indicating the number. 'Seven.'

He pulled open the screen door and led them through to the kitchen. The house was thick with the smell of dogs and Esther felt her nose prickling ready to sneeze. She was relieved when Frank suggested they all sit outside.

Tommy took four mugs from the draining board and spooned in International Roast instant coffee from a tin. He lifted the kettle onto the stovetop and clicked the ignition button. Nothing happened. He swore. 'Gas bottle's empty. Have to use this.'

He plucked an electric frying pan out of the sink. It was slick with fat and egg. After a cursory rinse under the cold tap, he filled it with water and switched it on. Esther watched the scum gathering on the surface as the water boiled, and dolloped sugar into her mug. She gritted her teeth against the sweetness but it was better than drinking bland greasy water.

Tommy dragged chairs together on the veranda. He slumped into an armchair. Frank's bulk spilled over the seat of a deckchair, and Kent and Esther balanced on folding stools.

Esther slid her notebook out of her rucksack. 'Do you mind if I make some notes while we talk?'

Tommy shook his head.

'And I've got a tape recorder with me. Would you mind if I recorded you?'

'Nah. That's all right.'

'OK. Thank you.' She put the tape recorder on the arm of Tommy's chair. It was ready to go with fresh tape and batteries. She'd already checked it, not wanting to give him time to change his mind while she fussed over setting it up. Esther pressed record. 'Try to ignore the tape recorder if you can,' she said. She glanced at her notes, reminding herself what she wanted from the interview. 'Can I start by asking you where you were born?'

'Red Gum Station,' said Tommy. 'My father was a stockman.'

'And you were a stockman, too?'

'Worked all over this area.'

Esther prodded his memory, getting him comfortable with talking about stations and bosses and his duties as a stockman. It helped establish his familiarity with the area. They would build their case on the credibility of his knowledge. When he was warmed up and chattering about other stockmen, Esther asked, 'Did you know any old Aboriginal people on the stations?'

'Course. All of them.'

'Did they talk about country?'

'All the time. Never stopped talking and singing. Taught me lots of things.'

Her ears pricked up at this but she kept her voice casual. 'Did they tell you any Dreaming stories?'

'Yeah. Them and the Lawmen.'

'I know you can't tell me much about that,' said Esther carefully. 'So I'll try not to ask you questions about it.'

'Uncle Tommy was one of the last people to go through the Law here,' said Frank, using the name 'Uncle' as a mark of respect to the old man, both for being an elder and for having gone through Law business. 'Now the boys and men have to go up to the Pilbara for Law.'

'Is that where you went, Frank?' asked Kent.

'Been there the past few years for Law. Uncle Tommy goes too, don't you?'

'I go all over for Law business.'

Esther paused. She wanted to ask about Mt Parker Dreaming stories but without it seeming like a question about Law business. Male initiation, coyly referred to as Law business, was a minefield for a white female anthropologist and she trod carefully, testing each word in turn. Lawmen like Tommy Possum, the elders who performed the initiation ceremonies on boys, were prickly and defensive, determined to protect their knowledge from inquisitive women. Especially an inquisitive white woman.

'I know you can't tell me about Law, but are you able to tell me any of the Dreaming stories the old people told you when you were a young stockman?'

'Yeah, some.'

'Did they tell you a story about Mt Parker?'

'Yeah, they talk about Mt Parker. Not just here but all over.'

'The story runs a long way,' Frank chipped in, anxious to demonstrate his own knowledge and status as an initiate. Usually Esther found his interruptions distracting, but with this querulous old man she was glad Frank was there to keep him talking. 'I've heard it at Law time. It's an important story for blackfellas.'

'Who does the story belong to?'

'It's our story,' said Tommy. 'Tjulpan story.'

'Can the story be told to women?'

'I can tell you some. Not all.'

Tommy picked at a scab on his arm. Scabies, thought Esther, noting the pattern of bumps, like Braille under his skin. Discoloured patches on his arms showed where old scabies sores had become infected and scarred. No wonder he keeps getting gangrene. She felt a pang of pity for the prickly old man.

Pretending to adjust the volume, she checked the tape was still running. Dreaming stories sometimes had their own agenda: she'd known fieldwork when video camera and tape recorder had seemed to be recording perfectly, but when she'd checked the footage the segment with the story was blank or crackled or was obscured. The rest of the footage would play perfectly; just the section with the Dreaming story was missing.

Esther sat back, forced her shoulders to relax and waited. Tommy breathed through his mouth for a minute, then started to speak.

'Back in the Dreaming there was a young man who lived out east of here in the country of war parties and featherfoots. Assassins they were. He caught his eye on a young girl in his tribe and decided he wanted her for himself. She was very beautiful and young and had firm titties, and he wanted her for his wife. And he said to himself, "I'm going to have her."

'But she was in the wrong skin group and he was forbidden to marry her. And she was already promised to one of the elders in the tribe. This young girl didn't like the old man she was supposed to marry. She thought he was wrinkled and ugly. She wanted a young man and she cast her eye about and it fell on the young man who fancied her.

'She knew it was forbidden but she paraded herself around until the young fella was so full of lust he couldn't stop himself. He sneaked up on the women's camp in the blackest part of the night and stole her away from her mothers and sisters, right from under their noses. He take her far away and have sex with her, and said she was now his wife.

'At first the young girl liked her husband and was happy with him and didn't think about how they done wrong. But she was a very young girl and after a while she begin to miss her mothers and sisters. She want to be back in the women's camp with the laughter and talking and for someone to groom the lice out her hair. When she thought about all she missed, she threw herself down on the ground weeping for days until the man agreed to take her back.

'When the runaways walked back into the camp, filled with shame, they were surrounded by the tribe, furious with them for breaking the Law. They took the girl away and the women beat her with sticks until she confessed she'd had forbidden sex with this man from the wrong skin group when she was promised to an elder of the tribe.

'Her promised husband was very angry that the pair had broke the Law and shamed him like this. He said they were to be punished. The girl had traditional punishment. Her mothers and aunties beat her head with their digging sticks until her scalp bled and the blood ran down her face.

'The young man was cast out of the tribe. He could not move from place to place, waterhole to waterhole, camp to camp with them any longer, but had to make his own way. He begged for mercy, and they let him take his spear and his dingo, but everyone knew he would soon die out there alone in the bush.

'The young man walked out of the camp with his spear in his hand and the dingo at his heels. With no men to help him with the hunting, and no women to collect berries and lizards, he soon grew skinny and weak. He was no one now, and he belonged in no man's country.

'He wandered across the land, moving from one tribe's country to the next, moving west all the time. But each tribe afraid of him. They say, "You're a featherfoot, you're here to assassinate us. You can stay in our country for a short time but then you must go." And they kept away from him, shaking with fear whenever he approached.

'Eventually he ended up here, near Moolya. He hadn't eaten for days and he was skinny and thirsty and tired. He was buggered. He lay down on the ground to sleep and died. The dingo had stayed with him all the time, following on his heels across sand and bush. He also was hungry and tired. The dingo lay down beside the young man's body waiting for him to wake up. He lay there crying, and his tears formed a waterhole that's still there today. The dingo is still there waiting, and you can see the tip of his nose, Mt Parker, which we Aboriginal people call Moolya.

'Now when whitefellas come here with their mines and say they've found gold, us blackfellas know that gold is the dingo's blood they're digging up.'

'And why are all these daisies golden?' asked Frank with a twinkle.

''Cause the dingo pissed on them.'

Frank guffawed and slapped his knee. 'Bet you don't have stories like that back in England, eh, Esther?'

'That we don't.' She exchanged a look with Kent. Frank and Tommy were still chortling over the dingo piss. She decided to plunge in. 'What about what Doreen said about a massacre?'

The laughter snapped off. 'She don't know.'

'What's she talking about? Was there a massacre near here?'

'She's a crazy woman. Don't listen to her, she's not an elder.' The old man glared at her. Unconvinced, Esther opted to leave it for now. She'd find out the truth eventually.

The barbecue spat and popped. A bored-looking young woman flipped the steaks with metal tongs and levered them into a roasting pan. The juices ran out pink. Another plate held a pyramid of sausages and a third had chops. Damper steamed in a jacket of tin foil on the edge of the hot plate. Two older women slathered it with home brand margarine from a container the size of a breezeblock. A line of trestle tables was set out with loaves of white sliced bread, dishes of blackened onions and rows of sauce bottles.

Esther took a paper plate and a serviette, squirted tomato sauce on two slices of bread and plonked sausages and onions on top. She rolled them into neat parcels and went to sit next to Doreen, a little apart from the others. The sauce squidged onto her hand as she bit into the hot dog. 'Think I overdid the sauce,' she muttered, licking her palm.

'Me too,' said Doreen, pointing at a sauce stain on her front. She wriggled a length of gristle out from between her front teeth and flicked it at a hopeful-looking dog prowling nearby.

A little girl sat on the fence post and stared at Esther. She'd seen the girl earlier, cowering away from the crowd during the community meeting, noticed her because the girl was wearing a long blue frock and wasn't scuffing after a football and screaming with the other kids. Esther waved her hotdog at the girl. 'You should get some tucker, it's good.'

The girl's eyes didn't flicker.

'Who's that little girl?'

'She's Tommy Possum's granddaughter. His daughter's daughter,' said Doreen. 'They call her Tamisha.'

'She was at the meeting earlier.'

'She hangs around, that one, like a ghost.'

'She doesn't play with the other kids?'

'Nah.'

'Shy?'

'Nah.' Doreen spat the word out. Esther glanced at her, surprised, and waited for Doreen to elaborate. When it was obvious nothing was forthcoming, she asked, 'What did you mean at the meeting when you said Mt Parker is a massacre site?'

'Just that. There was a massacre there.'

'When?'

'Over a hundred years ago: 1880 or 1890 something.'

'What happened?'

'There was a whitefella, Bilsom, and his family living on the station back in the early days. He's the one the town's named after. They had a lot of trouble with wild blackfellas spearing the sheep. Bilsom went out and found where all the blackfellas were camping and shot every one of them. All except a woman called Ruby.'

'Ruby? Who was she?'

'She worked at the station. Housegirl or something. Bilsom killed her family.'

'That's horrible.' Esther was suddenly conscious of how white her hands were. She shoved her hands between her knees, ashamed of being a whitefella and knowing what atrocities others had perpetrated because they considered themselves superior solely on the basis of race. 'Where did it all happen?'

'No one knows for sure. Blackfellas don't want to think about it and whitefellas don't like to be reminded.'

'You said it was at Mt Parker.'

Doreen shrugged. 'It could be. Course it might be in the other direction. Might already been dug up by the mine. But nobody knows for sure.'

'I asked Tommy Possum about the massacre.'

Doreen's eyes slid sideways to look at her. 'Oh yeah? And what did he say?'

'He says he's never heard of the massacre.'

'That's shit talk. Why's he think the town's called Bilsom's Grudge? It's 'cause of the massacre, that's why.'

'How do you know?'

'Why else would it be called that?'

'Places get names for all sorts of reasons, and later on people think they know but actually the story's got mixed up.'

Doreen pouted and huffed. 'Well, it's after the massacre.'

'So why doesn't Tommy know about it? He was a stockman round here for years. He would have heard the story even if he didn't know where the massacre site was.'

'You tell me. There's a lot of things going on in this community. You don't know the half of it.'

A Toyota Land Cruiser pulled up outside Tommy Possum's house and a white man in his late thirties stepped out. He went straight up to the door and inside.

'Who's that?'

'Mark Wright. He's community liaison for the mine. He's always here.'

'Oh? Meetings and things?'

'To see Mr Possum, mostly.' Doreen squinted at Esther. 'He's the sort of bloke who spreads to the edges, if you know what I mean.'

Mark Wright reappeared a few moments later and climbed back into the Land Cruiser. Tommy shuffled after him. He caught sight of Esther and Doreen talking and shouted, 'You shouldn't talk to her. She knows nothing.'

Doreen leapt to her feet and marched over to him, her face furious. Inside the Land Cruiser Mark turned to watch the fun. Esther cringed. Community slanging matches in front of outsiders could set back negotiations by months, even years, as the mine companies sought to exploit community divisions to pursue their own interests.

'Just mind what you say,' screeched Doreen. 'I've told her what you're up to, and there's more. Much more.'

'You're crazy woman!'

'Is that right? Maybe she should ask where you got that new car, eh?'

Tommy's mouth worked silently. 'What you know about it?'

'More than you'd like, old man.'

Tommy jabbed his finger in her face. 'This is nothing to do with you. You keep out of what you don't understand.'

4

They were kept waiting at the Caroline Mine Company offices in Bilsom's Grudge. Out of the window Esther saw ranks of units, temporary accommodation for the mine workers, each with its square air conditioning box on the outside above a window encased in flywire. Dog boxes, the miners called them. Basic but functional, they were home for fourteen day stretches, then the miners scarpered for four days of normality at home.

Esther fidgeted in a chrome and black leather chair while Frank and Kent studied the aerial photos of the mine flanking the walls.

'Bloody great hole in the ground,' said Frank. 'What a mess.'

'They say they have a "rigorous ecological policy of restoration",' Esther muttered, snapping the pages of a glossy brochure about the Caroline Mine and its social and ecological conscience.

'What's that mean?'

'It means when they've finished raping the country they'll do their best to fill the hole in and cover up the spoil heaps.'

'And until then?'

'Until then we are committed to regular ecological monitoring both of the mine site and the surrounding area, with a restitution plan already in place should our monitoring detect the slightest deterioration in native species' levels and habitats.'

They swivelled round to face a gaunt man looming in the doorway. He consulted a sheet of paper he held between trembling fingers. 'If you're from the Land Council, I'm expecting to meet Dr King.' His gaze snapped from Esther to Frank. Dismissing them, he advanced his hand to Kent. Wrong call, Esther thought, bristling. She stepped up to him and gripped his hand.

'I'm Dr King,' She maintained eye contact until he glanced away. His eyes were bloodshot and cloudy, set like pebbles in his face and making him appear older. He was like a sunburnt tortoise. A cranky one at that.

'And who are your sidekicks, Dr King? I wasn't expecting the Land Council to dispatch a posse.'

Esther introduced the men.

'Stuart MacKendrick,' he barked. 'You'd better come into my office.'

MacKendrick's office was littered with plans and rolled schematics, the walls busy with charts. Gold nuggets embedded in chunks of rock held piles of papers in place on the desk, and a walking stick leaned in one corner. MacKendrick scooped a stack of files from a chair and ordered them all to sit down.

Esther unbuckled her rucksack and took out her notebook. She flipped it open on her knee, foraged for a pen and wrote the date, time and location in block capitals across the top of a fresh sheet. 'So, Mr MacKendrick.'

He held up his hand. 'I'm waiting for someone to join us. I don't want to start before he gets here.'

Esther glanced at her watch and ringed the time she'd scribbled in her notebook. Keeping Land Council employees waiting was a familiar mining company power game. It said, 'We're more important than you, we're bigger than you and we can waste your time.' If only they knew. Esther had long ago persuaded the Land Council finance department to add on a "nuisance fee" to the invoices sent to mining companies. If a mining company wanted to start drilling they needed a heritage survey to clear the land. If the Land Council carried out the survey it added $100 for every minute employees were kept hanging around in these power games. Esther totted up how long she'd have to wait before the Land Council could afford a new laptop for Frank.

She was out of luck. Only a minute later the door opened and Mark Wright walked in. He dragged a chair across and sat next to Esther. 'Sorry to keep you waiting,' he said. 'I'm Mark Wright, Community Liaison for the Caroline Mine Company.'

'I saw you in Tjulpan earlier,' said Esther.

'Oh?' He frowned, then recovered himself. 'Yes, that's right. I've commissioned Tommy Possum to do a painting for our head offices in Perth.'

'Nice idea.'

'I hope so.' MacKendrick shot him a look, and Mark shifted in his seat.

Esther cast an appraising eye over him. Brown elastic-sided boots polished to conker sheen, with just the tips dusty; long legs in moleskin jeans. City boy, trying too hard, unable to conceal he's a new boy in the bush despite his account at R.M. Williams. Quite attractive. He grinned at her, flashing straight white teeth, and his eyes twinkled. Correction, very attractive. She smiled back and tucked her hair behind her ears.

Mark turned to Frank. 'Is this your country, Frank?' He was trying hard, all right, had evidently learned how to smooth his way into conversation with Aboriginal people.

'Nah, not mine, but Kent reckons he's got connections here.'

'That right? Which family are you from?'

'None of them that are still here, as far as I know, but my ancestor Mantitja was possibly from here. They say she discovered gold here.'

A look passed between MacKendrick and Mark. 'Actually, I think you'll find my grandfather discovered gold here,' said MacKendrick.

There was silence.

'The Aboriginal people say there's always been gold here,' said Frank. 'They own the Dreaming story.'

'And that's why you're here,' said Mark, looking relieved the conversation was flowing again. He launched into a slick PR spiel. 'My job as Community Liaison Officer is to get Tjulpan people involved in the decision-making, and to make sure they arrive at informed decisions based on impartial advice. Last thing we want is the community feeling it's been conned.'

'How many already work for you?' asked Kent.

'From Tjulpan? To be honest, not as many as we'd like. I started working here eighteen months ago; I'm the first Community Liaison Officer, and the Caroline Mine has developed a strong good neighbour policy. But taking up what's on offer will take time.'

'What is on offer?' Esther's voice was sharper than she'd intended.

'Jobs for people with the right aptitudes, a scholarship scheme to send kids to the School of Mines, assisted study, preferential weighting given to job applicants from Tjulpan.'

'Not a bad start,' she said, grudgingly. 'How about giving the traditional owners some shares?'

'The Caroline Mine doesn't issue shares,' growled MacKendrick. 'I own 50 per cent and I'm not about to undercut myself.'

'50 per cent?' said Kent. 'If there *is* gold under Mt Parker you're going to clean up.'

'If you can get to it,' Esther added. She looked MacKendrick in the eye. 'That's why we're here, after all.'

Mark hurried to break the tension. 'We got a tenement granted through the expedited procedure just over two years ago and started prospecting in the Mt Parker area. The geologist's report came back with a significant reef out there.'

'And there's only one way to get to it?'

''Fraid so. We've explored all the possibilities with our engineers, but with the shape of Mt Parker if we start drilling under it it's going to collapse. It's just not safe.'

'So you want to blow it up.'

'Yep.' Mark looked abashed and gave Esther a crooked smile. 'We're not keen on another open pit, but it's the best way to get to the gold, and we're committed to ecologically sound processes.'

As if blowing up the country could ever be ecologically sound, she thought. It would always be a big crater, like a massive dose of chickenpox, never mind the damage to the Aboriginal culture. 'You know it's a sacred site?'

Mark's head snapped up. 'I know there's a story but . . .'

'That's bull,' said MacKendrick. 'No one's ever said that it's a sacred site.'

'They're saying it now.'

'Typical. A sacred site miraculously appears every time gold or oil or uranium's found. They must think I'm stupid. I've seen what's happened in the Northern Territory; now they think they can try the same thing here. It's all a trick to screw more dollars out of the mining company.'

Esther let him bluster on like a grumbling volcano belching acid smoke. When he finally stopped she said, 'Nevertheless, we do have to investigate it.'

'And I suppose that's going to cost us?'

'I've been working in the community for eighteen months and they've never said it was a sacred site,' said Mark.

'Communities usually like to keep things quiet,' said Frank. 'If you don't know it's there you won't go messing.'

'There's something else, too,' said Esther. 'Apparently there may be a massacre site out there.'

'Where?' demanded MacKendrick.

'I don't know exactly. We'll have to find out more from the community.'

'I've heard rumours,' Mark admitted, 'but nothing with any weight.'

'And how long will this hold things up?' said MacKendrick.

'What's the rush?'

'The rush, Dr King, is that the Caroline Mine is producing more rock than gold right now, and a town of over a thousand people depends on the mine for its livelihood. If we can't open up the new reef soon Bilsom's Grudge will be a ghost town.'

'And Tjulpan will be dependent on welfare. That's if it can continue without the town nearby,' added Mark. 'Bilsom's Grudge is only there because of the mine, but it means Tjulpan has all those services on its doorstep: shops, bar, post office, the nursing post. Without all of that, Tjulpan will struggle to survive.'

'You can put these arguments to the Tjulpan community,' said Esther. 'Let them decide.' She snapped her notebook shut, signalling the meeting was ended.

MacKendrick refused to shake hands and snarled, 'You'll be very unpopular if you stop this mine going ahead, Dr King.'

'It's not up to me, or you, Mr MacKendrick. It's up to the Tjulpan community.'

5

'I wouldn't care if this became a ghost town,' said Esther in the main street of Bilsom's Grudge. Dowdy shop-fronts lined the wide main street; from the contents of their windows they sold only dead flies and curling brown paper. The yellow brick bank building on the corner boasted a date stone of 1912 and still looked imposing despite its crust of bird shit. Its windows and door frames were sealed with metal sheets: armour-plated against vandals and decay. It was impossible to tell when it had last been open.

'These are heritage buildings,' Kent argued, looking faintly shocked.

'Nonsense. My parents' house in England is older.'

'They're old for Australia.'

'That doesn't make it heritage. This town is barely a century old.'

'And your family lives in an ancient English castle.'

'Hardly.' Kent never understood that ordinary working-class homes could be old. She was irritated that heritage seemed to mean preserving relics of the past, however scungy their condition. It was obvious that no one much cared for the buildings in Bilsom's Grudge, but any hint that they might be abandoned if the mine closed would bring the heritage preservation lobby down on her, the Land Council and Tjulpan.

'So, do you want to stay at the Bilsom's Grudge Ritz or the Hilton?' said Kent.

'I thought the Bilsom's Grudge Waldorf.'

'Hm. That's booked out so we'll have to settle for the Grand.'

They went into the bar of the Grand Hotel, dazed by the gloom after the bright street. The bar was empty but a woman answered when they called.

'Hiya.'

'Hello. We've got three rooms booked. Names of Bell, Stevens and King.'

The woman flicked through the book. 'Right. Says here it's a Land Council booking.'

'That's right.'

'You've got to fill in a card.' She rattled a pen down on the counter. 'Yous here to stop the mine?'

'No.'

''Cause there'll be nothing here without it. Just a big dusty hole in the ground.'

Esther was tempted to make a remark about the mine's advertised "rigorous ecological policy" but bit it back. 'It's not up to us.'

'We'll all go under. Thinking of shipping out already before it's too late.'

'Like I said, it's not up to us.'

The woman took three keys from a board behind the bar. 'I've put yous in the units out the back.'

The Grand Hotel was built in 1910 of orange and cream brick, and was surpassed in ugliness only by the red brick box units behind the main hotel building.

'At least there's a bathroom,' said Kent, when they went to inspect their rooms. Esther was disappointed, having hoped to stay in the hotel. Though the rooms were basic, with a trek down the corridor to the toilet, there was character to them, with pressed tin ceilings and wide undulating balconies running round the upper storey. Faded grandeur, lurking in the dark sweep of stairs, embossed wallpaper and dado rails, was not quite obliterated by the sound of pinball machines and roars from the gamblers at the TAB. By contrast the new units were anodyne, each room reprinted in a line.

They had been allocated rooms spread out along the row. They dumped Frank's bags in the room on its own at the far end of the row of units: he'd slunk off to join the other men in the TAB, staking his wages on a horse race and screaming at the TV screen showing the racing in the hotel bar. Esther and Kent snaffled the adjacent rooms at the other end.

'Frank can get his key from me at dinner,' said Kent. 'You want a coffee?'

'Could murder one. Just let me wash my face and I'll come to yours.'

Esther splashed water on her face and the sink streaked orange. After only a few hours in Bilsom's Grudge her fair skin was filmed with dust. Orange fingerprints soiled the towel when she dried her hands. Dust clogged in her thick, short hair too. She dipped forwards from the waist and brushed it vigorously, then damped her palms and smoothed her hair back from her forehead.

Foraging in her backpack, she pulled out a pale blue cotton top and clean pair of jeans and changed quickly. She left her boots beside her backpack and wriggled her feet into a pair of pumps. The sudden lightness of the shoes after her clumpy boots surprised her.

She dug her mobile phone out of her pocket and switched it on, feeling apprehensive. Better check in case there were any work messages. There was one voice message from the office about an old lady suddenly taken sick: they wanted Esther to arrange for her to be interviewed soon, or her information would be lost. Her heart thumped when she saw there were five text messages from Rich, trying to make up for last night's scene.

'When RU back?'

'Miss U.'

'Rehearsals awful 2dy. Wish I cd tell U abt it.'

'Is it 2mrrw ure back?'

'Bad news. School choir will sing next week.'

Esther sighed and deleted all the texts without replying to them, and sat twisting her wedding ring round and round. She pulled it off her finger, wincing as it snagged on the loose skin on her knuckle, and examined her bare hand, flashing it in the mirror to see how it looked. Her finger felt naked without the wedding band. She shoved it back on, feeling abashed, then rang the office and spoke to her assistant.

'Hi, Gail, it's Esther. I got your message.'

'Oh hi, Esther. Sorry to bother you. I know you're back soon but Mrs Stone's daughter rang up and she was quite upset.'

'What's happened?'

'The old lady's had a mild stroke. She's all right, but her daughter's worried that she might get worse. She's in her seventies, after all. So the daughter wants to arrange for someone to talk to her.'

'Is she fit enough to be interviewed?'

'The daughter says so, but she wants to be present.'

'I wouldn't do it without her there anyway.'

'That's what I told her. But she's quite worried her mum might pass away without you getting all her information for the land claim. And you know her mother's the last speaker of the language?'

'Yeah.' Esther rubbed her temple. Another one about to drop off the twig and take all that heritage and culture to the grave. 'It's OK, Gail, the old lady did a lot of language work about ten years ago, but we need to make sure we've got her testimony for the claim. Is she at home?'

'She lives in Geraldton.'

'Trip up the coast for me.'

'Not bad this time of year. Not too hot. Though Gero's no great shakes: all wheat and crayfish.'

'Lots of lobster spaghetti on the menu, then. Gail, could I ask you to do something for me, please?'

'Sure. Fire away.'

'Please could you fix up with Mrs Stone's daughter that I'll come and interview her at the end of the week, if that's convenient. Then can you find me a flight up to Geraldton and a hire car when I get there. I'll stay overnight so I can do the interview in a few sessions, so could you book me a hotel room, please?'

'Any preference?'

'Do we have an account with the ones overlooking the ocean?'

'I'll check.'

'Thanks. Otherwise whatever you can get will be fine.'

'No worries. When you back?'

'Couple of days, I expect.'

'Well, you have fun.'

'Thanks, Gail. See you soon.'

Kent's door was ajar and the kettle was rattling when she went in. She paused in the doorway to watch him for a second. Straight back, wide shoulders, tall, wearing dark moleskin jeans, boots and a round-necked sweater in ghastly olive and red stripes. His dark hair was thick and wavy. He started when she came in and turned, his surprise morphing into a broad smile that crinkled his blue eyes.

He crossed the room, folded her into his arms and kissed the top of her head. She pressed her face against his jersey and the tension ebbed from her muscles.

'You've checked your phone messages,' he said, as Esther kicked off her shoes and flopped onto the bed, exhausted. Kent flumped down next to her. 'Budge up. How many?'

'The office about an old lady on the urgent list: she's had a stroke. I'm going to see her at the end of the week.'

'Where?'

'Geraldton.'

'Want me to come with you?'

'Better if I'm by myself. Just me, the old lady and her daughter. Be easier for them with just one stranger to deal with. All girls together.'

Kent paused, and she knew he was weighing up whether to ask his next question. She saved him the effort and volunteered the information. 'And lots of texts from Rich.'

'And?'

She ran her hands through her hair and groaned. 'Just stuff about music and rehearsals. And that he misses me.'

'Course he does. What is it?'

'We had a row last night.'

'What about?'

'Usual stuff. Me being away with work all the time. He just can't understand that my job isn't nine to five. It's so unfair. He's away on tour with the orchestra all the time, yet he seems to want me to be sitting at home pining for him.'

'And what do you want?'

She paused. 'This is so difficult, Kent.'

'I've told you: I'll wait. As long as it takes.'

'I can't make you any promises.'

'I know. I'll chance it.' He leaned towards her and kissed her on the cheek. 'As long as you know how I feel about you.'

She nodded. 'Me too.'

'I meant it when I said I'd wait. It's all or nothing, Esther. I don't want you to cheat on Rich.'

'Neither do I. I owe him that.'

He rolled off the bed. 'Coffee?'

'Thought you'd never ask.'

'International Roast?' said Kent, waggling the motel's sachets.

'Sod off and break out the good stuff.'

Kent withdrew a bundle of clothes from his rucksack and peeled off layers wrapped round a cafetiere. He spooned in ground coffee and poured over boiling water.

'I think this is what I like best about you,' said Esther, sipping the coffee. 'You insist on good coffee.'

'I'm very refined, me,' he said, through a mouthful of complimentary shortbread.

'Can you get TV here?'

'I tried the set. Crackly ABC and GWN.'

'Great. I can't get enough of those adverts for sheep dip and wheat and lime haulage.'

'See this.' Kent opened the bar fridge and took out two slices of bread wound in cling film. The bread was spotted with green patches. 'Tomorrow's breakfast.'

'No thanks. I'm going to try the diner.'

'A little token of their esteem,' said Kent, drawing rings round the mould patches with a marker pen and dating it.

'I bet it's still there next time we come.'

They drank their coffee lying side by side on the bed, sharing a pillow and chortling at regional TV offerings: adverts for tractors and lice treatments, and old soap operas Esther remembered from her childhood.

'We had this on the TV in England,' she said. 'I thought this was how Australia really was. I loved it.'

'Is that what made you come out here? The promise of country vets and flying doctors?'

'Yep. And Skippy.'

'I'm going in the shower,' said Kent. He left the bathroom door ajar and the room soon filled with steam.

Esther heard the water running, distracted by his proximity. It was six months since she and Kent had realised they were in love with each other. With humility she acknowledged how much faith Kent placed in her: trusting she would be honest with him, believing that one day she would resolve the problems in her marriage one way or another, and hoping she chose him.

She loved them both, Kent and Rich; she'd made that clear – but for a long time now her marriage to Rich had faltered. She wondered if she'd be so strongly attracted to Kent if she'd been able to talk properly to Rich. It was an impossible question to answer now: all she knew was that she trembled when Kent was near; he filled her thoughts, and she ached to melt into his arms.

But what about Rich? Even if Kent would allow it she couldn't live with the guilt and duplicity of an affair. Both men deserved better than that, though it would be so easy to do. With all those trips away from home the betrayal would be simple, but she recognised that the moment she gave into her feelings for Kent her marriage was over, and that thought hurt her like a knife wound.

Through the open bathroom door came the sound of water spraying against the tiles, and Kent singing in a deep bass voice while he clattered bottles in the shower. So easy to go to him, strip off and press her body against his under the jet, trace the grain of his skin under her palms. Esther padded to the door and gently closed it.

Later that evening they went to the bar of the Grand Hotel. It was filling up with mine workers and locals, and the bar was clogged with smoke. Frank bawled at a TV screen on a bracket in one corner, scrunched up a TAB slip and hurled it on the floor.

'Out of luck?' Esther asked.

Frank groaned. 'I reckon I ought to go in one of them card games at Warburton like Mr Possum.'

'Oh dear. How much?'

'Lost $100 so far, but I won $80 earlier.'

'So $20 then?'

'I can make that up.' Inwardly she groaned. Frank would never learn.

'You seen Kent?'

Frank shot her an odd look. 'You two pretty matey these days.'

Esther shrugged. 'Not really. You ready for dinner?'

'After this next race. I should win easy, have some to take back to Val.'

You hope, she thought. Frank's wife Val was less than impressed with his gambling. She locked him out of the house for a fortnight when he blew a week's salary on the trots. Coming home with the spoils was unlikely to change her mind. And if he went back with a deficit Frank's bad back would be tortured for another couple of weeks, sleeping in his swag on his brother's porch.

'Get you a drink, Frank?'

'Yeah. I'll have a coke, thanks.'

Kent was playing pool on the other side of the bar. She swigged her beer from the bottle and watched him lose three frames in a row to a scrawny truck driver in shorts, singlet and thongs. From what was visible it seemed the whole of his body was embroidered with tattoos.

'I'm beat!' exclaimed Kent, holding up his hands in surrender. 'Anyone else want to have a go?' He handed the cue over to the next punter and stood next to Esther. 'Get you another beer?'

'Thanks.'

There was a groan from the TAB.

'I hope that's not Frank,' said Esther. 'He's trying to make up what he's lost.'

'So that's what he was up to all afternoon. I thought he'd gone back to Tjulpan to talk to Mr Possum.'

'Can we get dinner here? I'm starving.'

It wasn't long before they were served with heaving plates of steak, mashed potatoes, vegetables and gravy. They ordered more beers and ate in the bar while the yells and moans from the TAB swelled and ebbed around them.

'It's amazing that you can get such good food out here,' said Esther. 'This is better than a lot of places in the city.'

'Miners like their grub,' said Frank. He wolfed his dinner in record time and rejoined his mates in the TAB like a doomed man.

Esther cleared her plate and ordered ice-cream and tinned fruit. She was scraping her dish when Doreen came in. She scouted round the bar, spotted Esther and Kent, and joined them.

'Hi, Doreen, like a drink?' Esther asked.

'Ta. A Malibu, please.' Esther hesitated. 'It's OK, they've got it. Get it in specially for me. They know I'll drink it.'

Esther gave Kent a glance that meant "make yourself scarce", and he melted away to the TAB to watch Frank inch closer to marital breakdown.

'You look nice, Doreen.'

'Oh, ta. These are me glad rags. Me pulling pants!' There was a twinkle in her eye as she smoothed down her black jeans and adjusted her patterned silk blouse. A large pendant snuggled between her breasts. Her hair was loose about her shoulders.

'Got time for a chat?'

'Sure. It doesn't really start up in here until later. The girls come in and we put on the jukebox and have a dance.'

'The girls?'

'They work in the mine canteen. Some of the blokes who come in are all right, too. I like having a boogie, let me hair down.'

'I might join you.'

'You should. They're all a real laugh in here. Now, Esther, what's up?'

'I've been worrying about what you said earlier, about the things going on in Tjulpan.'

'Oh yeah?'

'You said there was bad stuff happening.' She was reluctant to pry, in case Doreen had thought better of confiding in her. On the other hand, she had seemed insistent earlier, and she'd evidently sought Esther out this evening. 'Want to tell me about it?'

'Thing is, that community's sick. It needs help. I'm the only one who's prepared to kick up a fuss about what's going on there, and I need some help. No one's going to listen to a blackfella from the back of nowhere. It needs someone from outside to say it's not right.'

'Is this to do with the mine?'

'It's to do with everything. I don't like whitefellas nosing into blackfellas' business, but this needs sorting.'

'Why don't you start at the beginning?'

'I don't think there is a beginning.' Doreen took a deep breath and looked directly at Esther. 'You remember a while back those allegations about the Swan Valley Community? They closed the community down 'cause of it.'

'Child abuse?'

'Yeah. They's not the only ones.'

Esther paused carefully before she clarified what Doreen was hinting at. If she got it wrong she'd offend Doreen irredeemably. 'You mean there's child abuse going on in Tjulpan?'

'And no one's prepared to say what's going on and stop it.'

Esther groaned inwardly. Child abuse wasn't unique; many communities, Aboriginal and white, were infected with it, and it sickened her to think of Tjulpan being affected. But with Aboriginal communities it was difficult to point the finger; a whitefella interfering would certainly be accused of racism. Ultimately it was up to the community itself to stamp it out. 'That's not a Land Council matter,' she said, cravenly, despising herself. 'You need to go to the welfare people. Is it just one family?'

'Nah. All the kids are at risk, I reckon, but there's one person doing it.'

'Who?'

'Tommy Possum.'

Esther was stunned. He was an elder, a respected member of the community, a Lawman for goodness sake. 'Are you sure? It's a hell of an allegation.'

'Course I'm sure. We *all* know what's going on but the others are too scared to say anything.'

'What do you know?'

'You know his little granddaughter, Tamisha, who was at the barbecue?'

Esther recalled the little girl with her blue frock and huge unblinking eyes. 'Yes.'

'You know why she's so odd, always staring at people funny and shying away?'

Esther shook her head but silently guessed the answer. When it came it was much worse than she feared.

'When Tamisha was three her mother got appendicitis,' said Doreen, leaning in so close to whisper that Esther could smell the Malibu on her breath. 'She was flown to Perth for an emergency operation. She was really sick. She had to leave Tamisha with the other kids. Tommy Possum took Tamisha down the creek and raped her. Nearly killed her. Everyone knew he done it. He didn't exactly confess, but he said it was traditional culture or some bullshit and his right as an elder. Then he said it was his daughter's fault for leaving the girl behind and not looking after her.'

'But she was in hospital.'

Doreen shrugged. 'He said it makes no difference: it's the mother's responsibility to look after the child. The community took what he said, though they didn't like it, and when Tamisha's mother came back he said she had to be punished. He cut her and rubbed poison in the cut. She got blood poisoning and died.'

'My God,' Esther breathed, horrified.

'The community's too afraid to do nothing.'

'Why?'

Doreen ticked off the reasons on her fingers. 'One, he's an elder and you don't go against them, even if they're evil, lying, greedy, sick bastards. Two, he been through the Law so we respect him double. And he goes round catching the boys for Law all over WA so he's important. You say anything about him, there's all those Law men out there to protect him and shut you up.'

'But they wouldn't . . .'

'Three.' Doreen lowered her voice. 'He's been around, learned things from featherfoots. Y'know, assassins. He's a magic man. He knows how to cure people and how to make them sick. That's why people are afraid of him and not want to stand up to him, say it's all bullshit culture he's talking.'

'Do you believe he's a magic man?'

'I saw what he did to Tamisha's mother. And I've seen him take a piece of glass out of a man's arm, saw it move in a lump under the skin until he pulled it out, no blood or cuts, nothing.'

'Is Tamisha the only child he's hurt?'

Doreen shook her head. 'I don't know how many exactly, but Tamisha wasn't the first. He abused his daughter and the other grandkids. Probably other kids in Tjulpan, too, but nobody wants to talk about it.'

'I'm not sure I can do anything . . .'

'Aboriginal people are ashamed this kind of thing goes on, Esther, but they don't know how to stop it without destroying the community. You start undermining the elders, then what you got left? You understand me? It's not about whitefellas and blackfellas, it's about little kids.'

Esther drew her finger in the moisture sweating from her glass. 'Let me ask round a few people I know and see what's the best thing to do.'

'You promise? It's for the community.'

'I promise.' The look of relief on Doreen's face made her want to weep. She doubted there was much that could be done until Tjulpan itself was brave enough to speak out.

'Hello again.' A deep voice interrupted their conversation. Esther glanced up and met the smiling eyes of Mark Wright. 'Do you come here often?' he asked, with an ironic twitch of his eyebrow.

'All the time,' said Doreen, downing the remains of her Malibu. Mark took the hint and fetched a fresh round. Esther noticed how the barmaid simpered and tossed her hair when he went to the bar.

'Mind if I join you?' he asked her, already pulling up a chair.

'Sure.' Across the bar Esther saw Kent's head swivel in her direction. She flashed him a smile.

'So, Dr King.'

'Esther.'

'Esther. What do you think of Bilsom's Grudge?'

She shrugged. 'Sounds like you're talking work, and I'm off duty.'

'Fair enough. So, you married?'

'You don't waste much time, do ya?' Doreen spluttered.

'Why wait? I like to get to the point.'

'Yes, I'm married, to a guy called Rich. We've been married for seven years.'

'Any kids?'

'I thought I was supposed to be the nosy anthropologist.'

'She's got you there,' said Doreen, muscling in.

'I'm guessing you're not married,' said Esther.

'Divorced three years ago. I have a son I'm allowed to pay for but not allowed to see.'

'Ouch! How old is he?'

'He's six now. Lives with his mother in Sydney.'

A gaggle of women in short skirts and stretch tops pushed into the bar. Evidently regulars, they were met by a barrage of whistles and calls from the men propping up the counter.

'Here're the girls!' cried Doreen. 'Crank it up! Let's have some Shania Twain and get things going in here!'

Music suddenly blared from the jukebox. Doreen shoved through to the group of women dancing by the speakers. A few men were cajoled into the group and soon she was dancing with a drink in each hand. Lurching up to Esther's table, she bellowed above the jukebox and the roars from the TAB. 'Hey, look!' she called, holding up the drinks. 'I think I've pulled!' She beamed at a knotty-looking man at the bar.

'Good for you,' laughed Esther.

'Don't forget what I said earlier, about the community.' Doreen stared at Esther, her eyes already slightly glazed.

'I won't.'

'Only you can stop it.'

'All right. We can talk about it later.'

''Cause there's more going on there that only I know about.'

'Tell me tomorrow.'

'I will, don't you worry.' Doreen turned back to her conquest and bawled, 'Come on, Johnno, let's see you strut your stuff.'

'What's she talking about?' asked Mark.

Esther shrugged. 'It's nothing. She's worried about one of the elders, that's all.'

'Anything I can help with?'

'No.' Esther changed topic. 'She certainly knows how to enjoy herself.'

'I see her in here most evenings.'

'That means *you're* in here most evenings.'

'There's not much else to do round here. Doreen's always the centre of the fun. The blokes like her.'

'Course they do: she knows how to have a good time.'

'Want to dance?'

Esther met his steady gaze. 'Why not?' She was aware of the other women's envy as he took her hand and pushed her through to the group jigging by the jukebox. She was perspiring and tipsy.

'All right there, Esther?' asked Mark.

'I'm not much of a dancer.'

'Here, hold onto me.' He slipped his arm round her waist and held her hand outstretched as though they were about to break into a waltz. The ridiculousness of it made her snort with laughter. She placed her hand on his shoulder and let him lead. Up close he seemed taller. A whiff of classy aftershave wafted over her; Chanel. She recognised it, reviving memories of an old lover.

'Your dancing seems fine to me,' said Mark.

'Good enough for Bilsom's Grudge.'

He affected mock outrage. 'You come here with your fine city ways and look down on us poor country folks.'

Esther giggled. 'Well, exactly.'

'Hey, you know I'm sorry about Mack earlier.'

'Mack?'

'MacKendrick. He's pretty brusque.'

'You mean rude.'

'Yeah. No excuse for his manners to you, but he's worried about the mine.'

Esther groaned and pressed her forehead against his chest.

'What?'

'Do me a favour, Mark, and let me have a break from work just for a couple of hours.'

'Right.' He flashed her a grin. Esther caught Kent watching her and she pulled away.

'What is it?' Mark followed the direction of her look and she saw him and Kent lock eyes. She thrilled a little at the mute challenge they threw at each other, then was vaguely ashamed at herself. 'Fraternising with the enemy, eh?'

'Something like that. Thanks for the dance, but I'd better go now.'

'Shall I walk you to your room?'

'No thanks, I'll be fine.' Somehow she thought he wouldn't stop at the door.

The cold night air slapped her sober. Outside the hotel she recognised Doreen's car parked into the kerb at an angle. Esther stared up at the sky, trying to identify constellations and planets from the mass of stars. The noise from the bar followed her as she made her way round the back of the hotel to the units. It was dark there and she fumbled to get the door open, groping for the lock in the gloom. Something scrunched underfoot when she stepped inside. Snapping on the light she saw she was standing on an envelope that had been slipped under the door. Ripping it open she tore out a single sheet of paper. The lettering was crude, handwritten block capitals: 'KEEP OUT OF WHAT YOU DON'T UNDERSTAND, WHITE BITCH.'

6

She slid the envelope across the table to Kent. 'This was waiting for me when I got back to my room last night.'

Kent scanned it, his brow creased. 'Why didn't you come to me?'

'I don't know. It didn't seem sinister at the time, but then . . .'

Too proud to admit it unnerved her, she had spent an uncomfortable night, tangled in the sheets, alternately sweating then shivering, flinging off the covers then scraping them back, and thumping the pillows, trying to get comfortable. Her dreams jolted her awake and each time she plunged back into skittish unconsciousness. When she woke properly at 7am she was exhausted, and her head banged with more than the beers she'd drunk the night before. The envelope was the first thing to meet her gaze when she crawled out of bed, and the sight gave her a jolt.

Now she and Kent were breakfasting in the Miners' Diner in Bilsom's Grudge, steadily chewing through bacon, sausage, eggs, beans and toast, washed down with gallons of tea sloshed into thick mugs. Esther was ravenous. They weren't the diner's only customers. A stream of men in overalls and metal-toed boots came in and ordered sausage and egg rolls to take away at the counter, or dwarfed the wobbly plastic-topped tables and chomped through heaped platefuls.

Esther and Kent sat at the back of the diner, out of earshot. She didn't want anyone to know she was unnerved by the poison pen letter.

'Who do you think sent it?' asked Kent, reading the letter again.

'The awful thing is it could be anyone.' She glanced at a man at the counter wearing a shirt bearing the Caroline Mine logo. 'Someone working at the mine, someone in Bilsom's Grudge worried about the future. Even someone from Tjulpan. We've hardly had a warm welcome here.'

'But this is nasty. You should go to the police, Esther. A nutter sent this.'

She shook her head, instantly regretting it. It felt as though the Caroline Mine had started blasting for gold inside her skull. 'It's probably just someone trying it on, nothing serious.'

He was unconvinced, she could tell, but he covered her hand with his and gave it a squeeze, and dropped the subject. She was grateful he trusted her to deal with it herself.

She told him about her conversation with Doreen the night before, choosing her words and tone carefully, wary neither to allocate blame nor to offer patronising excuses. Her caution was unnecessary. On hearing Doreen's allegations, Kent instantly erupted in fury.

'When are these people going to get their shit together? No wonder nothing works properly if they're going to cover up atrocities like that, and then blame it all on "culture". No wonder your average Australian resents all the money that goes to Aboriginal people when bullshit like this goes on under their noses and they do nothing.'

A couple of people turned to stare as his voice carried across the diner. Esther shushed him and waited until he'd blown himself out, his anger receding into intermittent grumbles. 'You believe her, then?'

'Yeah, I do. I've heard similar things in other communities, too many times. It makes me sick. This is bullshit culture!' Kent thumped his fist on the table, clattering the crockery.

'What should I do? I promised Doreen I'd try to get her some help.'

'What *can* you do? You haven't seen anything and you've got no evidence, only what Doreen told you.'

'I thought I'd ask the lawyers at work for advice.'

'The Land Council can't do anything.'

'They might know who Doreen should contact. She might be able to report it anonymously, just to get it investigated.'

'Hell, Esther, these blackfellas make me angry sometimes.'

She squeezed his knee under the table. 'Thanks.'

'What for?'

'Just thanks.'

They left the Miners' Diner and walked up the main street of Bilsom's Grudge. It was a chill morning but the sky was lucid and the sun was already sharp. Esther snuggled into her fleece, aware that in a couple of hours she'd be glad to shed it. A few cars were parked nose-in to the pavement outside the mini-mart; early birds for cigarettes and milk. Esther pushed through the thick plastic strips in the shop doorway and bought large bottles of water and a packet of granita biscuits. Nibbling them would stave off the nausea of her hangover. At the checkout she bumped into Frank, grinning broadly. 'You look pleased with yourself.'

'Won $200 last night.'

'Excellent! Lunch is on you.'

They wandered back to the Grand Hotel. Doreen's car was still parked outside in the same position as the night before.

'She must have got lucky,' said Esther.

'The party was going strong when I left,' said Kent. 'Don't know how long it went on for.'

Frank's mobile rang. He turned away from them to answer it. 'No, mate, her car's still here. Yeah, dirty tomcat.' He snapped off the phone. 'That was Gavin, Doreen's son, wants to know if we've seen his mum. Boy, is she for it when she gets home. He sounds really pissed off – had to get his own breakfast.' Frank chuckled. 'Hope she turns up soon. She's supposed to be giving us a lift into Tjulpan.'

A bashed-up ute that would be white under the grot screeched up to the kerb, and Mark Wright jumped out. 'I'm glad I found you,' he said urgently. 'Something awful's happened.'

'What?' Esther saw with alarm that he was shaking.

'Esther, it's . . . I don't know how to tell you.'

'Mark, slow down and tell me what's happened.'

He visibly took a breath. 'I've just had a call from the mine site. They've found a body out there.'

'You're joking.' She caught his expression and turned cold. 'Who is it? Do you know?'

'Doreen.'

'Doreen?'

'The men who found her recognised her. I'm just heading out there.'

'I'll come with you,' said Esther, tugging open the passenger door.

'I don't think you ought. It won't be pleasant.'

Esther hopped into the cab and fastened her seatbelt. Mark climbed in beside her. His face was etched with fear.

'What did they tell you?' she asked, her voice shaky.

'Just that a couple of the men went to do a routine check of one of the drills and found a body there.'

'God, what a shock.'

'They rang me straight away.'

The ute left the main street and nosed down a side road and out into the scrub. The bitumen ended after a few yards and they bumped over corrugations. Esther grabbed the strap hanging above the door.

'Sorry about the state of this,' said Mark, looking grim. 'It was the only vehicle free when I got the phone call.'

'Does it belong to the mine?' she asked, glad to be distracted. Her stomach contracted when she thought of Doreen. 'What's all this for?' She pointed. There was a huge spotlight fastened to the tray and spotlights hung all along the bull bar. A winch was riveted to the front. The cab was littered with polystyrene cups and food wrappers.

'The blokes use it to go roo shooting after dark. One stands in the tray and works the spotlight while another drives and the third leans out of the window with the rifle. I've seen them hurtling through the scrub: you don't want to get in the way, that's for sure. They'll go down the pit one day.'

'Do they get many roos?'

'Some. They sell the tails to the store in Tjulpan. The rest goes for pet food.' He paused. 'There's not much for the men to do outside work.'

A chill prickled the back of her neck. 'What are you getting at?'

He coughed nervously. 'I'm thinking about the lives they lead out here. Hard working, hard drinking, not much to do. These aren't sophisticated men. A lot of them are only out here because they can't hack it in normal life. I can imagine one of them getting off with Doreen and things getting out of hand and turning ugly.'

'Is that what you think's happened?'

'I'm fearing the worst, I guess.'

There was a pause, then Esther asked, 'How well do you know Doreen?'

'I've met her in Tjulpan a few times, and seen her in the pub – like I told you last night.'

'What did you make of her?'

He hesitated. 'I don't like to speak ill of the dead and all that . . .'

'If it *is* her.'

'Right. I thought she was a good laugh but she rubbed people up.'

'Like who?'

'I've seen her and Tommy Possum fighting. They had a blue yesterday when I was in Tjulpan.'

Esther sighed, her muscles tightening as they drove further into the bush. Mt Parker, shaded purple in the early light, loomed ahead on the horizon. She gripped the corner of her seat as they rattled down a track past a huge mining vehicle, its tyres taller than the ute. Two men stood near a vehicle at the end of the track. Beyond them was scaffolding constructed round a drill rig.

One of the men approached Mark's window. 'She's over here, mate.' He nodded at Esther. 'You should stay in the car, love.'

'Where is she? I knew her.'

'Have it your own way.'

Esther clambered out and followed the men to the drill rig. As she rounded the scaffolding the men pointed. Doreen hung from the drill rig. A thick rope wound round her neck. Her tongue protruded, swollen and purplish black. Her eyes were open and bulging. Flies crawled over her eyeballs. Her legs dangled loosely beneath the bright blouse, which fluttered in the breeze like an obscene flag.

'Oh, Doreen, no,' Esther whispered, appalled at the thought of Doreen dead and alone all night in this eerie place. It might have been days before she was found. As she watched, the bulky body rocked in the breeze, pirouetting on the end of the rope. The rig groaned at the movement, the metal yawning and echoing across the scrub.

A thought nagged at the back of her mind, tantalisingly out of reach. Suddenly she washed cold. The scene was all wrong.

'I'll call the police,' said Mark.

'And everyone be careful what you touch and where you tread,' ordered Esther, aghast at the damage their footprints and tyre tracks had already caused. 'You don't want to destroy any more evidence.'

'What d'you mean?' asked one of the men. 'This is obviously suicide. She's hung herself.'

Esther rounded on him. 'Then how did she get here? Her car's still at the pub.'

'Guess she walked.'

'And how did she get up there?' She pointed to the scaffolding.

'There are irons up the outside of the rig,' said Mark. 'And there's a ladder up the scaffolding. She must've climbed up and jumped off.'

'Except Doreen was terrified of heights. She'd never be able to climb up there.'

'What are you saying?'

'Get the police immediately, Mark.' Esther's words trembled. 'She was murdered.'

Two hours later Esther shifted in an uncomfortable plastic chair in a dingy corridor at Bilsom's Grudge police station. Though the shock had started to recede, still her fingers trembled. She clasped her hands between her knees, trying to quell the shaking, and stared at a notice-board cluttered with curling police posters and leaflets.

A door opened at the far end of the corridor and a heavy-set cop came out, his low-slung heavily laden belt making him waddle. He scowled at Esther and beckoned for her to follow him into the interview room.

'I'm Sergeant Baldwin. We met at the scene,' growled the cop, pointing at a metal chair to indicate she should sit down, 'and I need you like I need a hole in the head.'

Esther scraped the chair back and sat down. Sergeant Baldwin faced her across the metal table. It was screwed to the floor, its surface scratched and dented. In the distance she could hear a man's voice shouting, the words indistinct.

Sergeant Baldwin rubbed his thumbs hard into his eye sockets. 'So, Miss King.'

'Doctor.'

'Eh?'

'Dr King. Not miss.'

He groaned. '*Dr* King. Tell me again what you said when we were at the scene.'

'I believe that Doreen was murdered.'

'And you have some evidence for this, do you?'

'I have some common sense.' She watched him bristle. 'Doreen was a large woman. There's no way she could climb up onto that rig.'

'Big people can be agile, y'know.' He squared his shoulders, typical fat country cop with an attitude to match. He yanked a biro out of his shirt pocket and sketched a hangman on a sheet of paper on the desk. His index and middle fingers were stained orange. Holding the pen between them, he champed away at the mangled end of the pen.

'Nicotine patches not working?' she commented, trying to be sympathetic, to make some connection with this awkward man, and he glared. 'Listen, sergeant, Doreen was terrified of heights. Even if she'd wanted to kill herself, which I refuse to believe, then she wouldn't choose that way.' The image of the body swinging from the rig intruded. Tears prickled behind her eyes and she fought to control herself. 'She was bright and happy when I saw her in the pub last night. She had some things on her mind, but nothing to make her . . . commit suicide.'

'What things?'

Esther realised her blunder. She'd have to tell him; there was no way out. 'Doreen told me that she believed there was child abuse in the Tjulpan community, and she wanted my help to try and stop it.'

Sergeant Baldwin threw his pen onto the table with a clatter. 'Who's she accusing?'

'Tommy Possum.'

'Oh, great. This just gets better.' He ground the heels of his palms into his eyes. When he looked up, there were strings of mucus linking his eyelashes. 'You want me to go and arrest him, a senior Aboriginal elder; a bloke of what? Seventy if he's a day?'

'No.'

'Good, because that's exactly what I'm not going to do.' He looked down at the sheet of paper, evidently realised what he'd doodled and scrubbed it out. 'What I'm going to do is take a statement from you, about when you met Doreen last night and exactly what she said. And then you're going to go away back to the city and let me do my job.'

'I just think you should know there's a lot of nasty things going on out there, and Doreen hinted she knew something.'

'And maybe she didn't know anything. Perhaps she was just trying to make herself look better. She never brought any of these allegations to me.' Baldwin paused, then adopted a conciliatory tone. 'It's a suspicious death, that's all anyone can say right now. I've got the big guns flying in from Perth. Yous can all wave at them as you fly past them on your way out. And the coroner's getting excited.'

His tone rankled more than the words themselves. Esther tried to see it from his point of view: his patch being overrun by smart city cops creating work and fuss; but all the time she heard Doreen's voice, confidential in her ear. *You gotta help the community, Esther.*

Sergeant Baldwin licked this thumb and flicked through the papers to extract a clean sheet. 'Now, I want the facts from you. No allegations, no hearsay. Think you can manage that?'

Esther nodded. The prick wasn't interested in Doreen at all; he just wanted her out of the way. She decided to keep quiet about the poison pen letter.

7

Rich was lying full length on the settee, the TV remote balanced on his stomach, when Esther arrived home, exhausted, that evening. His long bony feet were bare, jutting over the armrest. He was watching the 7.30 Report, and didn't stir when she came in.

'Hello,' he called, his eyes not even flickering from the screen. 'Good trip?'

'No.' It was impossible to begin to describe her day. Her mind rebelled at the thought of trying to explain all that had happened when he couldn't even be bothered to look up when she came home.

'Air sick?'

'No. I'm going in the shower.'

'Shall we get takeaway tonight?'

'If you like. Make it Thai.'

'I'll ring up when you're out of the shower. Esther!'

'Yes?'

'Is the menu on the fridge?'

Drooping with exhaustion, she lugged her bag into the bedroom and hurled the previous day's stinky clothes in the direction of the laundry basket. She stripped and padded into the bathroom. Only a couple of days in the bush and already her body and piss smelt wrong. Her urine was too thick, too yellow.

Esther yanked up the thermostat on the shower until it was very hot, enjoying the sensation of her skin prickling under the jet. Her skin was lumpy under her fingers, mosquito bites plumping in the hot water. As usual she hadn't realised she'd been bitten. Bites always took forever to fade, and the weeks of scratching inevitably left scars on her arms and legs. She gritted her teeth, fighting the urge to claw at the bites.

When the hot water was finished she muffled herself in a robe and padded through to the kitchen in search of ice. Rich heard her rummaging in the freezer compartment.

'Been bitten again?' he asked.

'Five big sods. There's even one behind my ear. It itches like mad.'

'Let me see.'

She scooped up a bowlful of ice cubes and went back to the bathroom, Rich following. She perched on the toilet seat and pressed ice to each bite in turn.

'Where are they?' He knelt in front of her, took an ice cube and rubbed it over a bite on her ankle. She shivered as the water pooled down to her instep.

'That easing it?' he asked, coaxing the bite with the ice cube.

'Yes, thanks.'

'So how was your trip?'

She looked at his bent head. 'Awful.'

'Usual awful or extra special awful?'

'Depends how you feel about finding the murdered body of one of your clients.'

'What?'

His shock gave her a stab of satisfaction, chased immediately by remorse. Let him think her work indulgent now. She continued her horror story. 'And being told in grotesque detail about systematic child abuse infecting a whole community.'

Rich collapsed back on his heels. 'Hell, Esther, what happened?'

Her account was flat and unemotional, just the bare facts of discovering Doreen's body and the police interview, as though she were a bystander reporting on her own life.

'We stood looking at her body hanging there until the police arrived and took photos and cut her down. And do you know the worst bit?'

He shook his head wordlessly, too stunned to speak.

'It was the sound her body made, hanging there. It moved, you see, very gently, but the drill rig moaned with it.'

'Oh, Esther.' He covered her hand with his. She flirted with the idea of flinging herself into his arms, letting him comfort her, but instead pulled away. He wouldn't understand.

'You didn't have to wait there with her.'

'I did. The others were convinced it was suicide and were trampling all over the site.'

'Maybe it was.'

'Listen, Rich, she was a large woman. Even if she wasn't afraid of heights she'd have had difficulty climbing up that rig. And how did she get there? It was stuck out in the middle of nowhere – she couldn't have walked there.'

Rich snorted. 'Obviously murder, then.' He caught the look on her face and said, more gently, 'But who would murder her?'

'She told me about some things going on in Tjulpan. Awful things. I can understand someone wanting to shut her up. If it was me she was accusing I'd kill her.' An image of Tommy Possum insinuated itself into Esther's mind and she shivered. The old man had given her the creeps even before she had heard Doreen's child abuse allegations. But could he have murdered her? And now she knew what was going on in Tjulpan, was she in danger?

'You're cold,' said Rich. 'Get dressed and I'll ring up for some food.'

'I was hoping you'd cooked.' With a faint laugh, she added, 'I've been fantasising all the way home about that wonderful curry you make with apricots in it.' He'd made it for her the first time he'd cooked dinner for her. It was his special dinner for her, hot and comforting and replete with memories. She ached for the ways things had been. If only they could talk, really talk, for once, maybe it could all be put right.

He took her comment as a reprimand. 'I didn't know when you'd be back. You didn't even say which day to expect you.'

'Give it a rest, Rich.' The distance widened between them. No point trying to be conciliatory now, if he was in that mood. Even in the middle of this horrific news he managed to turn the situation round to complain about how she had let him down.

'Are you home for a while now?'

'I've got to be in Geraldton the day after tomorrow, then back to Tjulpan.'

'Oh, Esther!'

The whine irritated her. 'It's my job, Rich. You go away with your job too. You don't expect me to sit at home all day while you go on tour, do you?'

The hurt look that puckered his face made her relent a little. 'So, how have you been over the past couple of days? Your text messages said something about rehearsals.'

He trailed after her into the bedroom and flopped on the bed, watching her pull on cosy trousers and a jersey. She felt chilled to the core. 'We've been rehearsing with the school choirs. Little buggers were smoking dope in the breaks. Total nightmare. They just won't watch the conductor. Probably can't see him. The whole orchestra's fed up with them.'

'When's the concert?'

'Tomorrow evening. Are you coming?'

'I expect so. I normally do.'

'Soon as this school débâcle is over we can get on and do some *proper* music. No more bloody Rossini overtures. I wouldn't mind so much if we played the whole opera. The conductor keeps calling it "The Thieving Magpie". I'm going to refuse to play until he says "thievish".'

Esther crawled with impatience. Rich's lower lip pouted when he grumbled and she yearned to poke it; to show him how childish he was being. It was all a bit much. Rich loved music, adored being a classical cellist and had fought hard to pursue his dream, but it didn't stop him from moaning with gusto now he'd got it. He griped about the choir a little longer, then sat up on the bed.

'Esther! Are you listening?'

'Yes,' she lied. 'Let me know when dinner's ready.'

Grabbing a beer from the fridge door, she went out into the dark garden to a seat set into the far wall. The twenty-eights had been stripping the foliage from the bushes again, she noted. Annoying, but it was still exotic enough for her to see parrots in her own back garden that she didn't really mind. Surrounded by lavenders and overarched by branches of frangipani and jacaranda, she forgot she was in the middle of

Perth. The bustle and the traffic were muffled. The city receded. This was her refuge, a place to gather herself before taking on the world again; a second of peace in the turmoil.

She closed her eyes and breathed deeply, focusing on her breathing and relaxing each muscle in turn from her toes to the top of her head. Part way through the ritual she realised her face was screwed up. Taking another breath, she smoothed her face with her fingertips. Her mind emptied of the horrors of the past two days. It was just her and the steady rise and fall of her chest.

A weight thumped onto the seat beside her. 'Esther? I've got to tell you something.' Rich's aquiline features glowed pale in the dark garden.

'What is it?' she sighed, checking her watch. Three minutes.

'Esther.' The furrow between his brows deepened.

'Rich? You're scaring me.'

'You know I love you.'

'What is it?' Esther's voice squeaked with impatience.

He gathered her hands in his and circled her knuckles with his thumbs. Staring at their entwined hands, he said, 'I've had an affair.'

Her heart thumped. 'What?'

He lifted his head and stared into her eyes. 'I've cheated on you. I'm so sorry.'

'Who?' Her voice croaked.

'A woman in the orchestra.'

'*Who?*'

'Philippa. She plays the viola.'

'How long?'

'Just one night. We went for a drink and got talking and it just happened.'

'You're saying you were drunk?' She spat the words at him. Even Rich couldn't be asinine enough to offer the oldest, most pathetic excuse.

'No. I knew what I was doing and I wanted it.'

The blood thrummed in her ears. 'Are you going to see her again?'

'No.' He gave a short, mirthless laugh, between a sob and a bark. 'I don't even fancy her much.'

'Then why?'

'Because for once I wanted something that was only about me instead of about you.'

She recoiled as though he'd slapped her. He continued more quietly, 'You weren't here. Again.'

'I've been gone for two days! You don't just jump into bed with someone, anyone, because I'm away for two days!'

Rich swallowed. 'It happened a while ago.'

It took a few seconds for the significance of this to hit her. 'When?'

'A couple of months back.'

'Two months? You've kept quiet all this time?' She flicked through the past two months, searching for clues, changes in his behaviour, and found nothing. The accomplished deception appalled her. What else had happened that she was ignorant of? 'Why are you telling me now?'

Rich looked away and she caught the flush creeping up his neck. 'You said you're coming to the concert tomorrow night. She'll be there and I don't know if she'll say something.'

'When would you have deigned to tell me if there wasn't a chance I'd bump into her?'

'Probably never.'

Hurt and fury seethed inside her. 'How could you, Rich?'

'Come on, Esther, things have been awful between us for ages. I've even wondered if you've been having an affair.'

Her heart knocked. 'What makes you say that?'

'You won't talk to me! Philippa just listened and understood and was interested in *me*!'

'Good for her! And *you're* so interested in *me* you drop this bombshell minutes after I tell you someone was murdered today. Just to save your own face. Thanks, Rich!'

'Esther, I . . .'

'There's no excuse. Now piss off!'

He slunk away with a hurt sigh. Esther thumped the seat in frustration, tears running unchecked down her cheeks. He'd desecrated her refuge, tainted it with the memory of his words. His guilty expression haunted it. She'd never forget him sitting there, squirming as he forced out the words. This was no longer her sanctuary.

Esther stared up the garden to the lighted house and saw Rich's shadow loping to and fro. A thin stream of misery trickled through her veins, poisoning her. She heard the engine of the takeaway delivery van, the doorbell loud in the still night. Her legs cramped and her head pounded but she remained outside. The lights went off in the houses along the street, and eventually the lights went off in her own house. Moths bashed their wings against a garden lamp in a neighbouring garden. She watched them for a long time, her body cold and numb, and only crept back inside when a lone mosquito droned past her ear.

8

The woman on the special collections desk in the Battye Library in Perth recognised her.

'Hello, Dr King,' she called. 'What are you investigating today?'

Esther handed over a sheaf of request slips.

'Hm. Mt Parker and Bilsom's Grudge. You want these for the 9.30 collection?'

Esther gave a rueful smile.

'Really you should have handed these in last night for the first morning collection,' the woman chided her.

'I know, but I was in Bilsom's Grudge yesterday.'

'Tell you what, as it's you and we're not busy I'll put them through for you. They'll be on the shelves at 9.30.'

'Thank you.'

After the past few days in bush clothing, today Esther had selected a cream linen dress and brown leather sandals. In an effort to lift her spirits she'd brushed on pale eyeshadow to bring out the gold flecks in her hazel eyes, coated her lashes with brown mascara and slicked on pink lipstick. She felt smart, competent and utterly wretched.

She perched at a desk nearby and reviewed her notes, scribbled on the train into work that morning.

Query: massacre at Mt Parker Station 1880/1890s? When, why and where did it happen? Any eye witness reports? Check for refs to Ruby. Check for links to contemporary Tjulpan people. Are they on the native title claim?

Query: early history Bilsom's Grudge. When/ how was it named? Named after the massacre?

Query: Mt Parker Dreaming story. Any early references to the story and to Mt Parker's status as a sacred site? Check sacred sites register.

Just before 9.30 the woman gave her a cheery wave and Esther collected two box files from the shelves behind the collections desk. The first held facsimile clippings from old newspapers and a handful of grainy photos. The second contained only a cloth-bound volume published in 1920, which purported to give 'A Fictional Account Based on the True Story of the Early Settlers at Mt Parker Station, and of the Ghastly Murders Committed There'.

'I'll start with the ghastly murders,' thought Esther, grimly, flipping the book open and leafing impatiently through it. Purple prose described the arrival of the Bilsom family at Mt Parker Station and their lives there, and she groaned at the romanticised portrayal of the family's early years at the station as times of sunshine and mild breezes, gambolling playtimes in daisy-filled paddocks, and sing-songs and storytelling round the fire at night. There was nothing of the brutal landscape, searing heat, basic accommodation and claustrophobic isolation that Esther imagined characterised real life on a nineteenth-century sheep station. Any Aboriginal workers on the station were faceless and nameless, the author insisting on referring to Aboriginal women by the offensive term 'gins', which made her wince each time her eye caught it.

Her interest quickened when it came to the murder of Hetty and Caroline Bilsom, and the ensuing massacre of the Aboriginal people assumed to have carried out the act. It was the first Esther had heard about the murder of the Bilsom family and she was hopeful of piecing together the early history of Mt Parker Station. But again the book disappointed her; there were few facts to be gleaned, only a blood-drenched scene worthy of a penny dreadful. Of the massacre itself the author lowered her eyelids and primly commented that 'such a heinous crime deserved a wrathful vengeance, and Mr Bilsom gave full vent to his grief and fury in a terrible visitation upon those who had slain his wife and daughter'.

However, the book redeemed itself with a less florid postscript, where the author set out the facts on which the novel was based. Taking it all with a generous dollop of scepticism, Esther nevertheless jotted a few notes to confirm later through more reliable sources. The Bilsom family, consisting of Charles, his wife Hetty and their daughter Caroline (known as Caro), took the lease on Mt Parker Station in 1885 and lived in very basic conditions until a rudimentary homestead was constructed. The station was stocked with sheep and enjoyed a couple of good years until wool prices plummeted in 1890, then remaining depressed for a decade. Throughout the period the Bilsoms lived there they and settlers on neighbouring stations were victimised by Aboriginal groups spearing livestock. In August 1891 Hetty and Caroline were alone in the homestead when an Aboriginal group broke in, raped and murdered them. When Bilsom returned and found their bodies he hunted down the culprits and shot them.

Esther rubbed her eyes. They felt gritty and dry. She hadn't slept for the past two nights. Two nights ago her mind had squirmed uneasily over the poison pen letter, and last night she had slipped into bed, knowing Rich was wide awake; they had both feigned sleep and meticulously avoided touching each other. That morning they had battered each other with silence.

Now a headache throbbed across her forehead and her stomach was queasy. She looked out of the window across the art gallery and beyond to where the blue skyscrapers sparkled in the Perth CBD. It was difficult to imagine the early city, constructed on fertile bush land and encircled by frontier territory. The Bilsoms were brave to leave the fledgling city and strike out on their own, pursuing a dream that turned into a nightmare.

She gazed out at the city. Rich was out there somewhere, his arms wrapped round his cello, encompassing it with his tall, slender limbs as though embracing a lover. He'd held her like that, once. She couldn't remember the point when they'd slid away from each other.

Esther replaced the book and spread the clippings and photographs from the other box file on the desk. Most of the photos were taken in the 1930s, too late to be of interest to her present investigation, but she made a note to get copies and see if any of the Aboriginal workers in the photos could be identified, in case it assisted the Tjulpan native title claim. The Aboriginal people stood in stiff groups, frowning into the lens, their arms and hands awkward. The men wore wide-brimmed floppy hats that had once been respectable but that months of mustering stock had turned lumpy. The women's pleated skirts bulged with the ghosts of many pregnancies. A toddler balanced on one woman's hip; another clutched a man's hand. Were they the grandparents of contemporary Tjulpan families? None of them resembled anyone she knew, but who really shares a likeness with their grandparents? And whose adult physiognomy is truly discernible in childhood photos?

Doing the maths, Esther calculated some of the adults in the pictures would have been children at the time of the massacre. Maybe the younger ones had heard about it from their parents, the story whispered through the generations, shameful but unable to be relinquished – keeping alive the memories of those who died, because they would only be truly dead when no one remembered they had ever existed. So why were some people in Tjulpan anxious to deny the massacre had happened?

Esther tapped her pen on her notebook and earned herself an irritated tut from a woman sitting opposite. She scowled back, half-hoping the woman would comment and give her licence to start a fight and release some of the tension pounding in her head. She dragged her attention back to the box files and worked her way through the newspaper clippings.

Outback Inquest Held

An inquest was held on Monday at Mt Parker sheep station into the deaths of Mrs Henrietta Bilsom and her 15 year old daughter, Caroline. The women were violated and murdered at Mt Parker Station some time between 27th and 29th August this year. Mrs Bilsom was expecting her third child.

Mr Charles Bilsom, the deceased's husband, bravely testified to how he and a prospector, Mr Henry MacKendrick, returned to Mt Parker Station on 29th August and discovered the women's bodies. Mr Bilsom told the court how Mt Parker Station and neighbouring properties had suffered repeated attacks from a gang of wild Aborigines for several years, and that attacks on livestock had been particularly troublesome and vicious in the months before the murder.

The coroner, Mr Wilfred Huby, recorded a verdict of murder and cited the wild Aboriginal gang as the culprits.

No inquest into *their* deaths, the 'wild Aboriginal gang', according to this source. No men in starched shirts and collar studs sweating in the middle of nowhere to see that due process was carried out for them: Bilsom's testimony was all the court needed to form its conclusions. No word from Henry MacKendrick, interestingly, giving his version of events. How many did *he* shoot? Judging by his grandson, the odious Stuart MacKendrick, he probably led the revenge party.

Esther ground her fingers into her eyes until her vision flashed with white spots. The image of the terrified women disturbed her. Who was killed first, the pregnant mother or the teenage daughter? And what of the one forced to watch the other die? An appalling crime. And then there was the massacre, an unspeakably horrific retaliation. The brutality of it all sickened her.

She sighed and stretched, put the clipping aside and reached for the next. It was a general account of atrocities perpetrated by Aborigines in the bush, calling for the authorities to turn a blind eye for six months while the station owners solved the problem in their own way.

Pastoralists Assert They Can Solve The "Aboriginal Problem"

The impositions against hard-working station owners has reached intolerable limits. For the past decade, stations throughout the region have been prone to attacks by bands of wild Aborigines, disaffected by their land being put to productive use, and wholly unwilling to work.

A recent example of violence inflicted by Aborigines on white settlers occurred at Mt Parker Station, where a woman and her daughter were stabbed to death by a group of blacks when the woman's husband, the station boss, was working in the far reaches of the property. Taking vengeance into his own hands, Mr Bilsom tracked down and executed the murderers. In a police enquiry, it was rightly considered that he had merely carried out the sentence of the law that would have been passed on the heinous culprits by a court of law.

Pastoralists' supporters commended Mr Bilsom's actions, deploring the activities of certain Aborigines against opening up of the country. They called for such lawlessness to be stamped out, stating that if the law was placed in the hands of the station owners for a mere six months, the situation would be totally under control.

However, the London parliament is less supportive and has asked why this brutal treatment of Aborigines is allowed to continue with impunity. Evidently being so far removed from the problem, they do not comprehend the extent of the situation and the hazardous conditions under which pastoralists are trying to contribute to the prosperity of our British empire.

Esther took the clippings to the photocopier, disappointed that the morning had been wasted. She'd learned little about the massacre. If it was committed near Mt Parker these articles wouldn't help her to prove it. Although the articles gave essentially the same story, the Aboriginal victims were nameless, ageless and genderless. She needed identities of the victims and an accurate location before this could possibly help to halt the expansion of the Caroline Mine and the destruction of Mt Parker.

She dropped the box files back onto the metal shelves and on impulse, but with little hope, asked the librarian if there was any other material on Mt Parker Station.

'Let me have a look in my database. There may be something.' A few keystrokes. The librarian bit her bottom lip as though she were still getting used to using a computer and feared the screen would go blank if she pressed the wrong key. Esther struggled not to drum her fingers on the desk. 'What kind of thing is it you're looking for, Dr King?'

'I'm interested in life on the station in 1891, mostly, but a few years either side would be good too.'

'Now that's unusual.'

Esther strained to see round the monitor. 'What's that?'

'Normally they don't let us have them, but there they are.'

'What?' She dragged her face into a pleasant smile and fought the urge to shove the librarian from her seat and check the computer herself.

The librarian swivelled the screen round for her to see. 'We've got the station records and diaries. May be no use, but we've got them from 1885 to 1915. Any good?'

'Could be. How do I get to see them?'

'I can't get these up from the stacks until 2pm, I'm afraid.'

'That's OK. I'll have a break and come back then.'

'You'll have to collect these from the reading room up the stairs.' The librarian pointed to a metal staircase leading to a mezzanine floor. 'And you have to read them up there: they're restricted, you see.'

'Two o'clock, you said?'

'That's right. Up the stairs.'

Esther took the lift down to the ground floor and retrieved her handbag from her locker. There was an exhibition of Australian poetry in the entrance hall of the library. She spent a few minutes browsing but it made her restless, so she stood in line at the café for a latte and a toasted Mediterranean vegetable panini. Just as she was about to hand over her money she threw in a violet crumble too. What the hell, she needed chocolate right now.

The squashy settee next to the newspapers was free but she took her lunch to one of the tables outside by a square pond, partly to avoid Mediterranean vegetable spillage down her cream dress and partly so she could spread out her papers while she ate. It was chilly there, overshadowed by the library, but she was glad of the fresh air after the recycled climate inside. The edges of her papers flapped in the breeze and she pinned them down with salt and pepper shakers and a bowl of sugar sachets. She reread them while she ate. Mrs Bilsom was expecting their third child, she mused. What happened to the other child? And who was the group who were attacking the stock? Have they got descendants in Tjulpan now? How many were killed? Did their families work on the stations?

The coffee didn't help her headache a jot, so she returned to the counter and bought a coke, hoping the sugar rush would get her through the afternoon. It worked, but she knew it was a short-term fix. I'll eat a proper dinner and get an early night for once, she promised herself, cheering at the prospect. Then she remembered Rich's concert that evening. Damn him, and his self-pitying fling.

At two o'clock she took the lift back up to special collections and climbed up the metal staircase. The woman on the desk in the reading room was a sturdy Australian battleaxe with flecks of crimson on her teeth, like a vampire caught mid-suck.

'You can't use a pen. You must use a pencil,' she barked.

'I understand.'

'Do you have a pencil? I can probably find one for you if you don't.'

'That's fine, I have one.' Which I'll thrust up your nose if you don't shut up.

'These are yours.' She slid a pile of leather-bound notebooks across the desk to Esther. 'You can't take them out of here. If there's a fire leave them on the desk. And you must wear these at all times.' She plopped a grubby pair of white handling gloves on top of the books.

Esther scooped up the pile and took them to the furthest desk, away from the harridan's beady eye. She felt like a naughty schoolgirl. That is, until she opened the station diary and flipped through the pages. And there, in tight crabbed writing, as though paper itself was at a premium, she found what she'd been looking for.

'Gotcha,' she said aloud.

9

Mt Parker Station Diary

December 1885
The new house is nearly finished, thank God. The heat is terrible even now. Another February under canvas would be unbearable. Hetty stays cheerful, but I can see how the heat tires her. She's toiled all this time with never a complaint; I told her it was a good thing her father couldn't see what I've brought her to.

She simply smiled and slid her hand into mine, saying we'll invite her father to stay with us when the homestead has twelve rooms and a piano and servants in white aprons, as if such a thing were possible. And she set her jaw in that determined way she has, and I remembered the girl I carried off, standing up to her father and insisting on her own way. We could go back to Perth straight away if she hates it here, but she won't hear of it, and chastises me for not giving our new life a chance.

Caro runs round like a wild thing, untroubled by the sun. I'm teaching her to ride. She has her own pony and gallops round the paddocks like one born to the circus.

Christmas 1885
Our first Christmas in the new homestead. Hetty pretends to be unaffected, but I know how relieved she was to move from the tents. Our two rooms are basic indeed,

but cool and dim, a welcome respite from the heat and glare of the sun. The veranda runs round the whole house, so we can catch the breeze wherever it flows. Caro sleeps out there; she says she sleeps better in the night air. She is just outside our bedroom door, and quite safe.

She was pleased with her Christmas present, a doll Hetty sewed for her from calico, and has been dressing it in scraps and talking to it non-stop. She named it Jane, and already they are inseparable. Jane sleeps beside Caro at night, and rides in her pocket during the day. If only my girl could have real companions, but the children at Red Gum Station are schooled in Perth, like our son, Eddie.

February 1886
Rode out to where the Aborigines camp at the waterhole near Mt Parker. I gave them beef and jam, and asked them to work on the station. Poor creatures didn't know how to cut open the tins until I showed them. Later I took out blankets and tea, and set the men to building fences. They are very slow.

Hetty is offended by their nakedness, and is fashioning tunics and breeches to cover them. They will look a raggle-taggle bunch indeed once she's finished with them.

July 1886
Good rains this week, and there is water in the creek at last. We sank another water bore in the far paddock and put up the windmill. One of the old Aborigines showed me a water pan. It only fills after rain, he said. I have told the boys to muster the sheep there.

August 1886
The stations neighbouring us are suffering with wild Aborigines spearing stock. At Red Gum Station, the homestead was surrounded by Aborigines for two days before the family was able to escape. We need some police out here, to put a stop to this sort of outrage. We whites are totally outnumbered.

January 1887
Found the Aborigines performing the most savage rituals on each other. Told them that if they did that again I would whip them with chains and put them off my land. A boy died at a station nearby as the result of their barbarism. I will not have that brutality at Mt Parker.

March 1887

My darling Hetty has suffered another miscarriage. She is being typically brave about it, but I understand how she grieves. She has been ordered to rest, and lies alone in her room with the blinds pulled half-way, reading and watching Caro through the window. I fear Caro and Eddie will be our only children.

August 1887

The paddocks are carpeted with golden everlasting daisies. I picked some to take to Hetty, who is unwell. She was propped against the pillows, looking very small and pale, when I brought in the flowers, her book face down beside her on the covers.

I promised to take her back to Perth as soon as she was well enough to travel, but she shook her head at me and pursed up her lips. I thought she was worried how we would live back in the city, but Munnings would have me back in a trice, and I could travel round selling seeds and farm machinery as I did when we first met. I think that's the main reason her father dislikes me: I'm not good enough for his daughter, being a mere hawker, not Perth gentility like Hetty's family.

Hetty laughed when I mentioned Munnings, and laced her fingers in mine. She reminded me of all the foolish dreams I had as a young man, of founding a station and living on the land. It's my pride and foolishness that have got us where we are now.

She looked so wan against the pillow that I told her a story to raise her spirits. Old Jimmy the yard boy told me the Aborigines call this place Tjoolpan. It means everlastings, Hetty's favourite flowers. She seemed so pleased with this that I didn't add that Maudie overheard my exchange with Jimmy, and sidled over to disagree, saying it means 'place of blood' or some such nonsense. She's a sly creature, and I distrust her intensely.

September 1887

Caught Maudie stealing tins of beef from the ration store. Whipped her over a sack of flour until she wet herself. That should stop her thieving, and be a warning to the rest of them.

November 1887

My dearest Hetty is confined to her room, very ill with a fever. Caro sits beside the bed reading to her. She is showing great maturity for a girl of eleven, though her doll, Jane, grimy beyond belief, keeps vigil with her. Seeing Hetty so ill fills me with despair: the nearest doctor is hours away. Last night I prayed for her to be well again, the first prayer I've uttered since I was a boy.

November 1887

My prayer was heard and answered. Thank God Hetty is on the mend, sitting up in bed and able to drink some beef tea. Caro and Jane continue to nurse her.

January 1888

More wild natives have come to work on the station. I rode out to them at the waterhole near Mt Parker and gave them stores. Amazing that the waterhole is still full after this long drought. I brought the Aborigines in to the homestead. They live in their own camps and keep away from the house. The boys are good horsemen, once they have lost their fear; but the gins are lazy, and don't wash the linen properly.

February 1888

I am thirty-five today. Half-way through my life's allotment. I own a large station, and 5000 sheep. I have a beautiful wife, a pretty daughter, and a scholarly son. My life is blessed indeed.

April 1888

Hetty has brought another of her waifs and strays from the native camp into the house. The girl has some unpronounceable native name, but we call her Ruby. She is about the same age as Caro. Hetty is training her to be a house girl. She started by giving the girl a good scrub. Underneath all that grime and matted hair emerged a pretty girl, for a native. Hetty has dressed her in some of Caro's old frocks, and is teaching the girl to speak English. She seems shy, which is good. I've had too much insolence from disagreeable creatures like Maudie.

June 1888

I found Hetty with the orphan Ruby at her elbow, teaching the girl her letters by writing in the sand with a stick. I laughed at how the girl's lip stuck out with the effort of concentrating. Hetty immediately chided me for laughing, because the girl is learning fast and already speaks very good English, much better than some of the others. At her earnest expression I asked if she would be sending the girl to the university, too, incurring her wrath, which she demonstrated with a soft pout. This is no place for such a gentle creature.

September 1888

Hetty and I are once again anticipating a happy event. I wish she would go to her father in Perth, with Caro; they'd be safe there, and I'd be happier knowing that medical attention was close by, should Hetty need it when the baby arrives. I tried again to persuade her to go, thinking that she could visit Eddie while she was there, and that Caro could get a proper schooling. The girl runs wild out here. She's too old to be a tomboy, and needs taming.

Hetty set her mouth in a perfect imitation of her father and wouldn't listen to reason. She insists that Caro should be allowed to enjoy these years of freedom, before she's grown and has to settle down. I have to agree that life here has made Caro strong and healthy; if only my dear Hetty could also be well. This is no place for a woman in her fragile condition, and I worry almost constantly for her and the baby.

Hetty seems to think that because the Aboriginal women manage to give birth out here without any problems, she should be able to, too. But they're born to the hardships on the land; they're not fragile creatures like her.

Seeing I still intended her to go to Perth, Hetty accused me of wanting her out of the way. I spun to challenge her, and found as usual she was teasing me, so I kissed her rosebud mouth, and whispered she'd guessed my secret: I was sick of having my two beautiful and clever girls cluttering up the station and taking my mind from my work.

It was a moment before she realised the bluff, and she let out a squeal of delighted outrage that thrilled me. I dodged the cushions she pelted me with, and scarpered, chuckling.

October 1888

The wild Aborigines continue to kill the stock and terrorise the neighbourhood. I taught Hetty and Caro how to load and fire the rifle in case they should need it, God forbid. They mocked my fears, but I feel happier knowing they are able to protect themselves.

January 1889

Another child lost. Hetty is very ill, but will not hear of going to Perth where she can be nursed properly. I am sleepless with worry for her. She lies in her room weeping for much of the day. It is very hard for women, much more than men. It is eleven years since she carried a baby to full term and I am gloomy thinking we shall never have another child. I had hoped for another son but this now seems impossible.

February 1889

Hetty is in low spirits today. I caught her in the shade of the veranda looking towards Mt Parker, with tears rolling down her cheeks. She showed me a letter that had arrived earlier, brought with more supplies of flour and cloth and lice powder for the sheep. Eddie's writing looped across the page.

It's a year since she last saw him, and she misses the boy. Although we both know it's better he stays in Perth and gets his proper schooling, it's hard on a woman to be separated from her son. In her lowest moments, Hetty has confessed she wishes he knew less algebra and Shakespeare and was here with us.

She handed me the letter. It was a schoolboy's letter, not saying much, except a boy had been caned for putting frogs in the inkwells and boasting that he had filched a pint of custard from the larder.

I laughed. If he carries on like that, we'll get a letter asking for more clothes because he'll have outgrown the others.

Hetty gave me a tight smile, and silently folded the letter. I sent Ruby to fetch the mistress a cup of tea, and went to check the shearing sheds.

December 1889

The stations neighbouring Mt Parker have been badly affected by a group of blacks spearing stock. Over 100 sheep have been killed in a week, and left to rot in the paddocks. The Taylor family is terrified. They daren't leave the women and children alone even for an hour for fear of what the Aborigines might do. I say we should take the law into our own hands to protect ourselves.

I tried to persuade Hetty to take Caro to Perth until the blacks settle down. After much arguing, she finally relented and they left today. The homestead is very quiet without their chatter.

A very queer thing happened this evening as I sat alone on the veranda enjoying a smoke and the cool evening breeze from the mountains. Mt Parker loomed ahead, a denser dark shape against the night, poking up into the Milky Way. Beyond the cookhouse and the shearing shed, pricks of light came from the native camp, and the eerie sound of their singing drifted across to the homestead.

Ruby slunk out of the door and sat down beside me at my feet. She leaned her head against my knee and stroked my hand. I assumed this was just a girlish *whim of hers until she tried to kiss me. I leaped to my feet and pushed her roughly away. She followed me, and draped her arms round my neck, and pressed her lips to mine. I took hold of her arms and unwound them from my neck, and told her sternly that she mustn't behave this way. She walked away, leaving me unsettled.*

March 1890
Hetty and Caro have returned from Perth. I was more relieved than I can say to see them back. They are full of stories of parties and concerts they attended in society. I suppose they have entertained our friends in Perth with stories of the adventurous life they lead here at Mt Parker Station. Hetty says little of her father's response to her tales; no doubt his disapprobation was manifest.

September 1890
Hetty, Caro and I rode up to Mt Parker today. Hetty was enchanted by the red rocks covered with golden everlastings, and picked handfuls of them to decorate the homestead. The waterhole was overflowing after the winter rains. Caro tore off her boots and stockings and hitched up her skirts, and paddled in the water. Suddenly a wild old native burst out from behind the spearwood bushes and jabbered at her in his language, waving his arms around and looking menacing. She was terrified, and ran back to Hetty and me in tears. I went back to the waterhole, but he had gone. Later, I told Ruby what had happened and asked her what he meant.

'Water not wash. Drink,' she said. I suppose the old Aborigine thought Caro was sullying the drinking water by paddling in it. I've warned her to be careful in future. I dread to think what would have happened to her if I had not been there to protect her.

April 1891
Hetty told me that she is pregnant again. She looks blooming: her cheeks are rosy and her appetite is good, though she is very tired. The baby is due in October. I have ordered her to rest, and make sure that Ruby and Caro take on the daily household tasks.

May 1891
There has been trouble from three young Aborigines. They worked as stockmen on the station until last week when they walked off with their families, taking stolen rations

with them. They returned this week and asked for rations, but when I insisted they work for it, they ran away. Later, I found a sheep had been taken and four others speared. One was still alive, but with such wounds I put a bullet through its skull.

June 1891

The three blacks continue to make trouble. I caught Ruby taking blankets to them. When I challenged her she said, 'They my brothers.' I told her to put the blankets back in the storehouse, but did not have the heart to punish her. Her brothers speared another three sheep for my pains.

July 1891

We have a visitor at Mt Parker Station. He is a young prospector called Henry MacKendrick, barely twenty years old from the fluff on his chin. I fancy Caro is already half in love with him. She flutters her eyes up at him, and plays the coquette when he speaks to her. Where does she learn these tricks? Even dear Hetty gets a fond look in her eye when she talks to him. The young adventurer reckons to find gold on Mt Parker Station. He has come out from Perth all this way to seek his fortune. The government is offering rewards to men who strike gold and register the find.

We sat on the veranda smoking last night and I asked him if he thought this country would make him rich. The arrogant young pup is convinced of it. He's not alone in his madness: hundreds of men are streaming out of the cities and heading inland in search of gold. At least MacKendrick has some sort of a plan in that wild head of his. He's struck a bargain with his father to spend a year seeking his fortune (wasting his time in idle adventure, I call it), then if he hasn't struck gold by then, he's given his word of honour to slink back to Perth and settle down getting a shiny backside as a clerk in a shipping firm, and put all this nonsense behind him.

He'll forget this scheme soon enough, I reckon, for all he's convinced he can sniff gold out. Humouring him, inspired by grog, I admit, I've made a pact with him: if he finds gold on my land, we'll register the find together and build the mine. He can run the mine, and I'll take my share of the profits. He liked my plan well enough, and declared he'd call the mine after Caro. Says she'll bring him luck. I wasn't happy with that remark, and remained silent. He and Caro are getting too moony eyed over each other, and she's too young for him, despite his fluffy chin.

August 1891

MacKendrick is certainly a determined fellow. They say nothing will shake the convictions of the mad. He has been out for a fortnight at a time to different quarters of the station, hunting for riches. He returns, dirty and empty handed, but never downhearted, has a good meal and a bath, entertains Hetty and Caro with his nonsense, and then goes back out again.

He's out in the far paddock at the moment. Apparently Ruby told him to look there. She sidled up to him and pressed a gold nugget into his hand, and pointed to the eastern paddock. He's prospected all the other paddocks, so he might as well waste his time out there. At least it keeps him away from Caro.

I shall ride out tomorrow and take him more supplies, and check on the fences while I'm out there. I don't want to be away from the homestead for too long: I'm still having problems with Ruby's brothers attacking the stock, and I dislike leaving Hetty in her condition. I'll bring her back a handful of her favourite everlastings to cheer her. She is large now, and I hold my breath that at last she may be safely delivered after all our disappointments. We have only two months to wait before she is delivered.

August 1891
Hetty and Caro are dead.

September 1891
MacKendrick has registered the find. After the past weeks of horror I am glad of his company. The Aboriginals have all left the station, and I need his help with running the stock. I have taken on a few out-of-work jackaroos peddling their labour from station to station, and will have to see how I get on.

December 1891
The drought is very bad. Many of the stock have died, and the remaining sheep are scrawny from lack of water. Mustering them to what little water we have left is more than I can manage on my own.

A few Aboriginals have returned to the station, and I have put them to work. Ruby is amongst them. She is very large with child. The Aborigines are a surly bunch, but I do not care as long as they work. They camp a good way from the homestead, and I am glad.

January 1892

Ruby has given birth to a boy. She calls him Dennis. He is fat and healthy, but is very pale and obviously a half-caste. I caught one of the old gins rubbing the child with burnt sandalwood nuts to make him look black. Ruby seems fond enough of the lad.

February 1892

The other Aborigines shun Ruby and her baby. They have turned against her. MacKendrick says it is because she has a piccaninny. Whatever the reason, they will not let Ruby camp with them, and she is in a sorry state. I hate the sight of her. Each day is a reminder of what her brothers did to my family.

March 1892

The Caroline Mine opened today, and crushed its first rock. MacKendrick grinned so much I thought his head would split. It was a bittersweet day for me, wishing my Hetty and Caro could share in this excitement.

November 1892

Today, I saw how cruel the Aborigines could be to their own kind. Ruby left her child with an old gin while she went to fetch water. The old woman neglected the boy and let him crawl into the fire. He is badly burned but will live. He will probably bear the scars for life.

March 1893

The Caroline Mine has been in operation for a year, and already MacKendrick and I are reaping the dividends. I have decided to leave Mt Parker Station and return to Perth. I am a partner in the mine, and will manage the mine's export operations from Fremantle. MacKendrick intends to stay here.

June 1893

Men continue to flock to this area, looking for gold. Crowds of them are prospecting on Red Gum Station and in the paddocks here. MacKendrick is smug, knowing them all to be barren except for where we're mining ourselves.

Already a shantytown has sprung up near the mine. There are three public houses and many rough shelters of canvas or corrugated iron. It is a harsh life for the men who come out here for work. The stampede of men searching for riches was almost as ferocious as the whirlwind of low women who followed them. They all have their eyes on the main chance. They ply their trade from within canvas shelters, and are seen brawling and drunk in the streets as often as the men. They stand in the doorways, swishing their dirty petticoats, and hurling abuse as I walk past. I avert my eyes; they make me shudder.

Building has begun on a hotel, and MacKendrick has commissioned a house for himself. I hear they are to name the town after me, or some such nonsense. I shall be glad to leave this place. It has brought me little joy.

10

Esther closed the station diary feeling dazed. It was so easy, the proof she needed just there, in front of her. She'd found Ruby, the woman Doreen claimed was the only survivor of the massacre at Mt Parker. The old news clippings she had read that morning reported that Bilsom assumed the murders were committed by the same Aborigines who were spearing the sheep: Ruby's brothers. So Doreen was right: Ruby witnessed Bilsom slaughtering her own family.

Esther's brain thrummed with questions. Who were they? How many were killed? And did they have descendants in contemporary Tjulpan? Any descendants would be entitled to be on the Tjulpan native title claim. Ruby's descendants too, presumably, should be on the claim, but Ruby wasn't mentioned in any genealogies nor on the claim documents. The first Esther had heard of her was two days before; it was as if Ruby had been erased, only existing as a palimpsest in Doreen's mind. Now Doreen was dead, Ruby was just a scribbled name in an old diary kept in a library basement.

Esther scanned the notes she'd made from the diaries. Ruby had a son, Dennis. What happened to them? Aching with curiosity and frustration, she put the diary aside and picked up the next volume. It was the station records: a ledger of people, stores and stock. She turned the thick pages and read the now familiar crabbed handwriting.

The records started in February 1885, when the Bilsoms arrived at Mt Parker Station, bringing with them a thousand head of sheep. Their early workforce consisted of jackeroos and journeymen labourers, who set to work hewing the homestead out of local stone, fencing the vast paddocks and sinking water bores. An excruciating first year. The records showed supplies given to these men: leather boots, a jacket, blankets, a set of clothes to last a year. Some wages too: just a few shillings, but what was there to squander it on except gambling with the other jackeroos?

Then in September 1885 came the first mention of the Aboriginal workers. According to the ledger, Bilsom 'found' them in the southern portion of the station, gave them food and new names; but they walked off the station two months later and never returned. The names were unfamiliar to Esther but she made a note of them. They could be ancestors relevant to the native title claim, but more likely they were another group simply passing through Tjulpan land as part of their normal nomadic progress.

In February 1886 Bilsom recorded in his diaries that he approached a group camping at the waterhole, gave them supplies and set them to work. He listed their names and ages in the station ledger:

Jimmy, approx 60
Queenie, his wife, approx 50
Maudie, approx 20
Tommy, approx 45
Mary, his wife, approx 45
Sambo, approx 16
Charlie, approx 25

Some of the names appeared on the claim description. Esther scribbled down the others, despairing that she would ever be able to marry these people to their contemporary descendants. The contemporary Tjulpan people had short family histories: many of them only knew their family trees back to their grandparents, and some only knew their parents' names; it was rare for them to know their heritage back to their great-grandparents. The stolen generation had seen to that, casting its poisonous tentacles through the generations, decades after the whole sordid process had been condemned and shut away.

The Tjulpan family trees Esther had meticulously collected and researched only took the Aboriginal history of the area back to the turn of the century at most, yet native title law demanded that claimants had to show they were descended from Aborigines living in the claim area at the time of settlement. In the case of Western Australia that meant 1829, even though no whites were in the Tjulpan area to record the Aborigines until 1880. It was so unfair, the odds so stacked against her and the claimants, that she chafed at the injustice of the whole business.

Heart sinking, Esther ploughed through the ledger. Tins of beef, tins of jam, packets of tea, flour, blankets, clothing doled out to Aboriginal workers, who were expected to supplement these supplies with food they hunted and collected themselves. No shillings to gamble by the mulga fire, and no shelter either. Aboriginal workers lived in humpies away from the homestead, segregated there after their work was completed. The stockmen camped out under the stars, month after month, while the beasts cropped the ground around them.

In January 1888 Ruby's arrival at Mt Parker Station was duly recorded, muddled in with a long list of Aboriginal names. A few months later the ledger stated that Ruby, aged approximately thirteen, was removed from the native camp to be trained as a housegirl and to live at the homestead. No reason was given for this, although the diary suggested that Hetty 'adopted' Aboriginal children she thought needed nurturing.

Esther copied the list of Aboriginal workers brought onto the station at the same time as Ruby. Alongside their names were approximate ages, and some also had job titles:

Billy	*approx 30*	*Stockman*
Elsie, his wife		*Housegirl*
Walkabout	*approx 45*	*Stockman*
Reggie (boy)		*Stockman*
Maggie	*approx 20*	*Laundress*
Charlie	*approx 40*	*Trapper*
Old Bob	*approx 60*	*Yardboy*
Young Bob (boy)		*Ringer*
Possum	*approx 30*	*Ringer*

Lala his wife, one child		*Laundress*
Tracker	*approx 35*	*Tracker*
Dingo	*approx 15*	*Fencer*
Judy	*approx 70*	*Housegirl*
Ruby (girl)		*Housegirl*
Napa	*approx 30*	*Stockman*
Mary his wife, two children		
Blackboy	*approx 25*	*Ringer*
Bunya	*approx 25*	*Ringer*
Payla his wife, one baby		

Turning the pages, Esther saw their names repeated through the years, as they were given food, clothing, blankets, medicine. She looked back at the diary where Bilsom recorded Ruby's brothers walking off the station, and anxiously turned to the station records of May 1891 to see if the event was marked there. It wasn't. She flipped back and forth between the pages, itching to tear off the white cotton gloves so she could handle the pages properly.

Listing all the Aboriginal people who joined the station in January 1888, she put a tick next to each name whenever it was recorded in the ledger. Deaths of Aboriginal workers were marked in the ledger by a small cross next to the name; but there emerged a number of Aboriginal people who had been given stores regularly since January 1888 who suddenly stopped appearing in the station records, with no explanation given for their disappearance. She checked again. The names were recorded first in January 1888: the 'wild' natives who came to work on the station, whom Bilsom described as good horsemen but poor laundresses. Three men, three women, a number of children, with children added over the following three years until April 1891, which was the last mention of them in the station record:

Napa
Mary his wife, children 2 boys, 1 baby
Possum
Lala his wife, children 1 boy, 2 girls
Bunya
Payla his wife, children 2 boys

Could these be Ruby's brothers, the men whom Bilsom assumed murdered his wife and daughter? The men, with their wives and children, that he massacred somewhere on Mt Parker Station? Three men, three women, seven children and a baby. Fourteen lives taken, and Ruby the only survivor.

Possum. Esther chewed the end of her pencil and stared at the entry. It wasn't impossible for Tommy to be related to Ruby and her brothers. Maybe Ruby had sisters or other brothers who had survived. Did Tommy know of any connection? Is that why he was being cagey? She didn't relish confronting him with what she'd found, and made a mental note to consult Frank about the best way to approach the matter.

Esther copied down all the names and returned the files to the harridan on the desk. She sat in the empty café with a pot of tea cooling at her elbow and reviewed her notes. So many threads and strands that might tie up to contemporary Tjulpan claimants, but equally might just fade out to nothing, lost forever in the foggy tangle of Aboriginal family trees after the stolen generation policy.

She jotted down her main lines of enquiry:

> *Ruby's descendants – who are they and where are they?*
> *Aboriginal names in the records – are they related to contemporary Tjulpan claimants?*
> *Ruby's siblings – are they related to Tommy Possum?*
> *Where did the massacre happen? Near the site of the proposed new mine?*

An image of Doreen's bloated face swinging from the drill rig insinuated itself into her mind and goose-pimples prickled up her arms. Doreen knew about the massacre and she knew about Tommy and the child abuse. What else did she know? Her last words to Esther had implied there was much more to be told about Tommy Possum. Was that what had got her killed?

Esther popped into the Land Council offices briefly to collect some papers. Her assistant, Gail, followed her into the poky room laughingly called her office, a sheaf of memos and phone messages in her hand.

'And Ron Kelly has rung another four times insisting he ought to be on the Tjulpan claim,' Gail concluded.

Esther snorted. 'Only because he thinks they're in for a big compo payout with the new gold-mine. Six months ago he insisted he was from the Pilbara, when he thought he'd get some pipeline money. Last year he swore blind he was a traditional owner of Watarrka National Park until I told him to take it up with the Central Land Council. According to him, his traditional country is bounded by the coastline of Australia.'

'Greedy blackfellas,' said Gail. 'I know I'm Aboriginal, but I don't believe in native title. It brings out the worst in people. You've just got to get on with life, I reckon.'

'I reckon you're right.' Esther sat at the desk and flicked through the pile of messages teetering on her keyboard. Gail flopped into the clients' chair beside the desk.

'It's all organised for you for tomorrow, Dr Esther.'

Esther smiled. The name was Gail's way of showing affection. 'Thanks. I don't know what I'd do without you.'

'Only problem is getting you home. You can either come home straight after lunch on Friday, or the next flight is on Saturday morning. I've booked you on the Friday afternoon flight. You don't want to spend your weekend running round after blackfellas when you could be at home with that nice husband of yours, specially as you're off again on Sunday.'

'I like running round after blackfellas. Anyway . . .' Esther caught sight of a photo on her desk: her and Rich not long after they met. She was on a PhD scholarship at the Australian National University; he was playing in a Canberra orchestra. Both exiles from the homeland, they'd met at a uni party. A mutual friend brought him 'to stop him being so bloody moody and homesick', she'd said, dumping him with Esther to cheer him up. Esther liked his uncompromising angular frame, too gaunt to be handsome. They'd spent the evening swapping gripes about being foreign in a country that seemed so much like home.

'And why do they call it Weetbix instead of Weet-a-bix?' Rich grumbled, but with a twinkle in his eye.

'Gladwrap caught me out,' Esther confided.

'Gladwrap? What's that?'

'Cling film.'

They'd gone home together after the party and had drunk beer out of proper glasses and talked until the morning.

The photo had been taken by one of her uni friends; Rich had few friends and most of them he made through work. She and Rich had adopted cheesy smiles for the camera, and he was giving her a piggyback; it was the early days, before he complained she was too heavy. Almost ten years ago. Happy then. When had that stopped? She couldn't pinpoint it, but suspected the decline started horribly soon after they married. It was a tense year, the year they married: gaining her PhD, marriage a few months later. She insisted she wasn't going to change her name twice, becoming and remaining Dr King. Rich didn't object at the time; maybe now he regretted her independence.

'Esther? What is it?' Gail said, concerned.

Esther rubbed her hands over her face. 'Oh, nothing.'

'You and Rich had another row?'

'Yeah.' She gave a rueful smile. 'Nothing new there, eh?'

'Everyone rows, Esther. You should hear me and my old fella. Just you make it up before you go to Geraldton tomorrow, huh?'

'Sure.'

'I'll get you a coffee.'

'No thanks, Gail, I've got to go out again. Is there a car free that I can borrow? I've got to go out to Guildford to see someone about the Tjulpan claim.'

'Yes there is, but you'll have a coffee first,' Gail insisted. 'You look wiped out and you're going to be busy the next few days.' At the door she turned. 'You've got to take care of yourself, Dr Esther. You work too hard.'

Esther waited until the door closed behind Gail, then picked up the phone and rang SkyWest airlines to change her flight back to Perth from Friday afternoon to Saturday morning.

When Esther parked on the verge outside the house in Guildford, all the files, notes and scraps of paper she had stashed on the passenger seat slithered onto the floor. She was still cursing and scrabbling under the seat when David Liddle opened the car door.

'I'm always doing that,' he said cheerfully. 'I've made a special box I thread the seatbelt through to put all my stuff in. Stops it all getting mixed up in the footwell. I'd got 200 photocopied pages of Daisy Bates's field notes that landed in a heap one day, none of it numbered and you know what her writing's like. Took me hours to put it back in order. Never again.'

'I'm surprised you don't have all of Daisy Bates's field notes memorised by now, David,' said Esther, only half-teasing.

'Almost, but I still rely on my filing system. Come on in.'

David Liddle's house was as untidy as he was. The room Esther was shown into held no furniture, only ranks of filing cabinets and a set of old ink-stained library card index drawers. A scungy carpet was covered with piles of papers held down with wooden artefacts and hunks of stone that looked suspiciously like pilfered petroglyphs.

In the middle of the chaos, beaming with pride, David Liddle sat cross-legged on the floor amidst a mosaic of papers. Esther tried to ignore his black toenails. She'd never seen David shod: even when he deigned to visit the Land Council offices in the heart of the Perth CBD he was barefoot, and his soles had grown a thick rind that curved up the sides of his feet. His hair was thin and greasy, longish, hooked back behind his ears. Smears and dust patterned the lenses of his glasses. His skin betrayed his lifestyle: staying up till the early hours poring over documents, fuelled only by instant coffee and snack food. Any meal that took longer than five minutes to nuke in the microwave was a waste of time in David's often-stated opinion.

And yet when it came to genealogies the man was a genius. He hungered to understand exactly how everyone fitted in in relation to everyone else, compiling a genealogy to encompass every Aboriginal person in Western Australia and many outside. He checked and double-checked names in station records, native welfare files and early anthropological field notebooks, piecing together identities and relationships with forensic precision. He was a godsend to Esther, who had neither the time nor the patience for this research. It was David's passion and it was how he made his living: squirrelling out facts and information from old documents all over Australia, and piecing it together to help prove or disprove Aboriginal connections to land through genealogy. Esther called him her 'library rat'. If David couldn't find it, it didn't exist.

She felt excited, presenting him with today's problem, and comforted to see the gleam in his eye, like an avid crossword solver recognising the genius behind a particularly fiendish clue. What was tedious, meticulous graft to her was a delight for him.

Esther briefly described what she'd learned about the massacre. She showed him her notes and photocopies and gave him a copy of the Tjulpan claim description. 'The claim is on the basis that contemporary Tjulpan people are the biological descendants of people who owned the area in 1829, when white men came into Western Australia. The descendants own the land today, just as their ancestors did, and that's what we want recognised in law. We've managed to find ancestors for all the contemporary Tjulpan people. We arrived at them after interviewing Tjulpan people and drawing up genealogies.'

'So you worked backwards from the contemporary group?'

'Yes. We've been able to confirm most of the ancestors from other sources.'

'I'm impressed: it's a tall order for that region. There weren't many anthropologists tramping round there in the early days recording Aboriginal culture.'

'The problem is, we could have missed some of the ancestors whose descendants should be included in the native title claim. Ruby isn't named as one of the ancestors and she isn't in any of the genealogies, and neither is her son Dennis. But I've found other names in the station records. Some are in the claim genealogies, but there are a whole load that aren't. They *might* be related to contemporary Tjulpan people and help us push back the ancestors a further generation.'

'And you want me to trace their descendants?'

'Yes, and find out whether they belonged in the Tjulpan area or were from somewhere else. I need to know that they were owners of the land, and not just from another Aboriginal group and passing through.'

'No problem.'

'But that's not my main priority. Actually I've got two problems. I've found some names who may be Ruby's brothers. One of them's called Possum.'

'And you think Tommy Possum might be a descendant from Ruby's family?'

'Yes. But if he is I don't understand why he's so reluctant to agree the massacre even happened, when it's clearly documented. And if Doreen knew, others must know about it too.'

'Would he have read the accounts?'

Esther shook her head. 'He's illiterate. Signed the claim documents with a cross.' She pointed to Tommy's wobbly mark at the bottom of the legal papers.

David nodded, flicking through the pages she'd given him and all too obviously aching to get started. 'I'll see if I can link up Ruby's siblings and find some descendants. I presume you also want some evidence that Tjulpan was Ruby's traditional country?'

'If there is any.' Esther smiled, grateful he understood the odds against finding documentary proof of Aboriginal ownership, yet also knowing it was critical to a successful native title claim. Frustration at the system gnawed at her again.

'And the other priority?'

'Can you trace what happened to Ruby and her son?'

'You think Tommy Possum may be directly descended from Ruby?'

'Could be. What do you think?'

'How old is he?'

'About seventy.'

'So Ruby would be his grandmother. I'll check it out. Ruby could have had lots of children. Dennis was her first child?'

'I think so. She was quite young, about seventeen or eighteen I think.'

'There's not much to go on, but at least we have a date of birth.' David scanned her notes. 'That's interesting.'

'What?' Esther perched on a tiny square of clear carpet and peered over his shoulder.

David jabbed at the pages with a chewed fingernail. 'Dennis was born in January 1892, so he was conceived in April 1891. Father a whitefella.' He looked up. 'Who was on the station then? Could his father be that prospector, what's his name, MacKendrick?'

Esther looked through her notes. 'No, he first turns up in July 1891.'

'One of the jackeroos probably.'

'Or Bilsom, the station boss.'

'Not unknown. Leave it with me. I'll see what I can turn up. If nothing else I've got some new names for my database.'

'There's one other thing,' said Esther.

'Go on.'

'I know you're not interested in whitefella family trees, but it seems Bilsom had a son, Eddie. He was at school in Perth at the time of the murder. I wondered what happened to him, that's all.'

David frowned. 'Hardly relevant to the claim, is it?'

'No, but I'm just curious to find out. Having your mother and sister murdered, then your dad committing that massacre. I'd just like to know what happened to him. And his descendants might know something about the massacre. They might be able to help us.'

'He'd have emigrated if he'd got any sense,' said David, drily. 'OK, I'll see what I can dig up. It'll be novel, at least, tracing a whitefella.'

'You never know, you might like it. You could find yourself advertising in the newspapers to do genealogies for rich whitefellas wanting to know about their convict roots.'

David shot her a sour look. 'When do you want this for?'

She hesitated. 'I know this is short notice, but I'm back in Tjulpan on Sunday evening and the community meeting is on Monday. I'd like some ammunition by then if possible. At least if you can turn up something about the massacre.'

He whistled. 'You don't ask much, do you?'

She shrugged.

'OK, better ring my mate Heinz.'

'Heinz?'

'Alphabet spaghetti.'

She was no wiser. 'If I've got four days max to get you this information I can't go to sleep. Need some of Heinz's letters to keep me awake.'

'I didn't hear that.'

He grinned at her.

'Usual fee rate?' she said.

'Tell you what, I'll halve my fee as you've brought me some new leads.'

'You don't charge enough as it is.' Esther waggled her finger at him. 'No charges for Heinz on your invoice!'

'As if I would.'

11

Rich's geriatric Mini was still on the driveway when Esther came home. She slunk past it into the house, padded to the kitchen and plugged in the kettle. She put on a punk CD, yanking the volume up full blast and howling along to it while she collected a tea-bag and mug. The music cut off dead.

'I don't know how you can listen to that racket,' said Rich. He was wearing a dinner suit; his shirt collar stuck up while he tied and retied his bowtie.

'"That racket" helps me relax. It's been a long day.'

'You and me both.'

Many of your clients get murdered this week? she thought, biting back the words. 'I thought you would have been gone by now.'

Esther had dawdled on the way home, reluctant to see him and face another argument. She was ashamed at how her heart sank to find him still there, fussing when she wanted calm, crowding her when she wanted space. She yearned to have the house to herself for an hour, to fill it with noise to blast away the day's stress.

'I was waiting for you,' said Rich. 'I just wanted to say, well, I'm sorry. That's all.'

'Not now, Rich, please.'

His mouth drooped into familiar sulky lines. 'We've got to talk about it, Esther.'

'Not now! Good God, Rich, I've just stepped in the door and you're yabbering at me!'

'I'm sorry you think that trying to mend our marriage is "yabbering" at you. Which, incidentally, isn't even a proper word. I'll leave you alone.'

He turned at the door. 'Oh, by the way, I spoke to Philippa today and asked her not to, you know, cause a fuss tonight.'

'Just so she knows we're both twitchy about it. Good move, Rich.'

He glared at her, picked up his cello case and banged through the fly screen. It clicked shut behind him with a rattle. Another reprimand. She watched him manoeuvre the cello case into the front seat of the Mini and fasten the seatbelt round it. He angled his lanky frame into the driver's seat and reversed full pelt down the drive and straight out into the road. A car horn sounded. The Mini belched a little puff of smoke, then careered out of sight.

Esther glanced round the concert hall. People milled to greet each other, braying across the rows. She ducked her head, feeling self-conscious and wishing she was invisible. The hall was chilly and she slipped her arms back into her jacket.

She'd dressed to the nines for the concert, in a long, slim-fitting skirt and silk blouse, and with strappy high-heeled shoes. She'd curled her hair into waves around her face, softening her features, and painted her lips a dramatic red.

I wonder if I'll have to meet *her* tonight, Esther thought, pretending to read her programme and determinedly avoiding eye contact with anyone. Be all civil and polite while all the time I'll want to shout 'You slept with my husband, you bitch' at her and then cut her head off. Philippa. She'll be tall and dark and willowy and a bit vague: the total opposite to me.

The lights dimmed and a spotlight made a cone of light on the stage. The audience continued to chat in whispers. The first soloist came on to applause and last-minute muttered conversations. Not her. Esther closed her eyes and battled to relax.

Rich came onstage with a quartet part way through the first half. Her breath caught in her throat as she darted a glance at the viola player, relieved to see a burly man in Rich's quartet. Probably better to get it over with quickly, this first necessary glimpse of *her*, but she dreaded the interval.

In the few seconds' pause between movements Rich's gaze searched the audience for her, and he sent a small smile into the dark auditorium. He'd never done such a thing before, always declaring such connection between performer and a specific member of the audience unprofessional, and railing against the children's orchestra for grinning at mums and dads. Her chest tightened at his smile, and she found herself meeting his gaze and smiling back, feeling simultaneously that her heart was breaking and that everything was somehow going to be all right.

The music ebbed away, she was no longer conscious of it, as she remembered the moment when she realised she was in love with Kent. It was so simple and extraordinary. One day she looked at him, and he looked back at her, and the jolt stunned her. Suddenly she couldn't breathe. Yet at the same time an objective part of her brain stood back, marvelling, 'So *this* is what all the fuss is about.' The intensity shocked her. And now, even though their relationship was unconsummated, the passion hadn't diminished and she loved him even more deeply.

It had happened when they were away together on a fieldtrip, dining in some outback pub in the middle of nowhere. Suddenly Kent had looked keenly at her across the table, his blue eyes serious. 'I need to tell you something I'm in love with you. I know that's not fair, because you're married, but that's how it is.'

Her heart jolted and a thrill warmed her. Tentatively she reached across the table and squeezed his fingers. 'I think I love you, too. But I don't want an affair. I can't do that to Rich.'

'I wouldn't want you to; I want you to be all mine.' He squeezed her fingers back. 'I wouldn't have said anything if I thought you were happy, but I get the feeling you've been unhappy for a while.'

She glanced down at her plate and smiled ruefully.

Kent continued, 'If there's a chance then I'll wait. Long as it takes.' And he picked up her hand and kissed it.

She and Rich had been unhappy for a long time, Esther realised, unable to pinpoint the time when they could no longer demonstrate their feelings for each other, spiralling away further with each careless word and act, but she feared it was over a year. A year of trying to get him to understand she loved him, that their marriage was precious to her, but seeing him slipping away, and powerless to bring him back. Each time she tried her words were clumsy; he took offence where she meant none; and being pushed away she cut back at him, slashing at his feelings with sharp words and selfish acts. Was it too late to stop?

When the lights went up in the concert hall she slipped from her seat and scuttled outside. It was a cold and clear night, though there were few stars visible. She remembered a friend telling her of the comfort of going into an old church to pray, knowing that whatever your problems they had all been brought to that building a thousand times before. It was the same with stars: weak humans had appealed to them for millennia. Esther's heartbreak wasn't anything unique. It was small comfort.

She lurked away from the bolt of light from the doorway and found a low wall to sit on.

'I didn't think you were a smoker.'

She spun round. To her astonishment Mark Wright grinned back at her.

'I'm not. Just getting some air. What are *you* doing here?'

'I like classical music, believe it or not.' He perched next to her on the wall, very dashing in his dark city suit.

'I meant, what are you doing in Perth? You were in Bilsom's Grudge yesterday.'

'So were you.' He inched closer to her and she felt the warmth of his body seeping into hers. 'I had to come and register Doreen's death with the mines department, see all sorts of health and safety and insurance people. And I've had to speak to the police again.'

'Is there a problem?'

'Just formalities. But it's not good for the mine that someone managed to break in and get to the equipment so easily.'

'Why doesn't MacKendrick do all this?'

'With *his* people skills?' Mark laughed. 'No, it's easier on everyone if I do it. And I enjoy a few days in the city in addition to my four off.'

'Four off?'

'I work the same pattern as the miners: fourteen on, four off. I don't always come back to Perth, but mostly I do. Top up on city life and culture.'

'Going to concerts.'

'A bit of civilisation. A nice change. It's wild and woolly at times out in Bilsom's Grudge. As I'm sure you can imagine.'

'Yup. I'm the same after weeks of fieldwork, in scruffy clothes and no shower. When I get back I dress up in proper dresses and make-up, go to films, visit all the art galleries, hang around in bookshops. It's like mini culture shock.'

'It's astonishing how long it takes to adjust back to normality,' Mark said.

'Where were you before Bilsom's Grudge?'

'In Sydney. I went to uni there and then got a marketing job.'

She'd guessed as much, she thought smugly. That slick city life still showed. 'What made you come here?'

He glanced away. 'Wanted to get away from Sydney for a while, have a break.'

The vindictive ex-wife and the son he wasn't allowed to see. No wonder he had fled to the other side of the country to lick his wounds.

'How did you manage to get this job, though? It's a bit of a change from marketing.'

'To be honest, I don't think there were any other applicants,' he laughed. 'Who'd want to do it? But I did two anthropology modules at uni, and I blagged my way in on those.'

'Do you like it?'

He pulled a face. 'Ask me after a good week. If you can find one.'

'How do you get on with MacKendrick?'

'He's tough, all right. Ruthless when it comes to business. I wouldn't like to cross him.'

'Is that a warning?' She was only half-joking.

He shook his head. 'Anyway, how's your research going?'

'OK. A few leads from some library research, but it's painstaking work.'

'How do you mean?'

'Well, you pick up a name from a field note or station records, then you've got to find out how they fit into the scheme of things. Find out who their descendants are, where they came from, where they belong, what other records there are for that person and their family, if any. It all takes a long time.'

'So you'll be holed up in the library for the next few weeks?'

Esther shook her head. 'Not me. I'm an anthropologist, not a bookworm. I get someone else to do the digging: a researcher who's mad about genealogies and understands Aboriginal kinship systems much better than me.'

'One of your staff?'

'No, a consultant. I tell you, he's a godsend. He pretty much lives in the archives. If he can't find it, it doesn't exist. He's weird but totally dedicated and reliable.'

'Wish I could say the same about my colleagues at the mine. Most of them are weird all right, but not always dedicated and reliable.'

'Mining's a tough life. It appeals to mavericks.'

Mark sighed. 'Take no notice of me. I've spent all day explaining how Doreen came to hang herself on mine property and why it wasn't behind a locked fence. Seems like the most important thing is public liability insurance rather than that a woman died.'

They sat in silence for a while, Mark's shoulder pressing against hers. She shivered.

'You're cold. Here, have my jacket.'

Before she had time to protest he slipped his jacket around her shoulders. It was warm, and the weight of the fabric was instantly comforting. She caught a whiff of his aftershave. Bilsom's Grudge was no place for him.

'I'd offer to fetch you a drink, but the queue's so long you'd have no time to drink it,' he said.

'That's OK. I'm fine out here.'

'You look tired.'

She laughed mirthlessly. 'I'm always tired. I'm off to Geraldton tomorrow.'

'What does your husband think of you being away so much?'

She didn't answer; just stared at her fingers wound together.

'Sorry, it's none of my business. It must be difficult, but I'm sure you find a way, like couples in the forces.'

'The thing I find hardest,' said Esther, 'is that I can't have a pet or houseplants.'

He frowned at her, puzzled. She regretted sounding eccentric, and hurried to explain herself.

'I'm away on fieldwork so much, often at short notice. Like tomorrow, for instance, I only knew about that two days ago. I couldn't have a pet because it would always be in kennels. And houseplants, well, they've always ended up dying, so I don't even try now.'

'Do you have a garden?'

'It's more of a sandpit most of the time,' she said, ruefully. 'I don't have much time to spend in it, and I bless both the reticulation and the lawnmower man otherwise it'd be a dust bowl by now.'

Mark laughed. 'Yeah, you have to nurture things, or they die.'

Or run off with a viola player, she thought.

'Do you ever stop and wonder if it's all worth it? Working so hard for a home and garden you don't have time to enjoy?'

She was silent.

'Sorry, I've done it again. Being pushy. Tell me to keep my nose out.'

'It's a fair question, but right now, I don't want to start thinking about the answer.' Esther laughed to lighten the mood. 'I'm a coward deep down.'

Mark laughed with her. 'Sounds like it's time to go in.' He offered her his arm and she slipped her hand into the crook of his elbow. They walked together back into the concert hall. Rich was hovering in the foyer, searching the crowds of faces.

'There you are!' He looked relieved as he came over.

'Mark, this is Rich, my husband. Rich, Mark.'

'So you're the lucky man. Good to meet you, Rich.'

Watching the two men shake hands, Esther thought Rich could hardly look less lucky. His eyes were shadowed and his smile was fake and forced. He stooped a little, as though weighed down with worry. She was glad when the bell summoned them to their seats.

The full orchestra was assembled for the second half. Esther hardly heard a note, obsessed with deciding which viola player was Philippa. A couple of them looked likely candidates, and both sat near Rich in the orchestra. When the orchestra settled ready to play the overture to 'The Thievish Magpie', she saw Rich bend towards one of them and mutter a comment. The woman chuckled and whispered back. That must be her. She pushed away the images that soiled her mind, of Rich with this woman, shocked that the stab of jealousy was not that he'd been unfaithful, but for Rich experiencing the thrill of kissing a new person for the first time. When was the last time she was electrified by the touch of unfamiliar lips on hers?

She clapped until her palms stung when the orchestra rose to take its applause. Rich whispered to the woman again, tweaking the nut of his bow, loosening the horsehair. When he left the stage, his cello hoisted high, Esther imagined him dusting down the instrument next to the woman, sharing a joke, packing their music away together. It seemed unbearably intimate.

She tried to escape the concert hall, but she was out of luck. Hoards of people crammed the aisles and stairways, jabbering in falsely cheery voices about the performances and holding up the queue while they squawked at each other.

Just as she reached the lobby and could scent the night air, Rich touched her elbow.

'Got out the back way,' he said. Two spots of colour burned high on his cheekbones. He was always wired after a performance.

'Can we go?' she said. 'I've got to pack.'

The colour drained away and his feverishness popped like salt thrown on soap bubbles. 'Pack? You're leaving me?'

'No, Rich, I've got to fly to Geraldton tomorrow.'

'Why?'

'Work, of course. There's an old lady dying and I need to . . . Look, can we talk about this later? I'm exhausted.'

'Everything's always about you,' he said, hefting his cello strap onto his shoulder and elbowing through the crowd.

He yanked forward the passenger seat of the Mini and Esther clambered into the back. She perched amongst the folders of music, rags and sweet wrappers with her knees crammed under her chin. Rich handed his cello into the passenger seat and snapped the seatbelt in place around it. Was he so tender and caring with Philippa? Was it only with Esther that he was so careless and rough?

They brooded on the journey home. Esther stared at the city lights, determinedly ignoring Rich's pent-up anger. When the car jolted to a standstill on the driveway she waited for him to release her from the back of the car. Instead, he unclipped the cello and carried it into the house, leaving her to fumble with the release catch on the seat and crawl out. She slammed the door shut, an action guaranteed to annoy Rich, and stalked into the house.

In the bedroom she unzipped a holdall on the bed and selected jeans, shirts and underwear from her closet, folding them meticulously into the bag. She gathered toiletries from the bathroom and ordered them in the front pocket of the holdall and zipped it. She could leave. This is what it would feel like: packing her clothes, collecting her things, ending this life with Rich.

She snapped open her mobile phone and speed-dialled her usual taxi firm, arranging a cab to the airport for the following morning. When she turned, Rich was watching her from the doorway.

'Esther,' he started. He took a step towards her, hesitated, unsure what to do next.

'I don't want to hear it.'

'We've got to talk. We can't carry on like this. It's killing me.'

'Not *now*, Rich!'

'When? You're never here! You never talk to me. Half the time I don't know who you are. Sometimes I think I know nothing about you or what you think or feel any more.'

'Then leave.'

'I want to make everything better.'

'Sleeping with someone else is a novel approach.'

'You're not giving me a chance!' He flopped onto the bed. Esther's heart twisted at the dejected droop of his shoulders and she perched next to him, carefully not touching him.

'You've got to give me time for it to sink in,' she said, softly. 'You can't just expect me to say OK and everything be all right again. Give me some space. I don't know what to think right now.'

He nodded miserably. 'What're you doing in Geraldton?'

'I've told you. There's an old lady about to die. I've got to interview her before it's too late.'

'Your clients fall off the twig so easily.'

'They do this week, that's for sure.' She groaned.

'What?'

'Every month there's someone else gone. Or someone's child killed by drugs or petrol or drunk driving. We lost another language last month.'

'How do you mean?' He propped himself up on his elbow and looked at her.

'The last living speaker of an Aboriginal language died. Now it only exists in text books in libraries. It wears me down.'

'Do you ever wonder what it's all for?'

'You're the second person to say that today.'

'And?'

'And I think it's unwise to start answering those sorts of questions.'

'Esther?'

'Yes?'

'I love you.'

'I know you do.'

12

Esther had a late start on Thursday. Her taxi to the airport was booked for 8.30am, so she luxuriated in a rare lie-in. When she prised her eyes open Rich had left a cup of tea and a plate of toast and vegemite beside the bed. She heaved herself into a sitting position, wedged pillows behind her and reviewed her notes for the day while chomping the toast. It was cold and chewy, as he'd not woken her when he left it; but she so seldom had time for breakfast that she relished every mouthful.

Rich hovered in the background, watching her get ready. 'I could take you to the airport.'

'It's OK, I've got a taxi booked.'

'Cancel it.'

'Thanks, but I'm OK.'

'When will you be back? I could pick you up.'

'Saturday. But I'll just get a taxi home. It'll be simpler.'

'No, go on, let me come and get you.'

'Tell you what, I'll text you just before I leave. I'm not sure how long I'll be there; it depends how well I get on.'

Rich seemed mollified, but Esther had no intention of letting him meet her. There was no way she was going to arrive from an emotionally draining interview to plunge into his latest needy crisis.

The taxi beeped outside. Esther slung her computer case over her shoulder and grabbed for her holdall. Rich got it first and carried it out to the taxi for her. He pecked her cheek, his lips dry, a clumsy manoeuvre as she was already climbing into the car. He waved from the driveway as the taxi reversed out, looking so much like a lost child that she almost made the taxi turn round and go back to scoop him up.

The temperature change in Geraldton was distinct: Esther felt the heat pulsing from the runway when she disembarked. She collected a hire car and set off to her hotel. Although she'd requested a room overlooking the Indian Ocean, she found herself with a view of the empty swimming pool. Too early to go to her clients, she bought a Coke from a vending machine, let herself into the fenced pool area and lay on one of the recliners, enjoying the sunshine, seeing pink as the sun penetrated her eyelids. A few minutes' peace. Yesterday Perth had been chilly, though the sun was bright; here, the sun warmed her skin. She'd been so cold at the concert last night; Mark Wright's jacket had been very welcome around her shoulders. She wondered what he was doing. More appointments about the safety of the mine after Doreen was killed there, presumably. He seemed genuinely upset by it all. A nice man.

After a while Esther dragged herself off the sun lounger and went to the hire car. She tuned the radio to a popular music station and sang along to the cheesy tunes as she drove through the town and out past the cemetery to the old lady's house.

She pulled up on the bare grass strip outside the house. The walls of the fibro house were stained orange from rusty water. In the front yard there was a huge bougainvillea, its branches crowded with purple papery flowers. A washing line hung with T-shirts and children's pyjamas. Esther took her time getting her gear out of the car, giving the old lady time to get ready for her visitor. Brown faces appeared at the next-door windows. Esther smiled and waved; they glared back.

The front yard was baked hard and cluttered with children's bicycles and garden chairs. She started calling 'hello' as she pushed through the front gate, dawdling up the path.

The old lady's daughter, Barbara, beamed at her from the front door. In her sixties, her hair was dyed patent black and scraped back from her face with a sparkly Alice band. Earrings drooped to her collar. 'Thanks for coming to see Mum,' she said. 'Bin driving long time?'

'No, I flew up from Perth this morning.'

Barbara chivvied her into the lounge. The room sweated under the tin roof, and when she pressed against the wall to allow Barbara to pass it was warm to her touch. In the summer it would be like living in a microwave. The old lady was perched on a red leatherette settee. She swivelled milk-clouded eyes towards Esther and grinned when she said hello.

'Nice to see you, Elsie. How are you keeping?'

'Not bad. Come to talk about the old times? Sit next to me, girl.' Elsie pulled her down beside her. The settee squeaked like a fart and the old lady giggled.

Through the kitchen door Esther heard Barbara swearing at the flies and clattering tea things. Esther was ashamed to be presented with a pristine china beaker for her tea; Barbara and Elsie drank from tin mugs.

Esther squashed between them, her notebook open on her lap and her tape recorder churning on the table beside them. Both women peered over her shoulder as she scribbled a note, watching the pen move, correcting her if she wrote something they didn't understand. Barbara's bulk joggled Esther's arm every time she sipped her tea.

Esther started by asking about recent births, helping Elsie to relax by talking about grandchildren and great-grandchildren, getting her comfortable talking to a stranger with a tape-recorder. Both women joined in, Barbara prompting her mother when the old lady faltered. It was a familiar routine, and Esther felt drowsy with the ebb and flow of words – drawing the relationships in her notebook, adding the names and dates for each new person, stitching the family tree together with lines and circles and triangles. She remembered learning this anthropological convention at university, admiring the ease with which even a complicated family tree could be set down, using circles to denote women and triangles to denote men.

Then Esther worked back, asking about Elsie's parents and grandparents. That was the important stuff: how the culture worked three generations back, and how it compared with contemporary Aboriginal culture. When she thought Elsie was ready she asked, 'Did your grandparents ever tell you about before the whitefellas came?'

Elsie was silent a long time before mumbling, 'My *gami*, my grandmother, she told me. They thought they were ghosts! Blackfellas didn't know about whitefellas then.' She chuckled at their naïvety, inviting Esther to share the joke. Barbara chortled along beside her, making the settee wobble.

'What else did she tell you?'

'About fishing. We're salt-water people, live next to the sea. Dolphin Bay and inland along the river little way, that's our country. My totem, he's a turtle, because my mother ate turtle when I was in the tummy, and I got a turtle birthmark, here, on my hip.' Elsie slapped her side. Barbara nodded in confirmation of the birthmark's existence. 'My *gami*, she was a dolphin.'

Esther nodded and jotted a note.

'My *gami*, she say they all fishing in the river near the sea when the white men come. White men gave them tins of sugar and jam and beef. Good tucker! They thought the whitefella was being friendly. Then they gave them grog, got them all drunk, being silly fella, and they took some of the women away, the young pretty ones.'

'And your grandmother?'

'She little girl, ran away and hid in the bush, saw them blackfellas try to take their women back. Saw the whitefellas get mad and whip them like horses. Then whitefellas sat down on our country and say, 'This our land now. We gonna grow sheep here. You blackfella gotta work if you want to live here'.'

'Then what happened?'

The old lady shrugged.

'Mum worked on a sheep station,' said Barbara. 'Didn't you, Mum? She was born on the station and worked as a house girl for years. Got tea and beef and a blanket instead of wages; they all did. I grew up on that station.'

'Were all your children born on the station?'

They both nodded. Esther flicked through her notes. 'You had nine children, Elsie. Can I check their names?'

Barbara reeled off nine names, then paused. Elsie pursed her lips. Esther's pen hovered over the notebook. She waited. Barbara glanced at her mother. 'I have another brother. But don't write it down. Mum doesn't want people to know. She's ashamed.'

Esther folded the notebook and put it on the floor, then switched off the tape recorder. 'Do you want to tell me about him?' she asked, gently.

'He was my second baby. Big fat baby. Called him Victor. He was dolphin totem, same as my *gami*. I saw dolphins jumping in the bay and then I found I'd fell for him. When him born, he too pale. His father was a whitefella, jackeroo on the station, rode the horses. I had an Aboriginal husband, an old man. I was given to him when I was young, but I didn't like him. I liked the white man! But my husband say Victor was his and grew him up proper blackfella way.'

'Mum taught all of us the old ways,' said Barbara.

'When Victor about twelve the welfare men came with the police, looking to take the children away,' said Elsie. 'They took the half-castes, so I painted Victor with burnt gum nuts, make him look dark. No good. They took him anyway, took him to the mission near the city. I had little baby at the titty when they got him, couldn't do nothing.'

'What happened?'

'He live in the mission, long way away. I wrote the welfare asking if he could come home.'

'They never replied,' said Barbara. 'We wrote and wrote and wrote, begging them to let Victor home, and they never wrote back.'

'It come near Christmas,' said Elsie, 'and Victor wrote us saying he was homesick and he want to come back. He escaped out the mission and ran away. The police went after him and shot him. Shot him dead, for running away.' Tears plopped into her hands.

'I'm so sorry,' Esther said, helplessly. Shame and pity pricked her eyes. She slipped her hand into Elsie's and gently squeezed the old lady's fingers.

'She doesn't want people to know,' said Barbara.

'Because Victor's father was a whitefella?'

'Naw. She ashamed because he was killed by the whitefellas.'

'It's us whitefellas who should be ashamed,' Esther said, conscious of how pale her hand was in Elsie's.

'You didn't shoot him,' said Barbara. 'You're here helping us get our land back.'

The door crashed open and the room filled with children. They hurtled into the kitchen and fought over biscuits and fizzy drinks. A huge woman in a floral print dress lumbered into the lounge, calling, 'We're here, *Gami*, you got anything to eat?'

'I'd better leave you in peace.' Esther stood, and prised her slacks out of the rucks around her bottom and thighs. 'Thank you for talking to me.'

'Thanks for coming all this way to see Mum,' said Barbara at the doorway. 'She knows she hasn't got long, and she wanted to record her story before it's too late.'

Esther squeezed her arm, called goodbye again to Elsie and left them with the rowdy family.

She drove along the coast road to Dolphin Bay, the old lady's country that they were fighting for. The Indian Ocean glittered silver. Two men fished from the end of the pier. Dolphins arced and plunged in the warm water. Esther watched them, weeping. Sometimes the job was simply too much. Too much grief, too much horror, too sad. She remembered Mark Wright's question the night before, 'Is it all worth it?' and asked herself if the sacrifices were in vain.

Esther turned the car and drove to her hotel. She took the laptop out to the poolside and balanced it on her knees, feeling the heat burning through her linen slacks. She flicked through her notebook, amending Elsie's genealogy, adding children and dates of birth and death. When she got to the end she paused, wondering what to do about Victor's story. She clicked on the family tree program and added another child to Elsie's family tree. Victor Stone, born 1936, died 1948. She adjusted the program to conceal the information, then sketched in what Elsie and Barbara had told her about Victor. It was all recorded, accessible to other Land Council researchers, but not made public – and it wouldn't be used in the native title claim without the family's permission. There were so many records like that: true biological fathers, concealed pregnancies, children given away and taken away, lost strands of families who may, or may not, resurface in the future.

Her mobile rang just as she was finishing. It was Kent.

'Hey, how're you?' he said. Her spirits lightened at the sound of his voice.

'OK. How are you?'

'Busy. How was Mrs Stone?'

'Lovely family, but you know what it's like: they tell you such intimate stories that wrench your heart out.'

'None of it's your fault.'

'Maybe not, but sometimes it's hard to be detached from it.'

'Don't beat yourself up, Esther. These blackfellas round here know how hard you work for their native title claims, and they admire you for it.'

'Thanks, Kent.' She was grateful he always understood how hard it was for her.

'It's true. They think you're pretty good, for a pommy white woman.'

She smiled. 'Praise indeed.'

'So, are you going back tomorrow?'

'We talked for a couple of hours today, but I'll go back tomorrow and see if she can remember any Dreaming stories for Dolphin Bay.'

'When are you back in Perth?'

'Not sure. Probably Saturday. I'll see how it goes with Elsie tomorrow.'

'You know we're off to Tjulpan on Sunday?'

'How can I forget!' Her stomach squirmed with dread.

'Can you come and pick me up from my mum's on Sunday? I'm off to hers for lunch.'

'Sure.'

'We'll drive together. Frank's making his own way.'

'Typical.' She chuckled. 'So I'll have you to myself for a few hours.'

'Esther?'

'Yes?'

'Be gentle with me.'

'Get lost! See you tomorrow.'

'Love you.'

Depressed, Esther closed up the laptop and went for a walk along the foreshore, trying to trick herself into cheerfulness by admiring the evening light spangling the Indian Ocean. It didn't work. Her mind picked at Elsie's story. Too much anguish in her job.

She sat alone in a restaurant near her hotel nursing a large glass of white wine. Palm trees rustled in the courtyard and along the foreshore. A persistent memory prickled, made her squirm, wouldn't be banished by walking or drink. She glared at the palm trees, mired in gloom.

'You started it,' she muttered.

England, 1979

'Palm trees in your own back garden,' Nanna said, casting a wistful glance at her backyard with its blackened walls and sooty hydrangeas. 'Look at how blue that sky is, and that's in their winter.'

She slid a photograph across the table to Esther's mother, who studied it and murmured, 'Wonderful! Just imagine.'

They were in Nanna's cramped sitting room, huddled round the oak drop-leaf table, its top sticky with orange squash and crayon. Esther swung her foot against the gate-leg, hoping to 'accidentally' scuff her hated new school shoes and so force Mummy into buying her some nicer ones.

She could hear children playing in the yard next door. She didn't know them and wasn't allowed to make friends with them. Nanna had given her a puzzle book to play with, but she was restless, anxious for Granddad to come home and take her to the swings. Bored, she counted the dancers on the carousel supporting Nanna's carriage clock, twirling endlessly, and wondered if Mummy would be cross if she asked to watch *Hong Kong Phooey*.

Nanna held an envelope open in her hand. She pulled out another photograph and sighed. 'It's like a tropical island.'

'That deep blue sea,' said Esther's mother. 'Are there sharks there?'

Esther's ears pricked up. 'I want to see!' She knelt on her chair and craned over her mother's arm. 'I can't see!'

'There!' Her mother slapped down a photograph. 'Don't get grubby fingermarks on it.' The familiar note of irritation made Esther's eyes prickle with tears.

She clutched the photo. A man in long shorts and a woman in a sundress posed in front of a low, squat house. They both squinted at the camera, hands held up to shield their eyes. A line of palm trees stood in stark relief against the cobalt sky. Behind them the sea glittered silver.

'Who are they?'

'Uncle Des, Granddad's brother, and Auntie Myrna. You won't remember Uncle Des. You were a baby last time he visited.'

'Where do they live?'

'In Australia,' said Nanna. 'A place called Geraldton.'

'I've never heard of it,' said Mummy. 'Is it near Sydney?'

'No, it's on the other side of the country.'

'Where's Australia?'

'On the other side of the world where kangaroos live.'

'Like Skippy?'

'Just like Skippy,' Nanna said.

'Why don't the people in Australia fall off the world?'

Esther's mother rolled her eyes. 'Everything's 'why' these days. Take no notice of her, Mum, it's just a phase she's going through.'

'But I want to know!' Esther whined.

'Talk properly! And stop making that silly noise.'

'It's because of gravity,' Nanna explained. 'Have you done gravity yet?'

'She's only eight, Mum.'

'Nearly nine,' Esther corrected.

Nanna and Mummy exchanged smiles.

'Why doesn't Uncle Des live here?'

'He went to live in Australia after the war,' said Nanna. She turned to Esther's mother. 'Your dad and I thought about going with the £10 passage, but we decided not to in the end.' She glanced at a flimsy blue sheet of airmail paper. 'Des has certainly done well for himself. I don't think he would have thought to join the police if he'd stayed here, but he seems to like it out there. And he's doing well. Myrna says he's been promoted again and next year they're going to buy a boat. This year they had a swimming pool put in the garden. Wouldn't have the space here.' Another glance through the net curtains.

'They must have a big garden.'

'All the houses do,' said Nanna. 'I suppose they've got a lot more space.'

'Can we go and visit Uncle Des in Australia?' asked Esther.

'No.'

'Why?'

'It's a very long way, and you know you're always travel sick. Honestly, Mum, I had to stop the car four times on the way here, and it's only an hour.'

'I'm going to go to Australia and see Uncle Des and kangaroos when I'm grown up.'

'That's nice, dear,' said Nanna. The back gate scraped. 'That's Granddad back for his dinner.' She scooped up the photographs and wedged them in their envelope behind the carriage clock on the sideboard. Taking the photo of Uncle Des and Auntie Myrna, she propped it up against the fruit bowl. 'I'll get a frame for that.'

Tanned faces grinned across the miles at Esther as she gathered her crayons together and helped Nanna set the table. The palm trees were impossibly exotic, fanning the deep blue sky. But although Esther peered hard and scrutinised the photo every time she visited Nanna, she still couldn't make out a shark in the sea behind them.

Geraldton, Western Australia, 1994

It was the most soulless town she'd ever visited. The foreshore looked out over the sparkling waters of the Indian Ocean, the view obliterated by the heavy rail freight thundering along the seafront, the rail tracks a long scar. Container after container, dozens of them made up each train. Once she counted seventy wagons. To get to the beach she had to scuttle over the train tracks, and once on the beach, if she looked along the coast, the white sand dunes like cascading icing sugar were obscured by hulking silos and conveyor belts pumping wheat into cargo ships lurking at the docks.

The main street looked inland, turning its back on the sea. There was nowhere to sit and relax and enjoy a drink and gaze out over the waters, where the sun bounced so hard it hurt the eyes. The whole place was a missed opportunity, a town planner's depression made concrete.

The palm trees were there, though. Hundreds of them, all the same, a job lot of cocoa palms littering the town. Each garden boasted several, even if the rest of the garden was concreted over and studded with fibreglass swans and lions with orange plastic eyes. Cocoa palms formed hedges, pierced the pavements, waved brown fronds in front of shops and hotels and the town hall. Esther detested them.

Uncle Des met her at the airport. Now seventy, his hair was grey and he stooped: a long way from the proud man in uniform who had beamed at her from the photographs in her childhood. His thin legs poked from shapeless shorts; his T-shirt was ripped at the shoulder. Like everyone else meeting the plane, he scuffed along in rubber flip-flops. Coming from the cool Canberra climate, Esther had embarked on her journey in the company of government officials and businessmen in suits and ties. She felt the change of culture keenly.

They stood awkwardly outside the square airport building, more shed than terminal, waiting for the suitcases to be unloaded, peppering each other with bursts of conversation.

'How long you been over here?' asked Des. He'd lost all trace of the Yorkshire accent of his youth and sounded like a true Aussie bushman. He spoke through closed lips, shielding his mouth from the flies.

'I've been here nearly a year. I meant to come and visit you earlier but ...'

''Sawright. It's a long way to come. You in Sydney?'

'Canberra. I'm at ANU there.'

'ANU?'

'The university.'

'Oh. Never been to Canberra. Heard it's no great shakes. Not like Sydney. You been there?'

'Yes, briefly. I'd like to go back.'

'What you studying?'

'Anthropology.'

'Studying the Abos, are ya?'

Esther squirmed. 'I'm away on fieldwork again soon.'

Des scratched between his toes where the rubber thong was chafing. His toenails were thick and long. They needed cutting, but looked as if they'd resist the scissors and need chiselling into submission. Esther glanced away, feeling self-conscious and awkward.

'Here's the luggage,' said Des, as a barrow appeared round the side of the terminal. The people waiting lunged for it, carting off surfboards and eskies and suitcases. Esther rescued her case and wedged it in the back of Des's station wagon.

Auntie Myrna was waiting at the door when they pulled up. She tottered down the steps and flung her arms round Esther.

'I've been to the hairdresser specially,' she said, patting her hair. It was set in brittle curls regimented into rows all over her head. 'Come in, come in! It's so good to meet you at last. I've been looking forward to it for years!'

She propelled Esther into a large open-plan living room with exposed brick walls. The windows were open to let in the breeze, and the room was filled with the crash and tang of the ocean. Esther perched on the edge of the settee while Myrna clattered around in the kitchen, chattering the whole time, though Esther couldn't catch what she was saying. Des flopped into the chair opposite and cracked open a can of beer.

Myrna appeared with a tea tray, looking flushed. 'How do you like Australia?'

'I really love it here. I've wanted to visit since I was little. Nanna used to show me the photos you sent over, and I always wanted to see it for myself.'

Myrna blushed with pleasure. 'D'you hear that, Des? Esther remembering those snaps and coming over for herself. I hope it's just as good as the photos, Esther.'

'I haven't been disappointed so far,' Esther economised with the truth.

'You been to WA before?'

'I had a couple of days in Perth before I flew up here. That's a beautiful city.'

'We don't get down there too often. We mostly go north for our holidays,' said Myrna.

'Esther's studying the Aboriginals,' said Des, glugging on his can.

'Are there any Aboriginals in Canberra?' Myrna turned astonished eyes to Esther, who shifted uncomfortably. 'They'd be half-castes, not full bloods,' she continued. 'Probably not even that, in the city.'

'Actually, some of the academics in my department are Aboriginal,' said Esther.

'Yes?' Myrna's eyes were round with incredulity.

'But I'm working with a community in the Northern Territory.'

'What do you do with them? Go out eating witchetty grubs?' asked Des.

'I'm researching how Aboriginal women's roles have changed.' She winced at the prim tone in her voice.

'I tell you one thing,' said Des, 'whatever you think about Aboriginals now, you'll have changed your mind by the time you finish your course.'

She'd heard this advice before and it was growing stale. To avoid unsolicited opinions about 'the Aboriginal problem', she fibbed to taxi drivers and told strangers on trains that she was a teacher. Otherwise she found herself pinioned by homilies informed by a potent mixture of media scaremongering, xenophobia and unadulterated racism.

'It's a complicated situation,' she said, neutrally, hoping to stall Des before he got into his stride.

'We've got Aboriginal families here, Des, haven't we? Quite a lot of Aboriginal people live in Gero.'

'Lines of them outside the dole office. They should get jobs, stop scrounging.' Esther braced herself, and was surprised when Des added, 'I used to feel sorry for them when I was a cop.'

'Why?'

'I had to help the welfare people when the kids needed to go into care. It was the only bit of the job I really disliked.'

'But if the kids were in danger, Des . . .' Aunt Myrna said.

'Hm.' The air throbbed with the rattle and suck of the ocean. Esther waited for Des to continue. He coughed. 'I was based in Northampton just up the coast from here when I first came to Australia, and now and again we used to get called in to help the welfare people if they were expecting trouble. Needed back-up sometimes. Sometimes the kids went on the run and we used to get sent to take them back. The Aboriginals weren't allowed to go in the towns back then, in the 1940s and '50s; they lived in camps outside the towns and on the stations. The welfare man had to remove all the half-caste kids and send them to the missions. It was the law. We'd go and help him take the kids and put them on the train, make sure they got there. Sometimes we had to drive them all the way down. The mission was near Perth. Moore River it was called. Lots of them went there.'

'I haven't heard of Moore River,' said Esther. 'I've heard about the children being taken, though.'

She'd cried and cried when she'd first been told, her tears dropping into her lap as an old woman described how she and her children had been bundled into a car and taken away to be incarcerated. The woman had escaped with one of the children, but wasn't strong enough to carry all of them and had to leave the others, including a baby, behind. She never saw them again.

'We weren't involved that often, but I hated it,' said Des. 'The camps were disgusting – filthy, dog dirt everywhere, only one standpipe, really basic houses. Some of them lived in humpies. The kids were better off out of there. It couldn't be good for them growing up in those conditions. They were shocking.'

'What happened to the children?'

Des shrugged. 'Most went to Moore River, some went to other missions and some even got adopted by white couples. I never knew what happened to them, unless they ran away. Then we'd get a call saying some kid or other had gone AWOL. We'd go and pick them up and take them back. They never got far.' He took another slug of beer. 'Yeah, they were better off, that's for certain. Proper education, jobs found for them, looked after and fed and kept safe. They could make something of themselves. You'd think the parents would realise it was for the best, but they took it real hard. A couple of times I felt really bad. When the parents really loved the kids, they were just poor, it felt wrong. They'd try anything to keep the kids with them: hiding them, sending them to live out in the bush when we came, painting them black so we'd think they were full bloods.' He shook his head. 'We always got them in the end, none too happy about being mucked around. The kids'd be screaming, the parents howling, all the other Aborigines crying and running after the car. But it was for the best, in the long run.'

'Was it?' asked Esther.

'You can't bring kids up in those conditions. We wouldn't let white people do it, so why should we let the Aboriginal kids grow up like that? And some people said that as they'd got one white parent they should have the same advantages white kids got: proper health and school and jobs.'

'But the law wasn't about making sure the children were looked after, it was about breeding them out!' Esther cried.

'Their own people didn't like the half-castes. Some of them killed the kids if they thought it was a white man's baby. We gave them a chance. That's what makes me so mad when I see Aboriginals causing trouble in town. I think, we gave you a chance to be better, so why're you wasting your life like this?'

Esther dug her nails into her palm until she left a line of red, sore semicircles. 'I'll clear the tea things,' she said, piling up the tray and carrying it into the kitchen. She took deep breaths while she waited for the water to run hot, reminding herself that she was a guest in the house, that Des was from a different generation.

Myrna appeared behind her, looking embarrassed. 'Have you got a boyfriend? Or is there someone waiting for you back in England?'

The small talk was welcome. 'I've got a boyfriend in Canberra, but funnily enough he's English, over here studying too.'

'Another anthropologist?'

'No,' Esther laughed. 'He's a musician, a cellist. He plays with an orchestra over in Canberra. He was one of the first people I met out here.'

'A cellist! That would be lovely. Is he all deep and sensitive?'

'Yes, but he won't talk about his feelings much.'

'All men are like that.' Myrna sidled closer. 'What Des was talking about earlier, he was trying to brush it off, but I'll never forget how he looked after he'd had to take those children away. He used to sit like a stone out the back of the house, just staring into space for hours.'

'It must have been difficult,' Esther said, dismayed.

'He never said much. It was in the kids' best interests, but it was still hard for him, especially when our three were young. Made me realise how lucky we were. We didn't have a lot of money, but we lived like princes compared to those poor Aborigine kids.'

'You can't think it was better for them to be taken away?'

Myrna hesitated. 'Des wouldn't be able to live with himself if he didn't think it was right. And it was his job. It's what the law said back then.' She added in a sterner tone, 'Besides, I don't think it's fair to judge the past.'

Safely back in Canberra, Rich met her from the plane and she'd never felt so relieved to see anyone in her life. He could tell straight away that the trip to Geraldton had upset her and that she wasn't yet ready to talk, so he had taken her to his annoyingly neat and tidy flat and into his bed. And afterwards they lay in the damp, twisted sheets, and he coaxed it out of her.

'It was awful, Rich.' Esther nuzzled into the space between his neck and shoulder, comforted by his arms clasped round her waist. 'I couldn't believe what he was saying. It was so racist.'

'Lots of Australians say the same things.'

'That doesn't make it right. I didn't know what to say. I hated what he was saying, but I didn't feel I could object. I was in his house. He's my uncle! The women I've been working with talk about the stolen generation. They say it's not one generation but at least three who're lost: the parents who had their children stolen, the children themselves, and *their* children, who don't know where they belong. And now I find my family had a hand in it!'

'Shh!' Rich stroked her shoulder and wiped away the tears pooling along her collarbone. 'You can't take responsibility for your uncle.'

'I'm a coward,' she sniffed. 'I should have spoken up and I didn't.'

'Here, this will cheer you up.' He swung his long legs out of bed and pulled on underpants and trousers. He padded across the room to his cello case and took out the instrument.

'Why did you get dressed?' asked Esther, propping herself up in bed.

Rich faked shock. 'I can't play naked! It would be extremely disrespectful and probably get me thrown out of the academy.' He perched on the end of the bed and drew the bow across the strings. 'Sounds of Australia. Part one: the kangaroo.' He bounced the bow on the strings, close to the bridge. It made a loping, springing sound. Esther giggled and wiped her nose with her fingers. 'Part two: seagulls round the chip van.' He slid his fingers high up the strings, making a screeching, squealing noise just like seagulls. 'Part three: after a heavy night on the beer.' He thumped the bow down on the lowest string: a fart.

'So this is what you're learning over here,' said Esther. Her heart lightened and swelled with love for him. He understood her entirely.

'It's an essential part of my musical education. I could go far with this.'

'How far?'

'Probably as far as the chip van and the seagulls.'

'That far? You surprise me!'

'Good.' He kissed the end of her nose. 'Glad to see you smiling again. You're too hard on yourself, Esther.'

'Do you know the worst thing? It's that I'm related to him. I'm used to hearing bigoted opinions, but to hear them from your own family is awful. He seems like a normal bloke, but he had a hand in taking those kids and he can't see anything wrong with it.'

'You can't be blamed for what your relatives did thirty years ago.'

'Why not? Isn't that what the whole saying sorry business is all about? That we stand up and say it was wrong and we're sorry?'

'Come on, Esther, you didn't know. And if you don't cheer up I'll be forced to play part four: the barbecue, and part five: cricket.'

'I feel tainted,' she said. 'And ashamed. I couldn't bear it if any of the people I'm working with knew what Des did.'

'He didn't take *their* kids; he was working in WA.'

'It's the principle of it. I couldn't look them in the face, and I'm sure they wouldn't trust me if they knew.'

'Enough,' said Rich, putting down his cello and slipping back into bed. He pulled Esther close and kissed her. 'They're hardly likely to find out, are they? No one knows except us.'

Geraldton, August 2005

Esther awoke to the sound of the ocean. Over breakfast in the hotel's dining room she looked out of the window across the waves and watched a container ship coming into port. She couldn't face another night in Geraldton. She rang the airline and changed her flight again; she'd be back in Perth that evening. Then she called Kent.

'I need to see you tonight,' she said.

On her way to Elsie's house she pulled up outside Des and Myrna's old home. The house hadn't changed much. The palm trees Nanna envied so much still bordered the property. Des had died five years ago and Myrna had gone to live with their daughter. Even the whitefellas involved in the stolen generation were dying out now. Maybe one day the whole episode would be consigned to history, no generations tainted by its memory.

Elsie and Barbara weren't surprised to see her back again. They settled into their usual places on the leatherette settee and Esther probed for details of Dreaming stories that Elsie could remember. The old lady could recall only fragments of stories about Dolphin Bay, most of which Esther had seen in greater detail in a children's book of Dreaming stories. However, Elsie did know several stories connected with the waterholes and rocks on the sheep station where she grew up.

'I know that country best,' she said. 'That where I grew up. Old people told us all the stories for that country.'

'But not for Dolphin Bay? Why's that?'

'Got to tell the story on the country. We went to Dolphin Bay when I a kid, but the old people not tell little kids Dreaming stories. Too young. There are stories for that place. The old people try to protect them.'

'Did they tell anyone the stories?'

'Some people. They all finish now.'

'They're all dead, those people,' Barbara added.

'So no one knows the Dreaming stories?'

Elsie shook her head. 'My *gami*, she told me a song 'bout a turtle who lose his shell.'

'Can you remember it?'

Elsie started to sing. Esther cranked up the volume on the tape recorder to make sure she captured the song. Elsie's voice wavered, the words in her language sounding strange, the melody patterns ragged to Esther's ears. She wondered if Rich would be able to transcribe the tune. As Elsie continued to sing, Esther's skin prickled to think that this old lady was the only one left in the world who understood what she was singing. And soon she'd be gone.

'You teach me that song, mum?' asked Barbara, her eyes wet with tears. She glanced at Esther and they shared a moment of understanding, desperate to preserve what they could before a way of life was lost forever.

'Tomorrow,' said Elsie. 'It's about a turtle in Dolphin Bay who wants to swim free like the dolphins, so he crawls out of his shell. He leaves his shell on the shore. There's a rock there that blackfellas say is his shell.'

'Is the rock still there?' asked Esther.

'Yeah, it's still there. That old turtle he had a swim, but when he come out of the water he lay on the sand to dry off. He not used to the sun without his shell and he burned himself and dried out, and he died there.'

'Is he still there?'

Elsie shrugged. 'I think so, but I don't know which rock is him.'

On the way to the airport Esther drove to Dolphin Bay and looked for the rock in the shape of a turtle's shell, and took a photograph of it. She was late at the airport and had to sweet-talk the check-in girl into letting her onto the plane.

She switched on her phone as soon as she landed. There was a text message from Rich, reminding her to let him know when she was back so he could collect her. She deleted it without replying. And there was a voice message from Gail.

'Hi, Esther, it's Gail. I've got some bad news for you. David Liddle is in hospital. He was attacked last night.'

13

The face on the hospital pillow was purple and swollen. The left eye squeezed shut; the eyelashes tiny glistening spikes. His lank hair was combed back from his forehead, so greasy that the comb left furrows. The good eye popped open as Esther approached. Shock knifed through her at the sight of him.

'David, what happened?' she breathed.

'Oh, hi, Esther. Sorry I can't get up.' He waved a slinged arm. 'Have a seat.'

She perched on a plastic chair next to the bed, wishing she'd thought to pick up some fruit or chocolates. 'How are you?'

'You know. A bit sore round the ribs and head and general body and legs and arms. But my toenails hardly hurt at all.'

One bare foot peeped out from under the blanket. The toenails were clean, she noted. So this is what a spell in hospital did to you.

'What happened?'

David shifted, trying to get comfortable, his face screwed up with pain. 'I was on my way home yesterday evening when I got jumped on. Didn't see much, but I think he had a crowbar or something.'

'Jesus, David! Are you going to be OK?'

'Yeah. Lucky, really. I think something scared him off because just as I thought I'd had it, he stopped and ran away.'

'Then what happened?'

'I lay there bleeding in the gutter for a while, then some tourists came along, realised I wasn't an art installation and called an ambulance.'

'Thank goodness.' She looked at him helplessly, unsure whether to squeeze his hand. Only knowing him as a colleague, she feared any contact would embarrass him, yet not connecting with him physically seemed inhumanely distant. 'Can I do anything? Get you anything?'

'Actually, you can.' His good eye swivelled towards her. 'I wasn't entirely honest with the police.'

Esther's heart sank. 'Oh no. What have you done?'

'I didn't tell them whoever did this took my keys.'

'Your keys? Why?'

'That's the funny thing. And it's not the only funny thing.'

'I'm not with you.'

David heaved himself up against the pillows. His injuries were so grotesquely swollen she could hardly bear to look him in the face, afraid of betraying pity and shock. He grimaced. 'I started doing a bit of digging for that Mt Parker claim of yours. I got on OK with the stuff I've collected at home, but then I thought I'd have a look at the original station records. Your notes were all right, but I wanted to see them myself.'

'In case I missed something.' Typical of him not to trust her analysis.

'You don't spend all day looking at these things like I do,' he said, trying to mollify her but only succeeding in sounding patronising. 'It's easy to miss something.'

'And?'

'I've got a mate at the Battye library, so instead of giving me the official bullshit version they give the general public I got the inside story.'

'On what?'

'On why the Mt Parker Station records have disappeared.'

It took a moment to sink in. 'What? They've gone?'

'The diary and ledger you looked at the other day have been taken away, by someone saying they were a member of the Bilsom family.'

'The *Bilsom* family? Why would they remove the records?'

David shrugged and winced. 'No idea.' He paused. 'The timing makes me wonder if there's something in those records that would help you in the Tjulpan claim.'

'What's that got to do with the Bilsoms? They left the station a century ago!'

'These pastoralist families like to stick together. Most of them are against native title. Maybe that's why.'

Esther picked at the waffle blanket on David's bed, frustration churning inside her. 'So the whole of the station records have disappeared?'

'Yeah, but I'm hoping we still have your notes.'

'Of course you have. I dropped them off the other day.' A doubtful look shivered across his face. 'What is it?'

'I told you, whoever attacked me stole my keys. They took all the stuff out of my pockets, my wallet and everything, but only made off with my keys. I'm scared they've gone to search my house.'

'Why didn't you tell the police?'

'Because if *they* search my house they'll find more than genealogies.'

'Alphabet spaghetti,' Esther groaned. She could shake him.

'Could be. Maybe some other stuff too.' David had the decency to look embarrassed.

Her thoughts whirled. 'Do you really think you were attacked because of the Tjulpan claim?'

'What do you think? A woman was killed a few days ago after she tried to spill the beans about child abuse in Tjulpan community. You found the station diary, but when I go to read it suddenly it's missing. Then I get attacked and my keys are stolen. A coincidence?'

Esther prickled cold. 'OK. What do you want me to do?'

'Promise me you'll be careful. After what happened to me and Doreen, I don't want you to put yourself in danger.'

'I'll be careful.'

'Will you go and check on my place?'

'How will I know if anything's been taken?'

'That's not the point. I need you to fetch my laptop.'

'You're not going to work while you're in hospital!'

David held up his good arm to silence her. 'And I need another copy of your notes, the ones you made in the library, and as much as you can carry about the Tjulpan claim.'

'Why? What can you do?'

'All my genealogies are backed up on my computer. May as well be of use while I'm lying here. There's something going on with this claim and I'd like to get to the bottom of it.' He added in a lighter tone, 'And I'm pissed off stuck in here.'

Esther grumbled for a while but saw he was determined. 'OK,' she sighed. 'How do I get in?'

'There's a key under the concrete frog by the front door. It's tucked behind a big plant thing.'

'And the laptop?'

'It's in an old backpack at the bottom of the wardrobe.'

'Why do you hide it?'

'No insurance.'

'Anything else?'

'A two litre bottle of coke, not the diet crap, and some chips. No grapes.'

Dusk was settling when Esther bounced the car onto the verge. David's house sulked in the gloom; the windows stared blankly back at her like hostile youths. It was very quiet when she switched off the engine, and the ticking under the bonnet as it cooled paced her heartbeat.

David's front door was to the side of the house, up a path congested with overgrown plants. It was very dark away from the street lights. A thick creeper throttled the brickwork and snaked around the doorframe. Esther fumbled at the base of the creeper, squealing when her fingers brushed something slimy. It was the concrete frog. She lifted it and scrabbled for the key.

The door stuck, and she had to kick the bottom of it to get it open. She stepped into the dark hallway and groped for a light switch, then went into the lounge.

David's house was messy before, but that was nothing compared to the chaos that confronted her. Esther stared in dismay at the papers slewed over the floor. The neat piles and eccentric filing system were smashed to litter. Papers crackled underfoot. She scooped up a handful – a jumble of photocopied field notes, scraps of genealogies and interview notes. It would take David weeks to sort all this out again. Esther despaired at the thought. At least he was determined and obsessed enough to have the stamina to see through the task of reordering. But by the time he'd done that it would be too late for the Tjulpan claim, and without the proof that Mt Parker was a significant Aboriginal site it would be reduced to a heap of rubble.

A window banged at the back of the house. She froze, afraid the intruders were still there. A pulse hammering in her throat, she crept to the back of the house, poking her head into each room in turn.

The hallway was uncarpeted, and her feet clattered as she made her way through the dim house. She tried several doors before she found David's bedroom. The door grated on the carpet as she swung it open. The blinds were closed, the window a grey square against the black. She fumbled for the light switch, sighing with relief when the room flooded with light. It was sparsely furnished: a low bed in the middle of the room, a ringed coffee cup on the carpet beside it and a built-in wardrobe taking up the whole of the far wall.

Esther hesitated before sliding back the wardrobe door, fearful of someone lurking there. The door rocked off its runner, threatening to fall on her. She snapped it back into place. One half of the wardrobe was empty. The floor was littered with lace-up shoes and boots, all jumbled together, all scuffed and dusty. She wondered why David had such a collection of footwear when he rarely wore shoes. The rail hung with T-shirts, jeans and jackets. A shelf held two black sweaters bundled into heaps. Underneath the pile of shoes she found a canvas backpack with leather straps. She undid the straps and unzipped it, opened the backpack, and groaned.

The laptop was missing.

14

Rich started interrogating her as soon as her eyes flickered open on Sunday morning. Where are you going? Who with? Have I met him? When? I don't remember. Are you sure I know him? Until she wanted to scream with frustration. How could he be so jealous when he'd *screwed* someone else? Exhaustion fractured her into shards. Again she had barely slept that night; awoke feeling hollow and weepy, yearning for solitude and a dark room to sleep in until it was all over.

Rich plonked a cup of tea on her dressing table. When Esther reached for it she found he hadn't cushioned the cup, and it had burned a white ring into the surface. It was her grandmother's dressing table; cheap utility purchased during the war, but Esther had spent a lot of money and trouble getting it moved to Australia after Nanna died. Every time she looked at it she remembered childhood mornings, wriggling into bed beside Nanna and begging for a story or rhyme. The old man with the pig he took to market was her favourite, and she always joined in with 'Pig, pig, jump over the stile, or we shan't get home tonight.' She saw her reflection in the dressing table mirror, pink cheeks dewy from sleep, resting on Nanna's shoulder. Now the reflection that met her gaze was white and haggard. Black smudges ringed her eyes.

She traced the white ring as though it were a torture scar on her lover. Tears prickled her eyes and she swallowed hard twice. Silly to get so upset over a bit of cheap furniture, but the spoilt table made her feel sick and desperately sad. Nanna had always looked after her things, polishing and protecting them with pride, believing that if you looked after your belongings they would last forever. Esther had let her down.

She swung her legs out of bed and padded to the shower, letting the water scald her shoulders while she tried to scrub the tension out of her muscles. She was towelling her hair dry when the doorbell rang. Rich was evidently still sulking because he didn't deign to answer it, so after several rings she threw on some clothes and opened the door herself, astonished to find David Liddle on the doorstep, beaming at her.

'David! What are you doing?'

He pushed past her, his arms filled with cardboard files. 'I couldn't stand it in the hospital after you said my place had been trashed, so I discharged myself and went to clear up the mess.'

'But look at the state of you! You must be mad!'

'Probably. I don't suppose you could get me a coffee, could you? I haven't slept since I last saw you.'

Esther brewed the coffee thick and black – they both needed it – and carried it into the lounge. David perched cross-legged on the settee. His feet had returned to their usual grimy appearance, she noted, and he smelt stale and sour, like an old man.

'I think I've found something that might help,' he started.

'You've been working? You're mad! You should be resting . . .' She bumbled on for a few seconds until curiosity won. 'OK, what've you found?'

He grinned. 'Well, first I went through that mess at my place. I know pretty much what I've got, so it only took a few hours to scrape up the bits I thought might relate to Tjulpan. Then I went back through your notes from the station diaries, and then I called in reinforcements.'

'Who?'

'I palmed Bilsom's family off on a genealogist. Sorry, it'll cost you, probably quite a lot, but that was the best I could think of. I told him it was an emergency. This is what he came up with.'

David slapped a sheet of paper on the floor. It showed Bilsom's family tree: the normal muddle found in every family unnaturally ordered into neat lines and distinct generations. Esther picked it up and studied it. 'So he's got living descendants from the son, Eddie?'

'Yeah. Nothing interesting, but I thought you wanted it.'

'So the Bilsoms could have taken the station records from the library?'

David shrugged.

Esther scanned the genealogy. The names snagged at her mind, but she couldn't grasp the pattern emerging. The names floated, meaningless yet tantalising, while her tired mind tried to snatch at them. She sighed and set the sheet aside for later.

'But I did find this.' David's eyes twinkled with glee. 'I haven't been able to go through it properly, but I think this is the evidence you're looking for.'

'What is it?'

David handed over a sheaf of flimsy fax paper. 'I went through my records and found a Ruby and her son Dennis mentioned in some fieldwork fragments. An anthropologist called Elizabeth Roper-Jones did some fieldwork at Moore River Native Settlement in the 1920s.'

'Roper-Jones? I've heard of her. Hasn't she been discredited?'

'Yes, because she liked Neville's plans for Aboriginal assimilation. Say what you like about her politics, that's not the point. She wasn't a half-bad anthro. I've got some of the family trees she sketched at Moore River, and they include a Ruby and son Dennis but no other details. Here.'

He slapped down an A3 sheet covered with lines and scrawls. Esther peered at Roper-Jones's cramped squiggles. It was only when David jabbed at the place with a chewed fingernail that she could decipher Ruby's family tree.

'But there are only two names: Ruby and Dennis. They could be anyone.'

'Could be, but aren't,' said David. 'You see this funny sign here?'

'It looks like a doodle.'

'It's Jones's shorthand that means she did a longer interview with the person.'

'And you've got the notes?' Esther asked excitedly.

David shook his head. 'They're archived in Adelaide, at the state library. A few years back I met a researcher who's writing a book about Roper-Jones. I rang her and asked about Ruby. What she told me suggested this is *our*, your, Ruby. She's faxed through all the stuff she has. I've only skimmed it, but this is her. This is Ruby, here.'

Esther flicked through the pages, skimming over the words, hardly daring to believe they had found the woman who had witnessed the massacre at Mt Parker.

'Does it say where the massacre happened? Is it enough to stop them destroying Mt Parker?'

'Read it,' David said, simply.

Rich barged into the lounge. He glared at Esther.

'What are you doing?'

'David's brought over some notes I need for the community meeting tomorrow.'

'Working again?' Rich sighed. 'Esther, you only got back late yesterday. You're going to be exhausted before you even get to the meeting at this rate.'

'It was urgent.'

Rich wasn't to be mollified. 'It's Sunday,' he said, pointedly.

'Exactly. David, I can't thank you enough for the work you've done, especially as you're sick and after all that's happened. You're a star.'

David grinned and blushed. 'When are you back there, at Tjulpan?'

'Driving out there today.'

'I'd better let you get on, then.' He clambered to his feet, wincing when he bashed his slinged arm against a chair.

'Let me drive you home,' Esther offered, ignoring Rich's sigh.

'I'm going to a second-hand book sale at the uni. Hoping to get some old ethnographies.'

'I'll take you.' She scraped up the papers he'd given her and stuffed them into her bag.

After dropping David at the uni, Esther went to a café beside Lake Monger and smoothed the papers out on the tabletop. With the breeze ruffling her hair, she started to read.

Bilsom Family Tree: Direct Descendants of Charles Bilsom

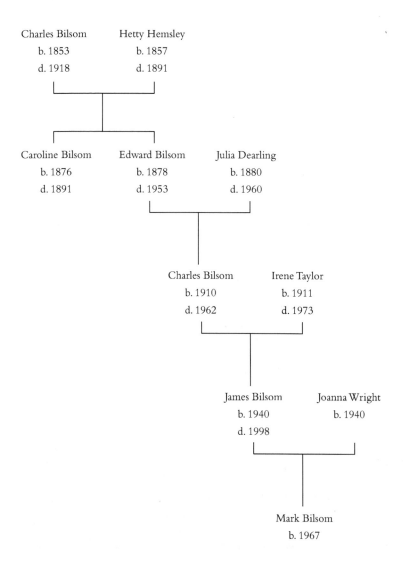

Elizabeth Roper-Jones: Fieldnotes
Interview with Aboriginal Woman Ruby, at Moore River Native Settlement
(MRNS), April 1928
Ruby: full blood Aborigine, aged approx. 50–55

Ruby came to the native camp in November 1926, after being rejected by her tribe. Almost starving, she was brought in by the local protector of Aborigines, and came to Moore River by train from Geraldton. Her height, build, physical description and skull measurements are recorded in MRNS papers.

I took a cursory genealogy from her when I visited in 1927, and interviewed her extensively in April 1928. She was then in very poor health with numerous weeping sores that refuse to heal, and with a persistent cough. Her clothes and blankets are very dirty, and I have requested the matron to supply her with clean bedding in the hope that removing the constant irritation of soiled blankets on her skin will aid her recovery. The matron also roasted her clothes with sulphur to kill the lice.

Ruby told me her story thus:

I was born at Moolya, that white men call Mt Parker. I am from the Tjulpan tribe. There's a women's cave round the southern side, part way up Moolya, that is a place where women go to give birth. My mother didn't have a midwife. She was alone when she gave birth to me. As is the custom amongst my people, she rubbed my palm with ochre and pressed it to the wall of the cave. She put her own handprint there, too. When I gave birth to my son, I went to the cave and made our handprints there. There are many prints of mothers and babies all over the cave walls. I do not know which ones are my mother's.

Moolya is my country. It grew me up. I learned the country from my mothers [R-J: Her mother and mother's sisters] and from other women in my tribe. I was the youngest in my family and the only girl. My mother died when I was a young girl.

We lived on our country all the time, moving between waterholes, hunting and camping and following the seasons. We heard about white men coming into our country from other Aboriginal people. They thought they were ghosts. Then people said the country was going to be a station, that white men were going to live on it and bring new animals. We thought there was no harm in sharing – we always share what we have with other tribes, and we didn't understand the white man meant to take our land and keep it for himself.

A white man came into our camp one day and gave us tucker – meat and bread and jam. I liked the jam. It was good tucker, sweeter than the sugarbag we snap from the mulga trees. He said he'd give us more if we worked for him. He asked us to sit down on the country. It was our country, so we said yes, and went to the homestead. I went to Mt Parker Station with my brothers and their wives and children, and we made our camp there.

I worked in the homestead for the missus. She was called Mrs Bilsom and she had a daughter they called Caro who was the same age as me. We both became women in the same month. Missus taught me to speak English and said she'd teach me to be a good housegirl. She made me clothes – dresses and skirts and drawers to wear, and she took me from the camp to sleep on the veranda near the house. That was good for me, as it was wrong for me to make camp near my brothers and their wives. I got blankets and tucker.

I had to wash the clothes and the linen and keep the house clean. I was always sweeping sand out of that house. One day I was pegging out the sheets when I dropped them in the dirt and had to start all over again. Missus was very angry with me.

Missus was always sick. She always had a baby in the tummy, and it always died before it could be born. I used to hear her crying in her bed when I was working. I scrubbed the blood from her sheets when her babies died.

Mr Bilsom, Boss, he hardly had a wife at all with her sick all the time. He was lonely for a wife and his eye fell on me. When I found out I had a baby in the tummy I was frightened. I went out into the far paddocks and collected plants the old women had taught me would kill the baby and make my bleeding start. Missus scolded me for being away from my work. I made up the medicine but it didn't kill the baby, I think because it was a white man's child and Aborigine medicine only works on Aborigines.

My tummy started getting big and I had to tell my brothers. They were more angry than I have ever seen anyone and they left the station and said they'd take revenge on the Boss for shaming me. It was wrong for him to take me and my brothers said they'd have revenge and they wouldn't work for him any more. So they went and camped on the station and speared the Boss's sheep and kept watch on the homestead. All the white people were afraid of Aborigines.

Another white man came to the station, looking for gold. He went all over the land, looking, looking, but didn't find any. To my people, that gold is dingo's blood. I told him where to find it. The Boss left the homestead and said he was going to check the fences at the far side of the station. He told me to look after Missus as she had a baby in the tummy again. She was very big with the baby and not far off her time. Caro was there, too, looking after her mother.

I was in the washhouse when I saw my brothers creeping into the yard with spears in their hands. They told all the other people to go away, and they all ran away to the bush – the yard boys and the old men and cook and the shearers – all went and left me.

The dog came out of the homestead barking, and my brother speared it dead. I knew they meant revenge and I begged them to go back into the bush. Missus heard the noise and came out asking what was going on. When she saw the dog and my brothers, I thought she might faint, she went so pale, but she turned and ran into the homestead. I ran after her. She was slow because she was so big. I stood between her and my three brothers. Caro was there, too, and she stood up and asked what was going on, her voice all shaky, and looked frightened out of her mind.

My oldest brother said that I had been shamed and they were here for revenge. Missus looked at me and at my belly and I know she understood, because she staggered back and fell on the bed and cried out for the Boss.

I tried to get my brothers to leave, go away and not harm the Missus. I beat them with my fists but they grabbed my arms and legs and carried me to the cupboard and locked me in. I hammered my fists on the door and screamed, but I could hear what they did to Missus and her daughter and it made me sick. I stopped beating on the door and huddled in a corner, covered with my own sick, and put my hands over my ears to block out the sounds of what my brothers were doing, and Missus screaming and Caro crying. I closed my eyes tight, even though it was dark as night in the cupboard.

I don't know how long I was shut in the cupboard, but when they let me out the homestead was silent. They grabbed me and took me to see what they'd done. When I saw how my brothers had butchered Missus and Caro, all in revenge for me, I was sick all over again and my legs gave way. They hauled me to the bed to have a good look, saying, 'If he takes our women, we'll take his.'

I spat on my brother and he punched me in my face. I hated him and what he'd done. They told me to go with them to their camp but I wouldn't. I couldn't leave Missus and Caro with no one to look after them. My brothers took their spears and left the homestead, cursing me.

The room was full of death and evil. I was very frightened to be there alone with the bodies. I didn't know what to do. I didn't want to leave them, and I was too afraid to sit with them, so I took my blankets to the cookhouse, where there was always a good fire, and waited for the Boss to come back.

I stayed there for two nights. All the time I saw the ghosts of Missus and Caro, their eyes burning in the dark. I heard them screaming as my brothers raped and killed them. I heard the dog barking and falling dead. I couldn't go near the homestead.

At last I heard horses coming near. I was relieved and terrified. I peeped out and saw it was the Boss and the other white man. Boss was stamping round the yard, calling for the men. He was angry when no one came, and suddenly I thought, 'What will he do when he finds the Missus and Caro?' And I was afraid for myself and for my brothers. Though I hated them, I ran to the camp to warn them the Boss was back, so they could hide in the bush and escape.

Their camp was at the waterhole at Moolya. I ran into the camp and heard horses galloping behind me. I screamed at my brothers to run away, but I was too late. The white men had guns. Boss started shooting at everyone. I hid in the spearwood bushes behind the waterhole, terrified he'd shoot me, too. He shot everyone, just kept shooting and shooting at my brothers, their wives and all of their children, even the babies, until they were all dead. I crawled out from my hiding place and he pointed the gun at me, too. I looked at him, and put my hand on my tummy to say there was a baby in there. When he lowered his gun I turned and ran to Moolya and hid in the caves until the white men had gone.

The waterhole was filled with blood. My family lay all jumbled up on the ground. I couldn't believe they were all dead. It all happened so quickly. I knew I couldn't bury them by myself, so I found where other Aborigines from Mt Parker were camping, and told them what had happened. They were too afraid to come to the waterhole, but one old man came with me and helped me bury them in the tribal way. We made the graves in horseshoe shapes and buried them sitting up facing the sunrise. And we built brushwood fences round the graves to protect them. It took a long time. There were many graves to dig.

I went back to the camp with the old man but the others were afraid of me because of what happened. I lived with them for a while but in the end I had to go back to Mt Parker Station. I had nowhere else to go and no one to protect me.

My son was born and I called him Dennis. He was very pale and everyone knew he was Boss's son – the Boss who'd killed my brothers and their families. The drought hit the country hard that year and there wasn't much tucker for people. They were forced to come back to the station to work and get rations, otherwise they'd starve out in the bush. One by one they slunk back onto the station. Some of the old people starved out in the bush, their skin hanging too big on their bones. When people came back to work on the land, Boss would spit and say, 'You need me now, but do I need you?' See he'd got a gold-mine on the country by then.

Life was very difficult for me and Dennis. Everyone hated him because he was Boss's son – not because Boss was a white man but because of the killings. Once I left Dennis with an old woman minding him, and when he rolled into the fire she just laughed. Dennis was scarred – all down his side the skin is burnt and twisted.

I left the station when Dennis was young. Mr Bilsom had gone and there was a new Boss there, and the mine was built for the gold. I walked off Mt Parker Station and went to Red Gum Station for a while, but it was the same there – my people cast me out because of the massacre and they hated Dennis. The Missus at Red Gum Station told me to leave – she didn't want any trouble.

I worked on a lot of stations, getting further and further from my country until I was in strangers' land. The white men started taking the children away. We'd paint them with burnt gum nuts to make them black, but they took them anyway. I saw lots of half-caste children taken away from the stations. Dennis went to the city and lived like a white man. It's easier for Aborigines and half-castes in the city. He went as soon as he was grown up. He sends messages to me but has not come to see me. I wish I could go and live with him, but I think he's ashamed having an Aborigine mother. Dennis has a wife, a half-caste woman called Rose, and they have a daughter called Polly. She's about ten now. I have never seen her.

I got sick on the stations and couldn't work. I was a stranger and the others wouldn't care for me. I had no family to take care of me. The welfare man came and brought me here on the train. I've been here a long time.

I want to go back to my country, to die at Moolya. That's the country that made me and it's where my spirit will go when I'm finished. This isn't my country here. Here, Aborigines are all mixed up. All people from different tribes together, the salt-water people and the red rock people all jumbled up. Young men and old men together. The half-caste children are in the compound, learning how to be whitefellas. I hear them crying for their mothers at night. The old women bang their heads against the walls and floors, trying to die. Everyone is lost, in here. We're all just waiting to die, so we can go home.

R-J: I paid a last visit to Moore River Native Settlement in 1930, and found that Ruby died a couple of months after this interview took place. She is buried at Moore River Native Settlement.

15

The breeze teased the surface of Lake Monger into waves. A lone jogger cranked along the far shore. Esther watched his elbows jerking up and down, lulled by the rhythm. Her mind chased shadows and scraps of thought. There *was* a massacre at Moolya, and now she knew where – a waterhole at Mt Parker. And the graves were there too. Lots of them. Shamefully many. Enough to stop the Caroline Mine Company destroying Mt Parker, even without Tommy Possum's evidence that Moolya was a sacred site. Stuart MacKendrick trounced. Mt Parker saved. She should be jubilant, but Ruby's story disquieted her. This wasn't a victory: it was a small step towards putting right ancient wrongs, and it ached like a defeat.

From the corner of her eye she caught sight of a family group: father, mother, two young children, squealing as the wind flicked away their picnic wrappings. She watched the father take his wife's hand, saw her responding smile as she gazed up at him. They were bubbled in their own happiness, cushioning them wherever they went, protecting them from the repellent outside world. Esther shifted, uneasy as a voyeur yet mesmerised. Happy families, they *do* exist. Sometimes. Wistfulness and yearning to be similarly loved and nurtured twisted inside her.

Brisk now, she gathered her papers together and stuffed them into her bag, then headed for home.

Rich was stewing when she returned, playing Mars from Holst's Planets so loudly the flyscreen door vibrated.

'A bit low-brow for you,' she commented, knowing he was being deliberately provocative and taking the bait anyway. What the hell, anything to release the tension.

'I don't know why you bother coming back,' he snarled. 'You obviously don't want to be here.'

'How can you say that?'

'Because you're never here.'

'It's my job, Rich. The job that pays for this house and the loan repayments on your sodding cello.'

He shot her a wounded look. 'And my contribution's worthless, I suppose?'

'I didn't say that. But I'm sick of you whingeing about my work. I can't win.' She stamped out to the garage, fetched a large eskie and lugged it into the kitchen. She banged open the freezer door and hurled ice blocks into the eskie, then piled frozen water bottles into the corners.

'What are you doing?'

'You know I'm going on fieldwork this afternoon. I'm getting my stuff ready.'

Rich put his hands on her shoulders and drew her round to face him. 'Esther.'

'I don't want to fight, Rich.'

'Neither do I.' He pulled her against his chest and mumbled into her hair. Her spine stiffened. 'We can't go on like this.'

'I know, I know. But I can't deal with this right now. I just haven't got the . . .' she waved her hands about, searching for the right words '. . . space to deal with your problems on top of everything else. I've got a big, mega-big case on at the moment. As soon as it's over I promise we'll talk.'

Rich's arms dropped from her waist as though she'd scalded him. His face hardened. 'Don't expect me to hang around that long.'

She thought at first she'd misunderstood. 'What?'

'I can't keep my life on hold forever while you sort out other people's.'

'You cheated on me! I trusted you and you betrayed me, and I'm not sure whether I can ever forgive you for that. I need some time to think, to see if there's any way we can get over this.'

Rich hung his head. 'It was one night, Esther! Just one night. It meant nothing.'

Her fingers itched to slap some sense into him. 'Don't you understand? It means *everything*.'

'Well, don't take too long to make up your mind, that's all.'

'Fine.' Esther turned away. Imminent tears clogged her throat. Her heart knocked in her chest and her hands shook as she took steaks from the freezer and stacked them in the eskie. She wedged in fruit, vegetables, salad and a carton of milk, then slotted a loaf of bread on the top, using the routine to calm herself. Into a cardboard box she piled tins of tuna and sweetcorn, tea, a jar of coffee, sugar, salt, pepper, UHT milk, cornflakes, a can opener, metal plates, cutlery, cooking utensils and a large red tin mug with her name scratched into the handle. She hefted the cardboard box onto her hip and took it to the 4WD, slotting it beside a water canister. She squashed her swag in the well by the back door.

Rich mooched in the driveway, fists balled in his pockets, waiting for her to react. She refused to play along. He cracked first. 'Here, let me help you with that.' He grabbed one of the eskie handles and together they lumped it into the back of the vehicle.

'Thanks,' said Esther.

'Make sure someone helps you lift it out,' said Rich. 'It's too heavy for you.'

She thought of the times she'd hauled tyres onto the holster on the back of the car, lugged full jerry cans onto the roof, and grappled with boxes, equipment and tools on fieldwork trips while male colleagues stood nearby, smoking. No concessions just because you're a girl. She finished packing the vehicle while Rich watched. 'OK, that's me done. See you when I get back?'

'Yeah,' he said, not looking at her.

Kent always had Sunday lunch at his mother's house, and Esther picked him up from there, hoping just to scoop him up and hit the road. To her annoyance he wasn't ready when she arrived, but Hazel ushered her inside and made a pot of tea while he crashed around in the background collecting his gear and fussing.

'Men!' said Hazel, shaking her head in mock-despair. Esther smiled complicitly, on her best behaviour. She'd never met Kent's mother before and was embarrassed.

'Are you married?' Hazel asked, settling in for a chat.

'Yes. Though I think Rich is more organised than I am.'

'That's what those men would like us to believe. Kent is just like his dad: it was always me waiting for *him* to get ready.'

Suddenly she said, 'Kent's always talking about you.' Esther started, apprehensive that she suspected they were more than colleagues, but she continued, conspiratorially, 'I think he's got a soft spot for you, though don't you tell him I said that. Good job you're married!' She paused. 'He says you're an anthropologist.'

'That's right.'

'He did archaeology at uni. I wish he'd done anthropology, then he could help me with my family tree.'

'How's it going?' Esther asked politely.

'Not bad, but I keep on getting stuck. Would you like to see?'

'Well . . .'

'Kent'll be ages yet. Wait there, I'll get my folders.'

Esther's heart sank. Once people got onto their family trees they could talk for hours. It was an occupational hazard of being an anthropologist: people just assumed you'd be interested in the intricacies of their family history. She was sure garbage collectors didn't find themselves dragged outside to review the contents of their friends' dustbins.

She glanced at her watch. Kent had better hurry up or they'd be driving the whole journey to Bilsom's Grudge in the dark.

Hazel returned with a box file and spread her papers out on the dining table. They pored over them together.

'I couldn't do anything until my mother died. She didn't like to admit she was Aboriginal. Both her parents were half-castes pretending to be whitefellas. Now she's finished, poor thing, I got the native welfare records and I've found Kent's great-grandfather. He was born at Moolya, where you're working now on that mine business. I've got native welfare records for the family up to 1945.'

'1945?'

'They became citizens then. It meant denying they were Aboriginal, but they lived in the city and it was easier there than in the bush. They could drink and vote once they became citizens.'

Esther picked up a piece of paper. It was a certificate of citizenship granted to Dennis Parker. She hardly saw it, her mind scratching over the row with Rich. Was he at home now, hurling his stuff into boxes and walking out of her, their, lives? Her stomach twisted.

'That's Kent's great-grandfather,' said Hazel. 'I'm not even sure when he was born, eighteen something. But we've always known where our traditional country was; it was whispered down to us. We always knew where we came from, really.'

'It's so hard trying to piece the bits together,' said Esther. She fidgeted, wishing Kent would hurry up and distracted by him moving about in the hall. Each time he passed the doorway she expected him to announce he was ready to leave. She skimmed over the pages. One of them showed Kent's extended family tree. At the top was a single name – Mantitja.

'Do you know anything about Mantitja?' she asked.

'Not really.'

'Didn't anyone talk about her?'

'No. Her son, Dennis, didn't see much of her. I think she neglected him.'

'Poor thing.' She put the paper down on the pile.

'See, here.' Hazel pulled out a low-quality scanned photo: an Aboriginal group standing stiffly together, the image too grainy to make out faces. 'See his arm there? All white. He got a nasty burn and it left a scar.'

Esther squinted at the print-out. 'Dennis?' she echoed, as the name clicked. She was reaching for the pile of papers to check when Kent appeared.

'Aren't you ready yet? Don't let Mum show you this stuff, Esther, she'll bore you to stone with it.'

'It's not boring! Esther's very interested. Aren't you?'

Esther was hurriedly flicking through the papers on the table. Where was the damn document?

'Give her a break, Mum. She does this all day at work; she doesn't want her weekends looking at other people's family trees.' He winked at Esther as she demurred. 'Let's get going, shall we?'

'I just want to look at one of these papers again . . .' Esther started riffling through the stack.

'He's in a rush now,' grumbled Hazel, shuffling the pages together and stuffing them into her folder. 'After you been waiting for him to sort himself out, now he's quick to be off.'

Esther looked at Kent. She couldn't ask to have another look at the papers without revealing what she suspected, and that wouldn't be fair to either Kent or his mother. They would be shocked if her suspicions were correct.

Feeling dazed that the chance had been literally snatched away, Esther shook hands. 'Thank you for the tea and for showing me your family tree, Hazel. It was lovely to meet you.'

'You come back and have yarn with me any time you like, Esther.'

'I might just do that.'

'Come on, Esther!' Kent called from the door. He flung his swag into the back of the 4WD and swung into the passenger seat. Esther climbed in beside him and waved out of the window as she pulled away. The long journey loomed ahead of her: hours of tarmac giving way to dirt corrugations thrumming pain into her spine.

'All right, Esther?'

'Bit tired.'

'You're not mad at me for making you wait, are you?'

'Course not!' She turned to him and attempted a smile, but to her horror felt her eyes flood with tears.

'What's wrong?' Kent's warm hand covered hers and drew it into his lap. 'Tell me what's happened.'

She rubbed the tears away, furious with herself. 'You don't want to know.'

'I do. Come on, out with it.'

'It's Rich.'

'Uh-huh.'

'He told me a few days ago that he's cheated on me.'

'He's having an affair?'

'Just a one night stand. It happened months ago and he kept quiet, then confessed because he thought the woman he slept with was going to confront me. We've done nothing but argue since then, even more than usual, and then today, just as I was about to go, he threatened to leave.' Her voice wobbled. 'He said he might not be there when I get back from this fieldtrip.'

'Do you want to go home to try and sort it out with him?'

'No.' She pinched her nose hard and sniffed. 'Rich can be petulant if he likes, but I'm not going to give in to emotional blackmail.'

'Will he leave?'

'I don't know.'

She wiped the tears from her cheeks with the hem of her T-shirt. They drove in silence for a few minutes, then Esther said, 'It's almost ironic, isn't it? He has an affair at the drop of a hat, and you and me . . .'

'Does he know about us?'

'There's nothing to know.' Even as she said it she knew that wasn't true, and that if Rich had an inkling of her feelings towards Kent he'd be devastated.

'Why didn't you tell me about this before?'

'I couldn't. It was too raw. I can't believe he's done this.'

Kent's hand rested on her thigh. 'You know, it was great to see you on Friday.'

'I told Rich I got the Saturday plane home. He thinks I was in Geraldton Friday night. After what happened to David I just couldn't bear to go home.'

'I'm pleased you stayed with me.'

After reporting back to David in the hospital she'd sought sanctuary at Kent's house. When he opened his door to her he looked so tall and strong that she'd flung herself into his arms and choked out the evening's events: David's injuries, going to collect his materials and finding his house turned over. Kent wrapped his arms round her and smoothed her hair while she rambled on.

'Stay here,' he said.

'I shouldn't.' Not while there was a particle of hope for her and Rich.

Kent understood. 'You'll be safe. Nothing's going to happen.' He stroked his finger down her cheek and gave a small smile. 'Least, not until you're ready.'

He forced her to eat something and ran her a hot bath. Then he put her into his bed and wrapped his arms round her to protect her, stroking her back until she fell asleep. She awoke once and turned to him in the night, aware of his presence beside her, and he whispered comforting words until she fell asleep again.

'Not now, not until you're ready,' he'd said, and she was glad.

Esther, remembering the sensation of his arms clasped around her throughout the night, said, 'I know it doesn't make any sense to be jealous of Rich, but I am.'

'He broke your trust.'

'We're both in the wrong. I shouldn't have told you how I felt about you.' She sighed and, almost to herself, said, 'Maybe we should stop kidding ourselves it'll ever work.'

There was a pause before Kent asked, 'Why not just move in with me?'

'You're not serious.'

'Leave Rich and come and live with me.' He turned to look her in the eye, and she saw he meant it.

She squeezed his hand. 'Let me think about it. Thanks for listening.'

'No worries.'

Kent switched on the radio for the cricket and they lapsed into silence, Esther swaddled in her own thoughts. As they drove further inland the wide freeway narrowed to country roads with uneven edges, littered with road kill. Neat blocks of suburban houses drifted into lonely farms. Green reticulated lawns and fruit orchards gave way to sand and jagged scrub.

After a few hours Kent clicked off the radio and said, 'Pull into this roadhouse. We'll swap over.'

Esther slid down from the driver's seat and walked round the apron of the roadhouse, stretching her legs and easing the kinks out of her spine. To the side of the building was a cage of native parrots and finches. She clucked at them, sorry to see them cooped in such squalor. A dead heap of feathers crumpled in one corner.

A beefy man slapped through the plastic strips in the doorway of the roadhouse and stamped towards the 4WD. 'Fill 'er up,' he stated.

'Cheers, mate,' said Kent.

The attendant hitched the nozzle into the petrol tank. His forearms flexed, and Esther saw the white scar where a tattoo had been removed. The ghost of it lurked beneath his skin. He and Kent went into the roadhouse.

A scar. Kent's great-grandfather had a scar.

She called out, 'Can you grab me a Coke, please?' and ran to the car. She jumped in the back seat and scrabbled amongst all the boxes and gear for her computer case. She yanked David's papers from the side pocket and scanned them, running her finger down the pages. She found what she was searching for and felt a worm of excitement wriggle through her. She had to know if she was right.

She pulled her phone out of her pocket: it was still in range. She jabbed out a text message and sent it to David Liddle. The envelope dissolved on the screen as Kent returned to the vehicle. Message sent.

Kent handed her a greasy paper carton. 'Hot chips made from genuine cardboard.'

'They smell good. Ug. Taste not so good, but the salt's nice.'

'I'm driving.' He swung his long legs into the 4WD and shoved the seat right back. 'Even with this girly appendage.' He prodded the miniature disco ball hanging from the rear view mirror. It joggled on its thread. 'I don't know why you put this in the car. Unless you're expecting a bit of a boogie on fieldtrips.'

'It's to stop Frank borrowing it and taking it to Jigalong for Law business,' said Esther through a mouthful of chips. 'It makes it too girly for his liking. Shame I can't do the same to the car fridges.'

'I hope no one thinks I'm a poof with this hanging there,' Kent said, darkly.

'I'll vouch for you.'

They exchanged smiles.

'You look knackered, Esther. Get some sleep and I'll wake you when we get to Bilsom's Grudge.'

She was convinced she'd never rest: her mind churned with possibilities and unresolved questions, and her stomach was queasy with jitters. She wedged her head in the nook between the seat back and the doorframe and closed her eyes. Kent switched the cricket back on. The steady thrum of the wheels lulled her, and when Kent shook her shoulder it was dark and they were passing through the main street of Bilsom's Grudge.

'Better?'

'Much better. Thanks.'

'You can make it up to me later.' He kissed the tip of his finger and dotted the end of her nose.

She massaged the crick in her neck, relieved to be in Bilsom's Grudge despite the difficult meetings ahead. There was nothing she could do about Rich while she was here. 'Any sign of Frank?'

'His car's there by the motel units. My guess is . . .'

'The TAB!' they groaned in unison.

They checked into the Grand Hotel and let themselves into the familiar motel units. The orange and brown doona covers were the same as last time. Esther wondered how often they were laundered. The nylon carpet tiles scuffed up static and she got a shock when she switched on the kettle.

She hefted her laptop onto the table and spread out David's notes. Her head throbbed but she had an idea that wouldn't wait. Beside her was the sheaf of papers David Liddle had given her. On the top was Charles Bilsom's family tree.

'Come on, Esther, you're rooted,' warned Kent. 'Leave it for a couple of hours.'

'I'll be right there. Just give me twenty minutes, I promise that's all. Just need to check something out.'

'OK,' he said, reluctantly.

She kissed his cheek. 'Order me a steak. Won't be long.'

As soon as the door clicked behind him she wired up the laptop to her mobile phone and logged onto the internet. She searched for the Caroline Mine Company and brought up the company website. Esther navigated to a link to the contemporary owners. It stated 'Ownership of the Caroline Mine has remained in the hands of the descendants of the original founders of the mine: Charles Bilsom and Henry MacKendrick', but it didn't give their names. She racked her brains for a minute, then typed Australian Stock Exchange into the search engine, and after lots of cold trails and dead ends found a list of the Caroline Mine's shareholders. There were two owners, each with a 50 per cent share in the mine. They were Stuart MacKendrick and Mark Bilsom.

Excitement rising and beating a tattoo in her throat, Esther went to the website of the West Australian newspaper and searched the images database, finally finding the confirmation she needed. Five years ago the newspaper had taken a photograph in the hospitality box of a major Australian mine at the Hopman Cup. The photograph bore the legend

'Joint owners of the Caroline Mine, with the Minster for Minerals and Energy, Western Australia'. The men were laughing and drinking champagne, heads tipped back as if they hadn't a care in the world.

'You!' Esther exclaimed.

16

'What's the hold-up, Esther?' Kent asked. 'The community's getting aggro.'

Esther scanned the rows of surly faces waiting under the Tjulpan bough shelter. There were already audible grumbles about the Land Council and several pairs of eyes glared at her.

'I need Frank to be here. The community's got a big decision to make.'

'We've done meetings without him before.'

'This is a tricky one. I think the community's been conned, and I want them to agree to take legal advice before they do anything else.'

'I'll ring him again.' Kent moved away from the group, scuffing the sand with his boot as he talked on his mobile.

'We're ready to begin, Dr King.'

Esther turned and met Stuart MacKendrick's eyes boring into her. 'I'm waiting for my colleague.'

'You're wasting my time. There's nothing to gain from these delay tactics.'

'Unlike your tactics, Mr MacKendrick.'

His eyes narrowed. 'I suppose you think you're clever, Dr King.'

'Bit cynical, isn't it, your choice of community liaison officer?'

He hesitated, caught off guard. She felt a stab of pleasure that she'd wrong-footed him. He recovered fast. 'Not cynical, more pragmatic.'

'But you didn't bother to tell Tjulpan community?'

'It makes no difference to them.' MacKendrick waved his hand dismissively at the people grouching under the bough shelter. 'I didn't want to confuse them with unnecessary detail.'

Esther snorted.

'Now listen here.' He loomed closer to her. His breath hit her cheek. A muscle flickered in his temple. 'The old seam is exhausted. We've been crushing rocks for months now. If that new mine doesn't go ahead this whole place is finished. And that means your precious Tjulpan community too. The new mine can give these people jobs, training, a future. Exactly what they're lacking now.'

'Very persuasive, Mr MacKendrick,' Esther said sarcastically, 'but I don't think they're going to destroy a sacred site and a massacre site just for the money, however much you offer them.'

'It's their decision,' he growled. 'Let's hope they see sense.'

'My feelings exactly.'

MacKendrick stumped off and took a seat next to the mine lawyers under the bough shelter. They looked incongruous in their smart trousers and ties, fountain pens hovering over yellow legal pads waiting to strike, briefcases resting on their laps.

Kent snapped his phone off and shook his head at Esther. He turned her aside so no one could see what he was saying. Cold foreboding sliced through her. 'I don't think Frank's going to make it,' he muttered.

'Why? Is he ill?'

Kent sighed. 'Don't go mad. He's on an accumulator.'

It took a second before she realised what he'd said. 'You're kidding me!'

'Nope. Soon as all the elders are here we'd better get started.'

Tommy Possum shuffled out of his house and made his way to the front row under the bough shelter.

Esther hesitated, swatted away a fly, calculating how much damage would be done if she stalled long enough for Kent to drag Frank out of the TAB.

'What are we waitin' for?' someone yelled from the back of the bough shelter.

'Mr Possum's here, so's we can start now,' another angry voice bawled.

If she wasn't careful the community meeting would break down altogether in angry exchanges and accusations against the Land Council – delicious fodder for the mine's lawyers. There was nothing for it. Esther moved to the front and started to speak. Her voice came out too high. She took a breath and started again, slowing her voice, making it deeper, in control.

'Good morning, everyone, thank you for coming to this meeting. I'd like to . . .'

Her words were obliterated by a voice that bellowed from the side of the meeting. 'This is totally wrong! My mother only died a week ago, and you're holding a community meeting!' Gavin forced his way through to the front and shouted at the crowd, pointing to people as he harangued them. 'Yous old fellas know better than this. You got no respect for my mother. And yous shouldn't let this happen.'

The mob shouted back with protestations and counter-accusations, slurs against Doreen and denials of Gavin's right to speak to the meeting. He was too young to talk to them like that; he hadn't been through the Law; he should show some respect to his elders. Esther glanced at Kent to see how he was reacting to the disturbance. He gave a tiny shake of his head. Don't panic yet, it meant: let them blow off steam and get the meeting back on track. She moved to the side while the argument tossed back and forth.

Tommy Possum heaved himself to his feet and the noise died down as he started to speak. 'This is shit talk. That woman was a troublemaker and she stirred up bad blood in this community, tried to turn blackfella against blackfella. Then she was shamed of what she done to Tjulpan people, and she hanged herself.'

'That's not true!' Gavin screamed, his face contorted with grief. 'She never!'

'All 'cause she crazy woman. And crazy woman doesn't stop important business in Tjulpan community.'

He sat down again. Tears streamed down Gavin's face and his mouth worked silently, trying to shape the words he needed. Everyone's eyes fixed on the ground, determined to avoid his gaze. 'This is wrong!' he cried. The impotent words battered against ears that refused to hear him. 'Yous all wrong to do this!'

He shoved out of the bough shelter and ran to his house. Esther paused, unsure what to do, aware that whatever she decided would somehow count against her. Her hands were shaking when Tommy indicated by a wave that she should continue. She shoved her hands in her pockets to hide the tremor.

'Perhaps we should have a minute's silence for the woman who died,' Esther said, conscious of the Aboriginal custom not to mention the names of the recently deceased and reluctant to commit another gaffe. They should have shown respect for Doreen right at the start. Tommy should have initiated it: it was his place to do so. If only Frank were here.

'No!' said Tommy. 'Get on with the meeting. We're not holding up business for that woman.'

Esther started again. 'The Caroline Mine Company want to build a new mine at Moolya, Mt Parker. Because the mine will mean destroying Moolya, they need Tjulpan's approval to go ahead.' She picked her words carefully. 'But I've found out that the mine people haven't been straight with you. One of the mine owners has been living here pretending to be someone else. They've been trying to deceive you.'

She paused to let her words sink in. Several people turned to each other in consternation, and incredulous mutters rippled through the crowd. The mine lawyers jiggled their tiny spectacles and held a muttered conference behind a legal pad. Stuart MacKendrick batted away their questions with an irritated flap of his hand.

'I think that it would be best if you had a lawyer out here to advise you before you make a decision on what to do about the new mine,' Esther continued.

MacKendrick stabbed at the grass with his walking stick. He looked as if he was about to rise and address the meeting, but Tommy beat him to it. 'This all whitefella talk,' he shouted at Esther. 'You think we're stupid, that we can't make a decision without more whitefellas.'

'I don't think that at all,' she protested. 'But there's misrepresentation here, and you should get legal advice.'

'More whitefellas interfering, telling us what to do. What's the difference between Land Council whitefellas and Caroline Mine whitefellas telling us what to do? No difference.'

'The Land Council acts in your interests.'

'No, no, we can decide now. It's our country. We say what happens here.'

The rest of the community nodded at his words. Deep-seated distrust pounded towards Esther: of lawyers, of the Land Council, of whitefellas in general. After what she'd learned in the past days about Aboriginal-white relations in the area who could blame them? It was never far from the surface, and needed only a minor incident to turn into full-grown hostility.

She backed off. 'OK, it's your country, you don't have to have legal advice. So the question now is whether you want to destroy Moolya: a sacred site and the site of a massacre.'

'What massacre?' Tommy Possum yelled. 'There was no massacre.'

'I've got evidence there was a massacre there.'

'More whitefella bullshit.'

Esther seethed. Hatred for the old man ripped through her. Couldn't he see she was trying to protect his country? All he saw was a whitefella, a white *woman*, to despise. 'I've got evidence,' she said again.

'What that crazy woman said? She didn't know anything.'

'Not just that but . . .'

'No!' Tommy roared. 'There was no massacre here!'

The community rumbled with unease but no one spoke up against the old man.

The Caroline Mine lawyer raised his hand. 'If any descendants of this alleged massacre were to come forward with evidence of the massacre we would obviously listen carefully to their views.'

'I tell you there was no massacre,' Tommy spat at him. 'This is my country, I worked all over it, and I know nothing about no massacre here.'

The community muttered in disbelief, avoiding his eye. Esther looked at Kent. He was as bewildered as the rest of the community. Why would Tommy Possum deny the massacre? It was obviously well known in the community; they'd all heard the rumours. Here was Esther with proof, and he refused to admit it ever happened.

One woman stood and shouted, 'Those were our ancestors who died there, our old people.'

The lawyer interrupted, 'Is anyone here related to the massacre victims?'

'That's not the point,' the woman cried. 'They were Tjulpan people who were killed. We all know that!'

Esther counted to twenty, then counted again. 'OK. The massacre is obviously too hard to think about. But we all know Moolya is a sacred site, so Tjulpan people need to decide how best to protect it.'

'Who said it's a sacred site?' Tommy demanded.

She couldn't have heard him right. 'You did.'

'I never.'

'You told me the Dreaming story of Moolya. Frank agreed with you. He knows the story from Law business.'

'This isn't his country! He can't speak for it!' Tommy's eyes bulged. Sweat rings stained his T-shirt underarms. 'It's my country and I speak here, and I say there is no sacred site!'

Horrified silence. The people in the bough shelter gaped, appalled, yet whipped and defeated and powerless to protest and defend their culture. They looked afraid and upset. Several wept. No one was brave enough to contradict the old man. One elderly woman stumbled from the meeting, her face wet with tears, sobbing audibly.

Esther looked helplessly at Kent. He had paled when Tommy Possum denied Moolya was a sacred site; now she saw the tremor in his hands and cheek as he visibly collected himself before addressing the meeting.

'Right,' he said, his voice shaky. 'If you say there's no sacred site and no massacre, the community still needs to decide about this new mine on its land.'

Esther was glad he'd stepped in. She was too shocked to speak. She'd heard of Aboriginal groups inventing sacred sites to stop a development before, but never of a group denying a site was sacred. A suspicion of Tommy's motives started to form, and sickened her. She looked at the old man: he was shouting and stammering, under stress, working hard. 'The mine will go ahead!'

'Tjulpan has got a set of agreements for how you reach decisions on your country,' Kent cut in, 'and one person can't decide for the whole community. You've got to vote on it.'

MacKendrick jumped up. 'The mine lawyers are here with a contract. You know what the mine is offering as compensation to the community. If you sign now that money will increase by 10 per cent.'

'We'll sign now,' said Tommy. 'This is good for Tjulpan.'

'You can't just push this through,' argued Esther. 'You need the minister's approval before you destroy a site.'

'It isn't a site, it's just a pile of rocks,' MacKendrick reminded her, glancing pointedly at Tommy. 'You don't need the minister's approval to blow up a pile of rocks.'

More people were drifting away from the meeting, washing their hands of the responsibility, too afraid to stand up to the old man and too ashamed to watch him destroy their culture and country.

Esther lunged at a last chance. 'There might be archaeological sites at Moolya. If there are, Tjulpan would be entitled to more compensation. But you won't get it if you sign now.' Tommy protested, but she spoke over the top of him, appealing to the mine lawyers. 'I'm sure Mr MacKendrick can let Tjulpan have until the end of the week before signing his contract. I know he'll want to see everything's fair and above board.'

MacKendrick scowled at her, but after a minute's conference with his lawyers he assented.

'We'll need an elder to help with the heritage survey,' said Esther. 'Usual rates of pay.'

The community members glanced at each other uncertainly. Esther smiled at them brightly, knowing what they'd say yet feigning innocence.

'It'd be right for Mr Possum to do it,' someone suggested.

'Wonderful!' She ached with disgust. 'Do you agree, Mr Possum?'

'Usual pay?'

'Yes.'

'All right.' He didn't look happy. Usually he was smug to get paid consultants' rates for visiting his own country and reminiscing about it. He was earning his money this time.

The meeting broke up and the people dawdled back to their homes and to the store, picking over the day's proceedings.

Kent grabbed Esther's elbow. 'What are you up to?'

'I just want to get that evil old man out on his country, out to Moolya and the massacre site, and see if he's so certain it never happened.'

'We don't know where it happened.'

'I do. At least, I know where to start looking and what I'm looking for.'

'But you can't just shanghai an elder to try and get him to change his mind.' Exasperation sharpened his voice.

She was hurt he didn't recognise how hard she was fighting to save

Moolya, wanting to end the deceit, trying to redress the wrongs. Stubbornness kicked in. 'I just did,' she said, pulling her arm out of his grasp.

Frank was perched in front of the TV screen in the TAB, flicking a betting slip with his thumbnail. He was wearing a grimy black singlet, showing off the full extent of the tattoos on his meaty arms. The hair on the back of his neck was greying, as was the pelt covering his chest. The bar smelled stale, layers of cigarette smoke and slopped beer mingling with hot bodies and greasy carpets. Dusty sunshine streaked across the bar. It was quiet in there. Just a few hardcore addicts mesmerised by the screen and lobbing occasional comments to each other.

Esther hurtled in and marched Frank out of the bar, and into the street, away from the amused grins of his fellow gamblers. They glared at each other, ignoring the interested stares of people going into the mini-mart. 'Where the hell were you?' she demanded, itching to shake him. 'We were crucified out there!' Frank swallowed and said nothing. 'The bloody community is now saying there wasn't a massacre and that Moolya isn't a sacred site. They've given the go-ahead to blowing the whole place sky high.'

Frank blanched. 'They can't do that! What are them blackfellas talking about? Everyone knows Moolya's a sacred site.'

'Not when there's money on the table it isn't.'

'Who says?'

'Tommy Possum.'

Frank swore. 'But he told us the story. I was scared he might tell us too much, you being a woman and that.'

'I know.'

'Blackfellas from all over know that site and that story. It's part of Law business.' Frank was babbling. Fear crumpled his face and she felt a pang of sympathy. 'It's in a chain of sacred sites. If they destroy it . . . oh fuckin' 'ell!'

'Exactly. But you weren't at the meeting. No one spoke up against him.'

'Jeez.' Frank rubbed his grizzled head. 'I can't believe these fellas. What's got into them?'

'Money.' She boiled with anger and frustration.

'Greedy blackfellas. But if you sell your culture you got nothing left.'

'Tell them that.'

'Dr Esther, I'm really sorry I missed the meeting.'

'Me too, but it's done now,' she sighed. 'I've persuaded the mine and the community to wait until Friday before they sign. That gives us a few days to convince them to change their minds.'

'That's not long.'

'It was difficult enough to get that. We're going out to do a heritage survey with Mr Possum, and hope he changes his mind about Moolya.'

'All right, Esther. I'll go and get the old fella and we'll have a bit of a chat on the way. See if I can't get some sense into his head.'

'Thanks, mate. Let's see what we can salvage.'

Frank stumped off to his 4WD and heaved himself into the driver's seat. He gunned the engine and hurtled down the dirt road to Tjulpan, sticking his hand out in a thumbs-up as he sped past. Esther watched the cloud of dust behind the car disappear, then slapped through the plastic flaps at the door of the mini-mart to stock up on groceries for the heritage survey. Dredging up optimism, she bought four days' worth of milk, bread and supplies, and shoved away thoughts of what would happen if this fishing trip failed. Even armed with Elizabeth Roper-Jones's field notes of Ruby's account about the massacre, she knew realistically she was unlikely to find any evidence of it, and even if she did there was little chance it would persuade Tommy to change his mind. It's their choice, it's their land, Esther thought on a continuous loop, unconsoled.

She was loading everything into the back of the 4WD when her mobile phone vibrated. She dug it out of the side pocket of her combat pants and opened a text message from David Liddle. It answered the question she had sent him the day before, a single word that confirmed her suspicions and sent her mind whirling: Mantitja.

She snapped the phone off, gnawing her thumbnail. Out of the corner of her eye she saw a bashed ute slide nose-in to the pavement outside the mini-mart. Mark Wright jumped from the cab.

Esther sauntered up to him, her face burning. 'Missed you at the community meeting.' She tried to keep her voice light, but the trap was sprung beneath her words.

'I don't think I was needed.'

'No, I guess your work is done.'

'What?'

'I'd have thought you'd be careful not to let the mine make an invalid agreement,' she said.

'Your point?'

'If the Tjulpan community is misled and signs Mt Parker over to the mine, it's an invalid agreement. Could cost you. Big time.'

'Yeah, it could. But we both know that by the time your lawyers crank into action it'll be too late.' He tipped his hat at her. 'Goodbye, Esther.'

She watched his straight back as he strode into the mini-mart as if he owned the place, and warmed with fury. She slammed the groceries into eskies and clambered onto the roof to check the swags were secure. The strap was fraying and she snipped off the loose end with her penknife and rethreaded it. She jagged her hand on a sharp edge; the pain pleased her. She sucked the metallic blood, rubbing her tongue over the wound.

She was still seething when Kent banged out of the hotel and slung his backpack into the back of the 4WD. He caught her dabbing at the cut.

'What have you done?'

'Just snagged myself on my knife.'

He took her hand and inspected the wound, chiding her about the heritage survey. 'I don't think this is a good idea, Esther. I can't see how this will change anything.'

'We've got to have a try at least. We can't just let them get away with blowing up Moolya without a fight.'

'But if it's what the community wants we can't trample over them and say we know better.'

'The community's been deceived. Shedloads of illegal stuff is going on here. If they sign now the agreement will be invalid.'

Realisation of the implications registered in his face. He gave a low whistle. 'Shit.'

'And I'm pretty sure Possum's being bribed to say Moolya isn't a sacred site.'

'Have you got any evidence?'

'Well, no, but remember when Doreen said there was something bad going on in Tjulpan? Straight after she told me I got an anonymous letter warning me off.'

'You think it was Tommy Possum?'

'It couldn't be. He can't write. His signature on the claim documents is a cross.'

'So who sent it?'

'My money's on Stuart MacKendrick.'

'Why?'

'Because he's basically a nasty piece of work, and he'd do anything to get the new mine. I think Possum's being paid by the mine to make sure the community votes the way they want. I want him away from MacKendrick, out on his own country, and then see if he's so certain that Moolya isn't a sacred site.'

'The community agreed with him.'

'No they didn't – it was just no one dared disagree. You saw them: they're terrified of him. He's using his status as an elder and a medicine man to beat them into submission. You remember what Doreen said about the child abuse? No one dares stand up to him. MacKendrick has found out through his sidekick Mark that the community will do anything Tommy Possum says. So all he had to do was get Possum on his side.'

'Blackmailing him over the child abuse?'

'Probably a mixture of blackmail and bribery.'

'What a bloody mess!' Kent flopped down onto the tailgate and ran his hands through his hair. He took Esther's hand and knit his fingers with hers. 'Do you honestly think the fieldtrip will make Mr Possum change his mind?'

She shrugged. 'Only one way to find out.'

It was their last chance.

17

Purple shadows strobed the rough dirt track. The sun dipped beneath the horizon, pooling last drops of amber light onto the eucalypt trunks. Grey and pink galahs screeched in the branches. The 4WD lurched as the track dipped towards the creek bed and rattled over pebbles, disturbing a flock of budgies and sending them up in a flurry of green and gold.

'Water,' Kent marvelled at the puddles dotting the creek bed.

Esther wondered at the optimism that termed a strip of dry sand a river; imagined the glee when the waters eventually unfurled along its length. When she first came to Australia she had been intrigued by the bitterness that named Lake Disappointment and Mistake Creek. Yet now, after living for years in this unforgiving landscape, she was surprised that the pioneers hadn't vented their frustration on more landmarks.

As the 4WD mounted the far bank a startled mob of grey kangaroos twitched in disgust and bounded into the scrub, their thick tails bobbing. The track snaked through the bush, twisting back on itself to cut round stately gum trees as old as the landscape. Wild goats skipped across the track, one at a time, playing chicken with the vehicles.

They stopped at a low, rough stone building. Frank's 4WD clattered to a halt beside Esther and Kent, peppering the running boards of both vehicles with stones. When the engines died the silence hung heavy on the air.

Esther climbed down from the 4WD and stretched up to the roof rack, grasped it and let go, her legs swinging and snapping her spine straight. Outback traction. Her vertebrae clunked into place.

She leaned in at Frank's window. 'Do you know this place, Mr Possum?' she asked.

The old man glanced at the ramshackle stone building. 'I haven't been here since I was a young man,' he said, slowly. His eyes flickered to the stone building and away again. 'I was a stockman here for a while.'

'Did you live at the homestead?'

'Nah. I was always camped out in the bush with the stock, mustering.'

'What we doing here, Esther?' asked Frank. Suspicion twitched in his face. Even with him distrust was never far from the surface; could turn in an instant.

'I thought we could poke round here for a while before we go up to Moolya. Thought Mr Possum might like a few days out on country.' And be paid for it. Corrupt system, she thought: who's to blame people for taking advantage of it?

'What is this place, Mr Possum?' asked Frank.

'Old Mt Parker Station homestead,' said Tommy. 'They built a new one further down the river.'

'This was the homestead when Charles Bilsom and his family lived here,' said Esther. 'It doesn't look much, does it? Let's have a look round.'

She set off for the homestead, the three men trailing after her. One wall of the homestead had collapsed into rubble. A door hung on one hinge, like a milk tooth ready to fall out. Grass and acacias sprouted from the stones. The roof was a patchwork of rusted iron.

'There were more buildings here back then,' said Esther. 'Shearing shed, cook house, wash house. Do you remember, Mr Possum?'

'All gone. Stones used to build the other homestead.'

'Strange they didn't re-use this too.'

He shrugged, hanging back, unwilling to edge closer to the corpse of the homestead.

Esther pushed at the door. It jiggled on its hinge, then settled, and she stepped inside. A feral reek made her gag. Something skittered in the corner of the room, invisible by the time she turned to look. In the gloom she saw the window shutters hanging at drunken angles, giving the room a lopsided look. The floorboards were caked with sand and animal droppings. Lizard and possum, she presumed. Snatches of sky peeped through the gaps in the corrugated iron roof.

Esther turned back and saw the men skulking in the doorway. 'Aren't any of you coming in?'

Kent stepped forward uncertainly. Tommy stumped back to Frank's 4WD and waited in the passenger seat.

'Why here?' Kent asked in a low voice.

'This is where the story starts. We're going to follow the story.'

Kent looked round the room. 'Shame about this place. If it was near Perth it'd be conserved and have a plaque outside it.'

'The whole station's a shambles,' said Esther. 'The land's being chopped to bits by goats.' She picked up a broken chair, disturbing a translucent gecko. It wriggled away on its sticky pads.

'Who owns Mt Parker Station?'

'No one. The property's been empty for years. You just can't make a living here.'

'Unless you find gold.'

Esther crossed to the shattered windows. 'You can see Moolya from here.' Moolya was dark purple in the seeping light. Behind it the sky darkened to navy, just starting to prickle with stars. 'It must have been wonderful looking out over it every day.'

'Hard life, though, for those early pioneers.'

Esther looked at the blank walls. 'How do we get to the rest of the homestead?'

'I think you have to come out and go round by the veranda.'

The veranda had collapsed on three sides of the homestead and a vine snaked over the remains. The second room consisted only of a doorway and a pile of rubble. It was difficult to conjure either the steadfast pioneering life of the Bilsom family or the brutal murder of the two women.

'You'd think that it would leave an impression somehow,' Esther muttered to herself. 'Not ghosts, just . . . an effect, a trick of the light, a sensation.'

'Come on,' said Kent, tugging her hand. 'Better set up the camp before it's too dark to see.'

Tommy was still in the 4WD, Frank beside him tapping along to a country and western tape.

'I'll put my swag over there.' Esther pointed to a clear patch of ground well out of danger from ant nests and falling gum branches. The men could fend for themselves. 'We'll stay here tonight then head to Moolya in the morning. OK?'

She threw her swag down from the roof of the 4WD and unfurled it on a prickle-free patch of hard earth. Kent and Frank dragged branches to the camp and made a fire. Soon the billy lid was rattling and the air was treacly with mulga smoke. Kent levered the barbecue grill over the flames, slathered it with butter and slapped down thick steaks. Only then did Tommy clamber down from the vehicle.

Frank glanced at him anxiously. 'All right, big fella?'

Tommy grunted and accepted a tin mug of tea. He flopped into a canvas chair and the tea slopped gently onto the sand.

Esther swigged her tea, burning her lip on the tin mug, and said, conversationally, 'It's odd this place feels so normal after what happened.' Kent stopped prodding the steaks and shot her a warning glance. Ignoring him, she continued, 'You know, I thought it would feel spooky here. Silly, really. Just because there was a murder, two murders, you expect it to change a place for ever.' She laughed. 'Humans are so self-important. We think our deaths will alter a landscape that's billions of years old. What do you think, Mr Possum?'

'There was no massacre,' he growled.

'I'm not talking about the massacre, I'm talking about the murder. You must know about that.' Her voice hardened. 'Or do you deny that happened too?'

'Esther . . .' Frank cautioned.

She carried on. See what the old bastard had to say to this. 'I was reading an account of the murder the other day. I've read all the newspaper reports from the time, but this was an eye-witness account.' Tommy stared at her, his face frightened. 'A young girl saw it all: the murder, the massacre.' Esther jerked her thumb at the tumbledown homestead. 'The murders were committed in there. This girl, Ruby, saw it all. The two women – the station owner's wife and their young daughter – were killed by Ruby's brothers. She stayed with the bodies for two days until the station owner returned.' She lowered her voice. 'She says she saw their ghosts the whole time, their eyes burning in the dark.'

She stopped and let her words sink in. The men exchanged uneasy glances. Night was complete, the dark surrounding them thick beyond the circle of light from the fire.

They ate their steaks in silence, then slid into their swags. Esther was glad she'd bagged the space close to the fire. The men's camp was a distance from her. Unwilling to sleep near the homestead, the men wedged themselves beyond the parked vehicles.

Esther placed her boots at the head of her swag and slid her torch inside one, ready should she need it in the night. She thumped her pillow and snuggled deep, hauling the canvas over her head to protect from the cold breeze whipping her hair.

She awoke some hours later. Rolling onto her back, she gazed at the star-crammed sky. A noise from the bush. She strained her ears to hear. Probably just a dingo, or one of those infernal goats. The scuffling came again. The fire had crumbled to ash and the only light was from the spray of the Milky Way. Propping herself up on her elbow, she fumbled in her boot for her torch. The torch's beam transformed the bush into jagged shadows. Slowly she swung the beam. Nothing.

Esther clicked off the torch and settled back to sleep. All was silent for a few minutes, then a scream sent her groping for the torch again. She sat bolt upright, and her hands shook as she clicked on the light and pointed it into the bush. Two yellow eyes glowed at her. She moved the beam, and a huge native cat sprang from a tree and slunk away into the night. Chuckling at her own jumpiness, Esther flopped down in her swag and fell asleep.

When she next awoke, Tommy and Frank were crashing about in the men's camp. Their voices skittered across the darkness. 'Can you still see it, Mr Possum?'

'This is evil place. There's eyes out there.'

Esther sat up, pulled her clothes from her swag and wriggled into her sweatshirt.

'I can't see anything, Mr Possum.' Frank's voice was hesitant. 'You sure it wasn't a dingo?'

'I'm leaving this place right now.'

'Wait up, old fella. It was just a possum or a dingo, that's all.'

More shuffling and thumping in the darkness, then the car headlights blazed. Esther scrambled out of her swag and squinted into the light. 'What's going on?'

'I'm going home,' said Tommy. 'You take me home now.'

'I can take you home tomorrow,' said Frank.

'No! Now! This is a bad place.'

Esther inched towards the men's camp, feeling uncomfortable, knowing that women should avoid approaching. She called out, 'What's wrong?'

'Mr Possum wants to go home because he saw something,' said Frank.

'I saw a native cat earlier,' said Esther. 'Huge thing it was.'

'This was no cat. I seen eyes out there in the bush, watching me,' said Tommy. 'It's not safe here. This fella taking me home. Now.'

Frank looked at Esther and shrugged. 'All right, old fella. Roll up your swag and we'll go back. OK, Esther?'

'No.' She folded her arms across her chest.

'He's made his mind up he wants to go.'

She recognised the edge in his voice that warned her not to contradict an elder. 'Fine. You two go back. Kent and I will stay here.'

'Why?'

'We've got a heritage survey to do.'

'You can't do it without Mr Possum.'

'He says there's nothing to find. I say there is. I want to have a look at that site before it gets blown to bits.'

'You're crazy,' said Tommy.

'Like Doreen?' She watched him struggling to roll up his swag. 'She cared more about this country than you do. You ought to be ashamed.'

She stalked over to her 4WD and rummaged in the eskie for a chocolate bar. She sat on the bull bar chewing it while Frank and Tommy scurried round in the darkness loading Frank's vehicle. Kent came and sat next to her. He took the chocolate bar out of her hand and took a bite. Caramel strung from his lower lip to his chin. 'You sure this is the right thing to do?' he asked.

'No.'

'Fair enough.'

Tommy Possum hauled himself into Frank's 4WD and stared grimly out as though he expected the ghosts of Hetty and Caro Bilsom to hurtle out of the blackness after him. Frank shrugged as he climbed into the car, yet looking relieved to be getting the hell out of there all the same.

It was eerie when Frank's 4WD had gone. They had a last glimpse of the headlights dipping along the track and the sound of the engine pulsed back to them long after the car was out of sight. Eventually all was quiet, just the throbbing of the bush, snapping branches and restless mammals rustling in the leaves. The night closed in around them, the wind whipping sand into their faces. Kent stirred the embers of the fire and fed in twigs and branches until it glowed hot and orange, and added a mulga stump to last the night. He dragged his swag next to Esther's and they clambered under the covers together, comforted by the closeness of the fire and each other.

Kent wound his arms round her waist and murmured into her hair. 'So what's the plan now, Esther?'

'I have absolutely no idea.'

She awoke to the sound of a crow barracking the dawn from the branches of a eucalypt. The mournful sound echoed through the dry leaves and cracking branches. Pale lilac light filtered through the leaves and lit up the ground in glowing pools. The air was cold; a persistent breeze lifted Esther's hair and she snuggled deeper into the swag. A fly crawled on her lip and she flapped it away, her bare arm emerging from under the canvas. The fly persisted, and she flung back the canvas sheet and propped herself up on her elbow. She raked her hands through her hair and scratched the nape of her neck. Flipping over, she saw Kent's swag was empty, the blankets in a crumpled heap. His pillow still bore the indentation of his head. 'Kent?' Where was he? Probably taking a leak. She scrambled out of her swag, slipped on her jeans and wriggled her feet into her boots. Laces flapping, she stamped to a doughnut of old spinifex and wrenched up a huge lump, grasping it close to the roots to protect her hands from the grass's razor edge. She shuffled back to the camp and prodded at the fire. A tiny ember throbbed underneath the ash, like a baby's heartbeat. Esther dropped the spinifex grass onto the ember and smirked at the whoomph as the fire surged into life again. It was a trick she had learned from an

Aboriginal woman when she was still a green postgraduate student out on her first fieldtrip, and it never failed to please her. She particularly liked doing it the first time she went camping with a new group: it helped to establish her credibility in the bush. A white woman anthropologist from England needed all the field tricks she could muster.

She fed in sticks from the pile by the fire, then when the fire was lusty and strong she insinuated a mulga stump into its heart. The flames curled round it, pulsing out the familiar thick smell that always reminded her of lapsang tea.

Last night's plates were scattered round the fire, brown with blood. Flies scurried over the smears. She scraped fat and gristle into the fire and stacked the plates, then went to fetch some water from the container that was tucked inside the back door of the 4WD. She inched it to the edge of the open door and held the billycan under the plastic tap. Water drummed into the billy. After she'd nestled it at the edge of the fire she knotted her laces and went to find Kent.

She found him scouring the orange sand under a stand of eucalypts. The air there was clean and menthol. 'See here?' He pointed to marks in the sand. 'That wasn't a native cat last night.'

'But I saw it.'

'Yeah, the cat was a cat, but the rest was human. There are shoe prints here: someone scuffling round in the dirt.'

She peered at the sand, barely able to make out the prints even with his help. 'They could be years old.'

'Could, but they aren't. They're fresh.' Kent indicated the traces with a stick. 'The sand hasn't blown over them at all. And there aren't any beetle or lizard tracks over the top of them.'

'That doesn't mean they were made last night, my dear Holmes.'

'Look.' He pointed at the sand, but she couldn't read it the way he could, amazed that he could deduce anything from the litter of curled leaves and sand. 'See how many prints there are, all in the same place? And see here, close by this tree, where the prints are clear and a fraction deeper? Well, over here he waited by the tree, standing dead still for a long time. And here he waited, moving around a lot, but staying in the same place.'

'So?'

'I think someone was watching us last night, maybe hoping to scare us off. After your ghost stories it wasn't hard. Tommy Possum was already jumpy.' Kent held her gaze. She was chastised. 'Who do you think is behind this, Esther?'

She didn't hesitate. 'Stuart MacKendrick. He didn't want us to do the heritage survey, especially after it seemed as though the Tjulpan community was going to do exactly what he wanted and agree to the new mine. And I'm pretty sure he sent me that anonymous note.'

Kent shook his head. 'But it couldn't have been MacKendrick here last night.'

'Why not?'

'Look at the prints. MacKendrick has a walking stick. There are no prints from his stick here. It was someone else trying to scare us off.'

She stared at the sand, willing it to reveal its secrets to her. A chill crept over her as she remembered David Liddle's warning about being careful. Yet she'd dragged them all out to this lonely spot, where there was a weirdo watching and trying to scare them away. All because she wanted to prove that Tommy Possum was evil, grasping and corrupt.

Kent carried on. 'I don't like this, Esther. I think we should go back to Tjulpan and let the community do what they want. It's their choice, after all.'

'I want to see if we can find the massacre site. We can't stop now. I'm not going to give in to bullying.'

'It's a long shot, and even if we did find it I don't think the community's going to change its mind. Possum has them whipped.'

She was desperate. 'But the descendants of the massacre might want to have a say. The mine lawyers said they'd listen to them.'

'There aren't any descendants. No one survived.'

'One person did. The girl whose family was killed. Her descendants might want to say what should happen to Moolya.'

'Who knows where they are? They could be anywhere.' Kent kicked the nearest trunk in exasperation. 'No one even knows if she had any descendants or who they are.'

'I know.'

'You? How?'

She paused. She'd gone too far. She'd have to tell him now, otherwise he'd insist on turning back and letting Tjulpan do whatever they liked.

Not his problem, not his country, not his guilt. Except. 'David Liddle's detective work, mostly, and a chance remark that helped me piece it all together.' Esther took his hand and rubbed her thumb over his knuckles, her mind chasing after the words she needed to explain it all to him. The right words, careful words, kind words, eluded her. They stood silently for a long time, then she held his gaze and said, simply, 'Kent, the girl whose brothers were massacred was called Ruby. Her Aboriginal name was Mantitja. Her son was called Dennis. He was your great-grandfather.'

Emotions chased across Kent's face. He dropped her hand and walked away. She didn't touch him or step towards him, but waited for him to gather himself and return to her.

She drew David Liddle's papers out of her knapsack. 'I think you'll find it's all in here,' she said, placing the papers in his hands.

Leaving Kent alone to read, Esther retreated to the camp, anxious for him but knowing to keep her distance. She cleaned the plates, her heart clenching with worry that he would hate her for knowing when he didn't, for confronting him with his history. A willie wagtail kept her company, flouncing its black feathers and promising not to tell. Aboriginal people feared it as a gossip. She remembered the women she'd worked with when she was a student warning her, 'Don't let it go near women's business, or it'll fly off and blab to the men.'

For the whole morning she ferried mugs of tea to him while he sat in the car and read on. They didn't speak. As she was prodding stir-fry steak and vegetables round a pan, he swung open the car door and stood in its shade, looking dazed. 'Who else knows?' he asked.

'No one. And I don't think even David Liddle could make the connection.' A dark thought slid into her mind. 'We're safe, Kent. No one knows Ruby's your ancestor, so there's no reason for MacKendrick to try and scare us off.'

He nodded and mooched round the camp, his hands thrust deep into his pockets, his jaw tense. She watched him, alarmed to find his expression inscrutable. Eventually he said, 'If the community accepts all this, my family stands to make a bit from the new mine. Compensation and future act agreements and so on.'

It was the last thing she expected. She'd never heard him so cynical about payouts for Aboriginal culture. But now it was his family that stood to gain. It was as if he'd punched her in the face.

'Could be handy, a bit of money coming in, help my cousin pay for uni,' he continued.

'Yes.'

'New car for me, one for Mum.'

'Yes.'

'Easy money. Step in at the last minute in a mining deal and prove you're part of the claim. Greedy blackfellas do it all the time.'

'They do, yes. But not you, Kent, you're not like that.' The phone calls every time a new agreement was reported – 'I want to be put on the claim. It's my country.' Esther was jaded by constantly fielding such calls, a weary repeated statement to each hopeful caller, like a recorded message. Many of them were fakes; others were Aboriginal people living on the other side of Australia, whose families hadn't set foot on their traditional country for three or more generations. Yet there they were, shouting the odds down the phone and insisting they get a share of the compensation for allowing someone to rape their country. A pitiful number were shreds from the stolen generation, lost people desperately trying to find an identity and a culture to fill the hole in their souls that had ached since birth.

She looked at him, hoping her expression didn't betray her.

'Except this was never about money for me and my family,' Kent said, bitterly. 'It was always about belonging, knowing our identity. And now I've finally found my place I still won't belong, because they'll all say I'm some Johnny Come Lately only there for the money, stepping in at the last minute to scoop up the cash.'

His acrimony scalded her. She was ashamed she'd ever doubted him.

'But she was my ancestor, Esther,' he continued, his voice muffled with emotion, 'and she saw her family killed. And because of that and everything that happened to her, my family hasn't known properly who they were. Now I do.'

'And?'

'Let's find that massacre site.' His voice was weary, worn down with the whole corrupting process, aware that he had no choice but to engage with it yet tainted by its contact. 'Out of respect for my ancestors.'

He unfolded a map onto the sand and weighted it down with rocks. He squatted on his heels beside it, suddenly brisk. 'We're here. Mt Parker is there. The waterhole is said to be at the base of Mt Parker somewhere. Ruby and her family were there when Bilsom brought them into the station in January. He says that in the station diary. That's long after the rains, so my guess is it was a permanent water source; the temporary ones would have been dry by then. A pool's marked here.' He stabbed the place. 'That's permanent water. Let's try there first.'

18

Kent insisted on driving to the waterhole. She didn't argue. It was his personal mission now, not hers. The vehicle lumbered along the track, jolting when it hit baked sand and termite platforms, the engine screaming when Kent gunned it to churn through deep sand ruts. They were thrown around inside, tipping from side to side as the vehicle lurched over potholes. Esther gripped the strap above the door and felt the seatbelt locking tight across her body, chafing her neck. She jumped when a branch whipped the windscreen and scraped down the side of the car.

The track narrowed and became increasingly overgrown, and Kent swerved expertly around mulga spikes, twisting the steering wheel with one hand and slamming through the gears with the other. The windscreen clouded with dust. Kent squirted the washers and flicked on the wipers. Dust smeared across the screen, then resolved into two clear semi-circles.

Eventually the track ran out altogether. Kent switched off the engine and they continued on foot, scrambling over boulders and scuffing through long grass. Moolya towered above them. Close to the rock face the scrub opened onto a wide, still pool flanked by white-trunked eucalypts, the bark peeling away like sunburnt skin revealing raw pink flesh beneath. As they approached a flock of zebra finches protested into the air.

'Is this it, d'you think?' asked Esther.

'Ruby mentions a spearwood bush at the back of the waterhole. Let's have a look.'

They inched round the edge of the waterhole towards the rocky flank of Mt Parker. It was streaked black with algae. Here the pool was shaded and so cool that Esther shivered. Jutting from behind a boulder they found a spearwood bush. Esther took her penknife from the pocket of her cargo pants and cut one of the twining stems, swishing at flies with it.

'Doesn't mean this is the place,' warned Kent, cautioning himself as much as her. They perched on the boulder and looked out over the still pool. It was hard to imagine horrors in this tranquil spot. 'Come on,' he said at last. 'Let's find some archaeology.'

They scoured the rocks and caves nearby, uncovering ochre paintings and grinding places. Esther rubbed her fingertips in the rocky indentations worn into smooth bowls by centuries of women grinding seeds and grasses for bread. A hefty grinding stone rested inside, as though waiting for a woman to come along and take it up again. She weighed it in her hand, pleased by its silky contours and speculating how many decades it had been since the stone was last used.

Walking away from the waterhole, they stumbled over a sparsely vegetated area dotted with a number of horseshoe-shaped raised mounds. Many were overgrown with everlasting daisies and grass; others were obscured by a tangle of dead brushwood. They exchanged glances.

Kent stepped gingerly between the horseshoes, his archaeologist's eye scanning for details and evidence. Moving systematically, tracing a grid on the landscape, he touched neither the mounds nor the ground around them, though from time to time he bent forward and pushed at the earth with the tip of his boot. Esther watched him making a mental inventory of the site, marvelling at his control. These could be the graves of his murdered ancestors.

He walked sombrely back to her. He took his hat off and rubbed his face on his sleeve. His hair was glossy with sweat. 'Yes, they're Aboriginal graves. At least eight of them, probably more. Too overgrown to tell exactly. The wild goats have trampled some of them and they're in poor condition. The others have been protected a bit by the brushwood fences they put round them.' He pointed as he spoke, his hand trembling. She touched his arm, offering comfort. 'It all fits Ruby's account. You were right, Esther, there *was* a massacre here, and there's a burial site right where MacKendrick wants to plant his explosives.' He slid his hand into hers and spoke so quietly she had to strain to hear him. 'They would have destroyed this. My ancestors.'

They looked out over the graves, Esther trying to imagine a young, pregnant girl and an old man toiling to hack away the earth and drag the bodies in, caring enough to build the brushwood fences and accord the dead respect. The only two brave enough to return to the site of the massacre. Tears prickled her eyelids, and she pinched her nose and breathed through her mouth until she could trust herself to speak calmly.

'We need to record the site,' she said. 'I'll go back to the car and get the equipment.'

Esther tramped back through the grass and everlasting daisies to the car, swishing the spearwood cane with a pleasing thwack as she went. She took her time collecting the equipment, squatting for a pee, glugging down a Coke snaffled from the eskie, giving Kent time on his own with the graves. She slung the strap of the camera case across her body and shoved the GPS into the pocket of her cargo pants. Carrying her notebooks and pens in her hands, she flapped them against branches and stalks that sprang in her face as she trudged back.

Kent leaned on a boulder looking out over the graves, completely still. Unsure whether to slink away, she lurked just beyond his field of vision until he turned, sensing her there, gave a half-smile as she approached, and folded her into his arms. 'I'm glad it was you who told me,' he whispered.

It took all afternoon to record the site: taking measurements, sketching the site, taking GPS readings and photographs. Once they had completed the graves they moved onto the waterhole and the caves. Kent found several artefacts close to the waterhole: hand axes and spearheads chipped from flint. As they were completing their records of the grinding stones Esther said, 'Let's have a last walk over the site while it's still light.'

They climbed over boulders and headed towards the peak of Mt Parker. Part way up they found a large shallow cave, the entrance partly obscured by brush. Inside, the walls of the cave were covered with red handprints, a jumble of large prints and tiny ones, overlapping each other and covering every inch of the cave walls, all over the roof and at the back of the cave.

'This is incredible,' Esther breathed. 'Is this the birthing cave Ruby mentions, do you think?'

'I guess it must be. Look at all the prints, all those women and babies,' said Kent, awed, shining his torch onto the walls and picking out clear examples. 'My ancestors' prints are here somewhere. Ruby's mother and Ruby when she was born, and Dennis and Ruby, all jumbled up here with these others.'

'She must have been so frightened, giving birth here alone. So close to where her brothers were killed.'

They photographed, measured and recorded the cave, then snapped the equipment back into the hard carry cases and returned to their vehicle. The sun was dipping below the horizon as they set up camp beside the 4WD, laying their swags side by side near the fire.

They sat cross-legged on Esther's swag, mesmerised by the flames, sipping tin mugs of smoky tea. Firelight danced over Kent's face, burnishing his skin, transforming his profile into hollows and crags.

'You OK?' asked Esther. 'This has been a hell of a day for you.'

He gave a short laugh. 'Not the usual fieldtrip,' he agreed. 'But you know, I feel peaceful, like it all makes sense at last. Though obviously I want to punch MacKendrick's teeth down his whitefella throat and have a pop at Tommy Possum too, if he wasn't an elder.'

Esther smiled to herself. Kent had never hit anyone in his life and she suspected that if he did he'd hurt his knuckles far more than the jaw they connected with.

'I've got everything now, nearly,' he said.

'Nearly?'

He held her gaze. 'Leave Rich and come and live with me. I love you, and I want everyone to know we're a couple. I'm thirty-five and living alone, and my family keeps saying I haven't met the right girl yet, but I have, and she's sitting next to me right now.' He lifted her hand to his lips and kissed her palm, folding her fingers over the spot to keep it safe. She turned her face to him and he kissed her deeply, drawing her close to his chest so she could feel his heart's steady thump against her breast. She wound her fingers in his thick hair and knelt astride his lap. He jerked his head back.

'Will you? Will you leave him and come and live with me?'

'I . . . Look out!'

She grabbed his shirt and wrenched him aside as spotlights blazed and a ute thundered towards them. Its tyres squealed inches away, peppering them with stones, as they scrambled for the trees and hurtled for cover. The ute's gears crunched as it charged.

Panic-stricken, Esther waved her arms and shouted, 'Stop! Stop! What are you doing?'

The spotlight snapped off and the ute reversed along the track too fast, smashing the scrub.

'He's got the message,' she said, catching her breath, her heart battering her ribs. 'It's a roo shooter. Probably drunk. Moron.'

Suddenly the spotlight blinded them again as the ute screamed forward, churning the sand and scattering the camp. Kent's eyes widened in alarm, and the breath was whacked out of Esther as he threw himself at her. They landed heavily on the ground. 'He's coming for us!' Kent yelled. 'Quick, get to the car.'

They dodged between the trees, circling through the scrub. The ute braked again, tyres squealing, and the roo light picked them out. They were like escaped prisoners caught by the wall. Esther squinted into the light and made out a figure standing on the ute's tray back. The light followed them as they scrambled for cover. There was no hiding place and their car was 20 metres away.

'Run for it,' Kent hissed, grabbing her hand and bolting for the car.

A shot rang out. He crumpled into the sand. Esther skidded onto her knees beside him. She tugged at his shoulder and rolled him over. Her hand came away red and wet. 'Kent! Kent, talk to me!' She flapped over his body, searching for the wound. 'Where were you hit? Kent! Don't pass out. Kent!'

His shirt was soaked with blood. Got to get him safe. Please don't die. Please don't die. She scrambled behind him and tugged his shoulders, trying to drag him to the car. Her feet slipped on the sand and she landed hard on her bottom.

'Come on, help me. We've got to get out.' She hooked her arms under his armpits and heaved. The roo light fixed on her. 'Kent, please try to move,' she begged, her breath a painful rasp. 'It's not far. We've got to get to the car.' Hauling with all her strength, she dragged him a couple of metres closer to the car. He groaned in agony. Please help me. Don't die. Tears and snot slimed her face. Got to get him out.

Another shot fizzed over the top of her head. She froze in the circle of light, then, panicking, grappled with Kent's arms and tried again to drag him to the car.

'Stop, or I'll shoot,' said a familiar voice. 'Time to end this charade, I think.'

19

Esther stared into the barrel of a rifle held loosely at waist height. Her gaze travelled upwards until she was staring into Mark Wright's eyes. His lips curled into a sneer.

'End of the road, Esther,' he said.

She squinted up at him. The rifle was aimed straight at her forehead, the muzzle inches from her skin. 'Kent needs help quickly. He's going to bleed to death.'

'Saves me shooting him again.'

'Don't be ridiculous! Help me get him into the car.' She watched his eyes harden, and thought furiously how to win him round. 'We can say this is an accident, but he needs a doctor urgently. Mark, for God's sake!'

'You really are a bit thick, aren't you, Esther?' Mark lowered the rifle. 'This isn't an accident. Didn't you realise that when you were running for cover?'

'All because of the mine?' White-hot anger flashed through her. 'Because of money?'

'Basically, yes.'

'I know you stand to lose a lot, but . . .'

'You think you're so clever, finding out all about me. Now, is Dr King clever enough to put the pieces together, I wonder?'

She knew she was taking the bait but couldn't stop herself. 'You didn't tell me about your *alter ego*. You're not Mark Wright, you're Mark Bilsom.'

He cocked an eyebrow. 'And you didn't tell me you owned 50 per cent of the Caroline Mine.'

'Why should I?'

'Didn't you think it relevant? Bit of a conflict, helping Tjulpan community to decide about the mine when you stand to make millions if it goes ahead.'

'And lose millions if it doesn't.'

'My heart bleeds for you.' Bastard.

'How did you find out?'

'I traced Charles Bilsom's family tree, and there you were at the bottom.'

'Clever girl.'

'You're a low life, Mark. It's in your blood.'

'You sound like my ex-wife,' he said, mordantly.

'Pretty nasty way to treat Tjulpan, tricking them into signing away their land like that.'

'You forget, Esther, this isn't your country.' He spoke lightly, as though admonishing a mischievous child. 'If Tjulpan's happy to see Mt Parker go, that's an end to it.'

'You bribed Tommy Possum to make the community agree to the new mine,' she spat.

'Yes. I soon found out what that old pervert was up to, abusing the children in the community and using it as his own sick playground. He knows it's wrong, but insists it's part of his culture.' Mark snorted. 'Even so, threatening to tell the outside world what he's been up to all these years was enough to make him, shall we say, pliant. The money was a little insurance policy on top.'

'So he'd persuade Tjulpan to let you go ahead with the mine?'

His jaw tightened and a pulse pumped in his throat. 'Until people started interfering. That bitch Doreen found out what was going on. I overheard her telling you about it.'

Esther's mind whirled. She recalled Doreen telling her about the child abuse and asking her to help the community. Her stomach lurched. 'You killed Doreen because you heard her talking to me?' She feared she was going to be sick. She gulped a couple of times, running her tongue round her teeth to stop the bile rising. 'It wasn't about you! All she cared about was what Tommy Possum was doing to the children. She wanted to protect the *children*.'

Mark raised the rifle again. 'Don't take me for a fool. That woman was always interfering. She was getting annoying.'

Hysteria sharpened Esther's voice. 'What did you do? Spike her drink, offer her a lift home, then take her out in the bush and hang her?'

'Something like that. You'll be pleased to know she didn't go quietly.'

He's lying, she thought, wildly. Doreen was unconscious. She couldn't bear the thought of him grappling with Doreen, the woman's terror and struggle to live.

'But you took me to her when they found her!'

'And now it's your turn.'

'You're going to kill us because we got in the way of your plans? The community will almost certainly say yes anyway, so what's the point?'

'The point is him.' Mark flicked the rifle towards Kent.

She was baffled. She glanced away from Mark to Kent, aware he was still bleeding, her lap sticky with his blood. 'What's he got to do with it? He's just doing his job. You're insane!'

'I know it seems a bit harsh, especially as we're related, but he's the only one who can stop the mine, so he has to go, I'm afraid.'

He pulled a mocking moue at her and shrugged in a parody of regret.

A second before she understood what he'd said. 'How do you know?' she breathed.

'You're not the only one who can work things out, Esther. I've known for ages, since I came here. Not about Kent but about Ruby. It took quite a bit of time, and money, tracking her down, but I wanted to make sure no nasty surprises were going to come out of the woodwork. Then Kent turned up at the mine, boasting about his ancestor who found gold here and helpfully giving me her Aboriginal name so there was no doubt who he was. It was obvious no one else had made the connection. I just made sure they never would.'

A horrible realisation came over Esther. 'You took the Bilsom diaries out of the library, and you attacked David Liddle and ransacked his house.'

'Yes. Thanks for warning me. I wouldn't have known what you were up to if we hadn't had our little chat at the concert that night.'

She cursed her own gullibility. All the time she'd assumed it was MacKendrick, just because he was hostile and cantankerous, even though she had no proof against him. Suave, sophisticated Mark with his good looks and charm had taken her in completely.

Kent's gaze flickered up at her. His blood ebbed into the sand. She was losing him while his blood clotted with the landscape. The sand was thick with it. She had to get him out soon. She shifted her weight and something jabbed her leg, something hard in her trouser pocket. The penknife. She slid her hand into her pocket and closed her fingers round it. Ducking her head, she pretended to sob. Her fingers worked to free the blade.

'Bit late for hysteria, Esther,' said Mark. 'Move away from him.' He grabbed her arm and hauled her to her feet. Unbalanced, she swung her arm towards his thigh, plunging the penknife deep into muscle. Mark squealed in pain and stumbled forward, letting go of her arm. She kicked him in the stomach and he crunched onto the sand. She stood on his wrist and wrested the rifle out of his hands. He smashed her face with his elbow and she reeled back, but anger plunged her onward. She kicked his head, pleased when he crumpled onto the ground. The rifle was still in her hands.

She sprinted to the 4WD and flicked the lights onto full beam. As she twisted the ignition key she saw Mark lumbering towards Kent, the stain on his thigh spreading. The penknife was clasped in his fist.

Esther hurtled the vehicle towards him. He ducked to one side, the penknife glinting. She reversed, spraying sand. Mark buckled against a tree. She barricaded the 4WD between him and Kent. She scrambled out and over to Kent, hauling him by his armpits and dragging him into the back seat.

'Kent, you're too heavy, you've got to help me,' she grunted, weeping with fear and frustration. 'Please, grab the seat and pull yourself in.'

She bundled his legs into the back of the car. He sprawled across the seats, moaning with pain. She slammed the door shut and climbed into the driver's seat. Ramming the 4WD into reverse, she surged back along the track, executed a swift three-point turn and accelerated away from the camp. In the rear view mirror she watched Kent's prone body on the back seat. Mustn't be too late. Hang on, don't die.

Esther leaned over the steering wheel, scouring the track, anticipating deep sand and mulga spikes. Mustn't get bogged. Don't get a flat. Just get out of here.

Lights blazed in the rear view mirror, blinding her. The ute gained on them, bumping from side to side on the track. She stood on the accelerator, her heart knocking as she flung the 4WD round a tight bend. The headlights made a tunnel in front of her, but it was too dark to see properly. To go any faster would be suicide.

The ute smashed into the back of the 4WD, flinging her hard against the steering wheel and thumping the breath out of her. She let go of the steering wheel for a second and the wheel spun wildly. The 4WD swerved and rattled off the track, crashing through scrub, the windscreen thwacked by branches. She grabbed the wheel and brought the car back under control. A crack zigzagged down the windscreen. Esther lost some speed so she could weave between the trees, the car buffeted by branches as she careered through the bush. The ute closed in behind, engine screaming as it gunned through the sand. A huge white gum tree glowed ahead, its trunk shimmering like a ghost. She sped towards it. Glancing over her shoulder, she saw Mark was gaining on her. A few feet from the tree she yanked the steering wheel hard to the left and accelerated, missing the trunk by inches. The ute braked and slewed, hitting the tree full on.

She brought the 4WD to a halt and left the engine running. Grabbing the rifle from the passenger seat, she stepped out of the car. Mark stumbled from the ute's cab. Blood trickled down his forehead. She approached, deadly calm, the rifle loose in her hands. He staggered and turned, tried to run away, fell to his knees and scrambled to his feet again. She paced closer and closer.

Esther nestled the rifle into her shoulder and fired. Again. And again. As the last shot rang out, she lowered the rifle.

'It's finished,' she said.

20

The recoil from the first shot stunned her; her shoulder was black for a week afterwards. She ran back to her vehicle and hurtled to Bilsom's Grudge. Kent curled in agony, blood soaking the back seat, his face grey.

'Stay with me, Kent,' Esther babbled the whole way, terrified it was too late to save him. She hardly breathed until she screeched up to the nursing post, pounded on the door and rattled out what had happened.

She clutched Kent's hand as the nurse packed the bullet wound and fed a drip into his arm. Shivering with exhaustion she sat by his bed, eyes glued to the monitor, watching his heart beat slug across the screen, willing him to live.

'I think I should take a look at you, too,' said the nurse.

Esther touched her face and winced. Her fingers came away smeared with blood. When she glanced in a mirror she saw her cheek and eye puffed up and purple with bruises. 'No, I'm all right,' she said.

The nurse brought her an icepack anyway, and insisted on cleaning up the cuts on her face. 'You won't win Miss World this week,' she commented.

Part way through the night's vigil Sergeant Baldwin strutted in. He was quieter and kinder than the last time they'd battled words across a metal table. He treated her like a traumatised child, gently asking her to tell him, as coherently as possibly, what had happened. Esther repeated her story, her voice a flat monotone.

He patted her shoulder and said, 'It's OK for now, but I'll need a proper statement tomorrow. Just tell me where Mark Wright is so I can go and get him.'

She told him with as much detail as she could muster. The cop nodded and said briskly, 'Don't go anywhere without telling me.'

'I'll be here, officer. I'm not going anywhere else,' and Esther turned back to Kent, feeling hollow.

Early the next morning Kent was stretchered into the back of the ambulance, a converted 4WD. Esther climbed in after him, and was slung around as the ambulance rattled out to the airstrip. The Royal Flying Doctor plane rumbled on the strip.

'What we got here, then?' asked the RFDS nurse, jaunty in trousers, sneakers and a ponytail.

'Bullet wound. He's stable, just. Lost a lot of blood, in and out of consciousness. I've contacted Perth.' The Bilsom's Grudge nurse gave a swift telegraphic report.

'They going to meet us that end?'

'Yeah. He needs that bullet out quick.'

'OK.' The nurse looked at Esther. 'Who're you?'

'I was with him when he was shot.'

'You coming with us?'

Esther shook her head. 'I can't. I've got to speak to the police. I'll see him at the hospital.'

'Best thing. Nothing you can do until he's out of surgery.'

They strapped Kent into the back of the plane. Esther kissed the tip of her finger and pressed it to his forehead. He didn't wake. She watched from the side of the strip as the plane taxied, blowing up a storm of red dust, then it was quickly in the air and out of sight.

She banged on Frank's door at the hotel.

'I said it was no good yous staying out there without Mr Possum.' He paused and squinted at her. 'What yous done to your face?'

'Shut up, Frank, there's been an accident.'

She quickly filled him in on what had happened. His face morphed from irritation at her impetuosity into fear for Kent's life and concern for her.

'Now listen to me, Dr Esther. We're going to have a big feed, then we're going to drive straight away back to Perth and make sure this young fella's OK.'

'I can go by myself,' she protested.

'No you can't. You're wiped out, Dr Esther. It's not safe for you to drive all that way by yourself. So don't you worry, we'll go nice and slow, and I'll be right behind you and make sure nothing happens.'

To her horror she burst into tears. He was being so kind to her; it was more than she could bear. Frank waited until the tears were over and she hiccupped away the sobs. In a small voice she said, 'I've got to see the police before I go anywhere.'

'It'll be all right, Esther. We'll go and talk to the police and then we'll get on that road to Perth. Reckon he'll just be waking up as we get there.'

She shook when she was shown into the frowsy interview room at the police post in Bilsom's Grudge. She took a seat at the familiar dented metal table dominating the room and waited for Sergeant Baldwin to come in.

He was crumpled and grey with tiredness. He slapped a folder down on the table and flumped into the chair opposite her. 'Well, thanks to you the big guys are flying back in from Perth.'

'The big guys?'

'Senior police. I'm not important enough to deal with a murder by myself.' He ground his thumbs into his eyes. 'So.'

'So. Did you find him? Is he all right? Mark Wright? Bilsom, I mean.'

'Yep, we found him. Mad as a cut snake and twice as nasty. He was still protesting his innocence as we slammed him in the paddy wagon.' A shiver of satisfaction shimmied across his face. 'You're a good shot.'

'Beginner's luck.'

'Though next time you're face to face with a deranged killer, just shoot the bastard instead of his tyres, eh?'

'I'll try to remember.' She glanced up and found him grinning at her. She smiled back. 'I just didn't want him to get away.' She recalled how she'd desperately aimed at the tyres, her frustration when a shot missed, and her elation when first one, then another of the tyres popped when she hit them, the ute lurching to one side.

'Let's have a look at this statement.' He slid a sheet of paper from the file: his notes, scribbled that night in the nursing post. 'Tell me about Doreen.'

'Officer, Doreen was a large woman. Mark boasted to me that she didn't go quietly. He would have needed help to kill her.'

'An accomplice?'

'Not who, what. The miners use an old ute to go roo shooting, the same one Mark used to come after me and Kent. He was driving it the morning Doreen's body was discovered. There's a winch on the front. I think he used that to ... to ...' She couldn't say the words. The image was too horrible. Baldwin was less sensitive.

'String her up?'

Esther nodded. 'Poor Doreen. All she wanted to do was help the children.'

'OK. We'll see if we can get some forensics on that.' The cop sighed. Another gang of city know-alls crawling over his patch. She almost felt sorry for him.

'Can I go now? Kent's been flown to Perth and I'd like to be there when he comes out of surgery.'

'Sure.'

'And will you let me know how things turn out?'

'I'll see what I can do. Now you'd better scram 'cause I've got VIPs here, all 'cause of you and your bloody gold-mine.'

He smiled as she shook his hand.

Frank slumped in the chair beside her in the hospital corridor, swigging over-priced coke from a vending machine. 'Get you anything, Esther?'

She shook her head. Her hands were clammy, clasped between her knees. She was reminded of people who were afraid of flying and believed they could keep the plane airborne if they only concentrated hard enough. It was the same with her and Kent. If she held her breath hard enough it would all be fine.

'You know, I reckon you two make a good couple,' said Frank.

She turned to look at him. He stared straight back. 'I guessed ages ago. However much you tried to hide it. Seemed like you two were made for each other. Blackfellas can see things like that. We're observant.'

Normally she would have teased him for this comment, but today, waiting for news of Kent's surgery, she only nodded. 'What about Rich? That's what I keep wondering. It's not fair on him.'

'Life isn't fair. At your age you should know that. You gotta do what you think will make you happy.'

A nurse came over to them, her shoes squeaking on the linoleum. Esther scrambled to her feet. 'How is he?'

'Pretty groggy, but you can see him for a couple of minutes.'

'I'll wait here for you,' said Frank.

She followed the nurse. Kent was hooked up to monitors and had a tangle of wires and tubes into and out of his body. She hesitated.

'Don't worry about all this,' said the nurse, gesturing in the direction of the monitors. 'He's going to be OK.'

Kent's eyes flickered open when she touched his hand.

'Hello you,' she said.

'Hello.'

'How are you feeling?'

'Terrible, thanks.'

She sat down, unable to speak. His fingers curled around hers and he fell asleep.

The sound of Rich's cello swelled to meet her when she let herself into the house. He carried on playing to the end of a phrase when she poked her head round the door, then sprang up and tried to hug her. She dodged. 'What the hell happened to you?'

'It's nothing.' She flapped her hands, batting his words away.

'Doesn't look like it. Esther, what *happened*?'

She sighed. 'Please, Rich, just listen.'

He hesitated, uncertain, tried to make the situation normal by babbling. 'Wasn't expecting you back so soon. It's great to see you. God, I've been such a prat. I've been worrying like mad that you wouldn't come back. I'm so sorry, I . . .'

'Rich, there's something I need to tell you,' she interrupted. Fear chased across his face. 'I've made a decision. About us. I'm leaving you. No, don't say anything. This is hard enough. The thing is,' she swallowed, unable to meet his eyes, 'I'm in love with someone else. I didn't realise until today exactly how much. Nothing's happened between us, we've not been having an affair or anything, but I can't keep on pretending.'

Rich shrank into himself. His mouth worked as he tried to frame a question, and after a while he whispered, 'Who?'

'Kent. From work.'

Rich frowned, trying to remember which one he was. 'How long?'

'A few months.'

'So what's changed?'

'Kent's very ill. When I saw he'd been hurt, all I could think was that if he died I wouldn't be able to bear it.' Esther's voice shook and she fought back tears.

'I couldn't bear it if *you* died.'

She shook her head. 'You'd be upset, but you'd live. With Kent, I felt as if I wouldn't survive without him.'

'That's just romantic crap! I suppose you're going to tell me he's your soulmate next?'

'No, but when I'm with him I understand how people can lose their heads over someone, risk everything, die for them.'

'But not me?'

'I'm sorry.'

Rich kicked round the room, raking his hands through his hair until it stood in a crest on his head. With his gaunt face he looked like a deranged parrot. The thought almost made her smile, and something outside herself reassured her that one day she'd be able to look back and not mind; but that this had to be borne first.

When Rich turned back to her his face was wet with tears. Her heart wrenched at the sight of him. 'Rich, I love you, I really do. Despite all the arguments and the fighting. But I love someone else more. We've lost our chance. Don't you understand?'

'What's wrong with him?'

'What?'

'You said he was ill.'

'He's been shot.' Esther sighed. 'The next twenty-four hours are critical.'

'So he might die?'

She mumbled affirmation.

'And then you'll come crawling back to me, will you, once he's out of the way? You'll put up with second best then?'

'No, I won't. It's not like that. I've realised I don't love you enough, and even if Kent . . . dies . . . I'll still leave you. What we have isn't enough.'

A sob broke from his chest. 'But I *love* you! I've always loved you. All I've ever wanted was for you to see how much!'

She took his hand, entwining her fingers in his. His right hand was sticky with resin from his bow. The fingertips on his left hand spooned at the ends. She rubbed her thumb over them in turn; so familiar, yet they still fascinated her. 'I know you love me, and I love you. But not enough. We've tried hard, we should be proud of ourselves, but it's time to admit defeat.'

Rich rested his forehead against hers and their tears dripped onto their hands. Eventually he pulled away, and in a hard voice said, 'So, you've told this chap all about yourself, have you?'

'Pretty much.'

'No secrets, eh, Esther?'

'Of course there are secrets.' The harsh expression on his face brought her up short. 'What are you talking about?'

'Just wondered if you'd confided the big secret, the reason you took this job in native title in the first place.'

She went cold.

'You think I don't know? Well, perhaps I know you better than you know yourself. Your sordid little family secret is what makes you work so hard, push yourself, risk your health and our marriage, isn't it?'

No answer. She stared at him, afraid, as he paced the room.

'But you'll have told your Aboriginal lover all about Uncle Des and his work with the welfare people, won't you? That must have been an interesting conversation. "It's so fascinating that your family has been torn apart by the stolen generation, darling, because actually my uncle used to take the children away. Just think, he might have dragged one of *your* relatives into the car, never to be seen again."'

'Stop it!'

Rich rounded on her. His voice was low and deadly, 'Or haven't you told him?'

'No.'

'No? Don't you think it relevant? Or is it that you're afraid how he'll react?'

Esther swallowed. Fear tightened the back of her throat and the swallow was loud, more a gulp.

'You can't trust him with that, can you?' Rich was suddenly shouting at her. 'You'll leave me for him, but you won't trust him with that secret, will you? And that's the thing that makes you tick. So all the time you're with him you'll been lying!'

'No!'

'Well, perhaps I'll tell him myself. Or you could stay with me and we'll forget this happened.'

'You don't blackmail me. I couldn't stay with you now if I wanted to.' Esther rose to her feet, suddenly calm and controlled.

She went into their bedroom and lifted a suitcase out of the closet. Her hands shook and tears poured unchecked down her cheeks as she took her clothes from their hangers and folded them carefully into the suitcase. She scooped all her underwear out of the drawer and plonked it on top.

In the bathroom she caught sight of her face in the mirror, her cheeks blotchy with weeping. On impulse she unscrewed the top on Rich's aftershave and inhaled the familiar scent. The rush of memories sent her mind reeling, and she almost turned to run back into his arms and plead for a new beginning.

But he'd threatened her, and she knew however much she still loved him she would never feel secure with him again. That he could think of hurting her so badly was enough, even without the past months of arguing, his affair, the sense of being two drowning people clutching for one another and slipping apart.

Esther blew her nose, hard, and splashed cold water on her stinging face and eyes. A last look round the bathroom, where they used to share a bath and a glass of wine, classical music playing in the background, flicking bubbles at each other. They had been so in love, once.

She grabbed a few of her favourite CDs and shoved them into her bag, then zipped it closed and lumped it to the front door. Her hands trembled as she dialled a taxi, and her voice was high and broken when she gave the instructions. Rich watched her, shocked, as she moved about the house. When the taxi pulled into the drive he ran towards her and tried to put his arms around her. She submitted for a second, her throat aching with emotion. 'Goodbye, Rich,' she whispered, and was gone.

'How long have you been sitting there?'

'Not long. I thought I should let you sleep,' said Esther. 'How are you feeling?'

'A bit like I've been shot.'

'Ah, that'll be the gunshot wound.'

Kent studied her face and drew his fingertip over her cheekbones. 'You look done in, Esther.'

'I'm OK.'

'No, you're not. I can tell.' He struggled into a sitting position, wincing as he jabbed his bandaged arm on the hospital bed. 'I did some physiotherapy this morning. At this rate I'll come out with more muscles than I went in with.'

'Sounds good. You'll need some beef to carry all my stuff around.'

Kent shook his head. 'Why?'

She clasped his hand. 'If your offer's still open I'd like to say yes.'

'Yes? You mean you're going to leave Rich?'

'I've already left.'

'Esther, that's fantastic.' His face cracked into a smile, then faded as she didn't respond. 'Must be odd for you, though.'

'You could say that.' She hesitated. His eyes were on her face. She dragged her gaze up to meet his. 'There's something you need to know about me, but after I tell you, you probably won't want to know me any more.'

'I can't imagine that.'

'Let me tell you first. I'll understand if you don't want to see me afterwards.' Kent's face was grave as she told him, hesitatingly, about Uncle Des. 'He was my grandfather's brother and he came out to Australia after the war. He was a policeman in Geraldton during the '50s and '60s. I met him after he'd retired. I was at uni in Canberra and I came over to Gero to see him. He seemed really exotic when I was a little girl, what with a swimming pool in the back garden and living on the opposite side of the world. But when I met him it was awful. He told me that he used to . . . used to help the welfare people when they came to take the children away. Aboriginal children, sent to Moore River. He said he thought they'd have a better life that way. I was appalled. I had no idea he did that. I was only just finding out about the stolen generation myself, and it sickened me. I hated what he'd done, was disgusted I was related to him. It was like finding out you were descended from Hitler or something. I was terrified that the Aboriginal people I was working with would find out. They'd despise me. So I never told anyone. But I got interested in Indigenous issues and thought I might be able to . . . oh, I know it sounds so trite and so naïve and pompous all at the same time, but I wanted to try to make things better.'

Kent lay silently squeezing her hand. 'And you want me to say it's OK, it doesn't matter, I forgive you?'

'If you can.'

'No, I can't.' She glanced up at him, anguished. 'Because there's nothing to forgive. You didn't take the children. You don't approve of what he did. And now you work harder than any blackfella *for* blackfellas. And fuck it, Esther, you don't have to. You could've just shrugged and said "It's in the past", but you didn't.'

She hung her head.

'Now do me two favours. One, go move your stuff into my place. And two, get some sleep. You look rooted.'

Esther badgered Sergeant Baldwin for information, ringing him repeatedly until she riled him sufficiently that he cracked. He called her into a Perth police station, and told her that forensic examination of the ute and the winch had found long black hairs attached to the metal rope. They matched samples taken from Doreen's body. When police searched Mark Wright's home in Perth they uncovered David Liddle's computer, and bank statements showing regular withdrawals.

'Can you tie them to Tommy Possum?' Esther asked. 'Is that the bribe money?'

'Tommy Possum never paid it into a bank account, so we haven't got a trail there,' he told her eventually, after grumbling that she was interfering with the way he did his job. 'But we've checked up on his story that he won that flashy Toyota in a card game in Warburton. We've got indigenous officers out there, and they say no one there's even seen Tommy Possum for nearly a year. He got the money from somewhere for that car, and we assume it was from Wright.'

'Can you make it stick?'

'We're going to have a go. Fact is, he came after you and Kent, so we've got attempted murder to add to the charge sheet.' The cop smiled grimly at her. 'Though I'm pretty sure he'll go down for murder. He's denying his confession to you, but the evidence is there to nail the bastard.'

An image of Doreen's body swinging from the drill rig insinuated itself into her mind. She comforted herself that she'd persisted with this, that she'd helped to find Doreen's killer, and would try to see justice for Doreen and her family.

It was poor consolation for a woman's life.

A few days after Kent was discharged from hospital the Tjulpan community held a meeting. Unlike the previous community meeting they were supported by a small army of lawyers, government officials and advisors. Stuart MacKendrick sat with his walking stick planted firmly between his knees, his face impassive as the community debated the future of Mt Parker and the Caroline Mine.

The Tjulpan community met, for the first time ever, in the town hall at Bilsom's Grudge. Ranks of chairs lined the walls; the elders, lawyers, advisors and Stuart MacKendrick sat at tables set in a square in the centre of the room. Esther sat between Frank and Gavin at the side of the room, watching the proceedings. The meeting was the most subdued she'd ever attended. No shouting, little swearing; everyone adopted an attitude of studied politeness and courtesy to everyone else. Yet the tension in the room was electric.

Still recovering from surgery, and too unwell to travel, Kent added his voice to the Tjulpan community via teleconference. This was a novelty for the Tjulpan people, who stood and bellowed into the phone every time they wished to address a comment to Kent. Despite the gravity of the meeting Esther smiled to herself.

After two minutes' silence to respect the dead killed during the massacre, and as a mark of respect to Doreen, Frank opened the meeting. 'There's been a lot of shocks over the past coupla weeks, and I know everyone's all upset. But you've got a big decision to make. Yous being asked to decide whether the Caroline Mine people can put a new mine at Moolya, Mt Parker. If you say no, that's it. But the mine people are here to make you an offer, so have a listen to what they say and then yous can have a talk about it.'

Stuart MacKendrick's lawyer was skilful, Esther conceded, and obviously used to talking to Aboriginal communities. He spoke clearly and straightforwardly, said the mine was upset at what Mark Wright had done and saying they wanted all dealings with Tjulpan to be honest. And then he put the offer to them: a lump sum for community development and investment, three scholarships to the School of Mines for Tjulpan youths, jobs in the mine and shares to bring in a regular income to support the community.

Esther leaned forward and whispered to the Land Council lawyer representing the Tjulpan community. He held a muttered conference with the Caroline Mine lawyer, who sprang to his feet and, alarmed that he may have made a cultural gaffe, announced, 'And of course, the mine will pay for the proper exhumation and reburial of the remains of the people killed in the massacre.'

The elders exchanged glances, using sign language to confer with the people surrounding the room. They asked the lawyers to explain a couple of points and then asked all non-community members to wait outside while they discussed what to do.

Esther walked to the mini-mart and bought a Coke and a Mars bar. She sat outside the town hall, listening to the drone of the voices within, her mind wandering in the temporary hiatus.

Two hours later they were all called back. All the Tjulpan people were serious and subdued. Some of them had obviously been crying. An old man with a shock of white hair sat at the back of the room and dabbed at his eyes with a piece of kitchen paper.

Gavin had been appointed spokesman for Tjulpan, as Doreen's son: the community felt this was a way to demonstrate their respect and grief for her; and so the young man suddenly found himself speaking for all of them. When he stood up to speak a mixture of sorrow and awe registered in his voice and face. 'This community has been through rough times. We need to respect the people who've passed away, and we need to build a strong culture for the future. We don't want to live on welfare forever, but we've got to look after country. This is a very hard decision for us to make.'

'You don't have to decide straight away,' cut in the Land Council lawyer. The Caroline Mine lawyer rolled his eyes. 'No one wants to push you into anything if you're not ready.'

Gavin shook his head. 'We want to decide now. We have all decided. But we're split even.'

'OK, let's have a show of hands,' said the lawyer. 'Those for the mine's offer. And now those against.'

All the lawyers counted independently, then turned to each other with the same answer: the community was evenly split.

'We've been talking to Kent all the time,' said Gavin, pointing to the phone on the central table. 'And we think that as it was his ancestors killed in the massacre he should have a vote too.'

'So he gets the casting vote?' asked the mine's lawyer.

Gavin nodded. He leaned into the phone and shouted, 'Kent, bro, you still there? You heard all our talking, everything in our minds, and we still can't agree. You speaking for your family and your ancestors now. What's your choice?'

Esther looked round the gathering. The lawyers clustered round the speakerphone; the elders stared at the table, their faces grave. A couple of women put their arms round each other's shoulders and wept together silently at the back of the room. Stuart MacKendrick stared straight ahead, looking like a crow perched on a dead branch.

Esther's palms were slick with sweat as Kent's voice came through on the speakerphone. 'It's time to move on, put the past behind us,' he said, his voice cracking with emotion. 'I vote for the new mine to go ahead.'

21

There was an oddly festive atmosphere in Tjulpan. It showed in the quick smiles of the girls perched on the fence, swinging their legs, and in the children brazenly hurling rocks at the store roof under the disapproving glares of their parents. Even the curs snarled with additional enthusiasm.

It was already warm and Tjulpan stank of rotting garbage and roasting dog shit, overlaid with the cloying sweetness of cannabis. The smell caught in the back of Esther's throat as she stood in line behind Frank. He was whiffy, too, in his singlet: a brew of stale sweat, worse when he lifted his arm and exposed a tangle of soggy armpit hair.

'There's always a sausage sizzle going on in Australia, whatever the event,' Esther commented, spearing two sausages and dropping them onto slabs of bread thickly spread with cheap yellow margarine. 'Jumble sales, church fêtes, outside DIY superstores, at sponsored car washes . . .'

'This ain't quite the same,' Frank interrupted grimly. 'Onions, Esther?'

'Thanks.' She held out two plates towards him and he heaped onions, looking like charred sliced worms, onto the sausages. They moved down the line to the table with the salad and sauces, and added to their plates. Frank eschewed the salad with a suspicious frown. Esther smiled at the two teenaged girls helping to set out the barbecue food and thanked them. They smiled back shyly. Like everyone else, they too seemed coiled up by the momentous day. 'Better take this to his lordship.'

Kent was balled up in a plastic chair in the shade under the Tjulpan community bough shelter, watching a group of youths and kids kicking a football against the wall of the community store.

'You comin' to play, bro?' one of the youths shouted to him with a cheeky grin.

'Don't want to embarrass you, mate,' Kent called back, grinning ruefully. He fidgeted in his seat, obviously uncomfortable. His shoulder was strapped up, his left arm fixed close to his chest in a sling. Only the tips of his fingers were visible, poking out of the dressing.

'Here you are, you lazy sod,' said Esther, plonking a plate of food on his knee. 'Do you want me to cut it up for you?'

'That's nice, isn't it?' said Frank. 'When you took a bullet for her.'

'He didn't take a bullet; he just got in the way of one.' Esther and Kent exchanged glances. She looked away, embarrassed by the intensity fizzing between them. Both sought to diffuse it.

'The bullet was OK. It was the surgery to extract it that nearly killed me,' Kent grumbled. 'All that hospital food; it nearly finished me off.'

'My hero,' Esther said, sarcastically.

'You did all right, too, Dr Esther,' said Frank. 'I never knew you could shoot.'

'Neither did I.'

Kent grinned at her and his blue eyes twinkled.

'What happened to Tommy Possum?' Esther asked Frank.

'He got scared and ran off to Perth. With him outta the way some of they kids and their families felt brave enough to tell the cops and the welfare what's been going on round here. Seems Doreen was right all along. No one dared stand up to that old man.'

'All Doreen wanted to do was stop the child abuse,' said Esther. 'Will he be tried?'

Frank shook his head. 'Not enough time. He's sick in hospital, not got long left. They reckon a magic man has put a curse on him 'cause of what he done. Next time he comes to Tjulpan it'll be for his own funeral.'

Esther frowned, and he explained. 'It is his country, after all. He belongs here, the sick old bastard.'

'And it'll be easier for all the kids he abused to dance on his grave singing "hallelujah",' Esther commented drily, relieved that the community could start to heal at last.

'Esther!' Frank looked shocked. 'What he done was wrong, but he's still an elder and still deserves respect.'

'Sorry. It just makes me mad, that's all.'

'Your number one fan's turned up,' Kent commented as a car drew up beside the community store. Stuart MacKendrick stepped out and leaned on his walking stick while he looked round, his head darting from side to side, making him look even more hawk-like than usual. His frame was gaunter and his skin looked sallow and pouchy, sagging on his skull. He spied Esther, Kent and Frank and drew his mouth into a thin line. He stamped across the road towards them, grimacing at the ripped nappies and curled dog turds dotting the path.

'Dr King. Kent. Frank.' He punctuated each name with a curt nod. 'A momentous day for all of us.' No one answered. 'All for the best, after what's happened.'

Esther choked.

'You know, I had no idea what Mark was doing.' He stumbled over the name, his face twisting as though he couldn't grasp the extent to which he'd been deceived. 'I admit I brought him here to advise the Tjulpan community, without letting them know he owned part of the mine. And I still think that was the right thing to do.' His blue eyes blazed in his battered face and he thumped the ground with his stick.

'Did you know who I was?' Kent asked. 'Did you know Ruby was my ancestor?'

'Yes, I did. I had her family traced years ago.'

'Why bother about an old Aborigine woman?' asked Frank. 'You mining people don't think about the ancestors.'

'We do when they have the potential to threaten our mines. Forewarned is forearmed, as they say.'

'How did you trace Ruby?' Esther was curious.

'Anyone's history can be bought.' MacKendrick grinned wolfishly. 'There's a whole new industry out there: people who spend their entire lives trawling records and piecing together family trees. But you know that, Dr King.' The pressure of Kent's fingers on hers stopped her retort. MacKendrick turned to Kent. 'And then you marched into my office and declared yourself. A bit of a shock for me, it's true, but it was obvious you didn't have a clue who you were. I just prayed to get the go-ahead for the new mine before you worked it all out.'

'And you thought you'd help things along by trying to scare me off with a poison pen letter?' said Esther.

MacKendrick had the decency to look discomfited. His grip tightened on his walking stick. He turned to Esther. 'You and me will never see eye to eye about Aboriginal rights, Dr King, but I admire your tenacity.'

'Patronising git,' Esther muttered as the old man stumped away.

The bough shelter was filling up with people, and the women organising the barbecue started clearing away the empty plates and bowls. Frank glanced at his watch. 'Not long now.'

'Do you think they've made the right decision, Frank?'

'It was their decision, not some whitefella interfering. No offence.'

'None taken. But after all the community's been through it all seems so pointless.'

'Time for these people to move on, Esther. Gotta build something good out here on their country. Can't live on the dole forever.'

Esther turned to Kent. 'You had the deciding vote. Still think it was the right one?'

'No. I think it was the only one.'

'Tell you something might cheer you up, Dr Esther,' said Frank. 'Young Gavin is going to train to be a community policeman. Means he can stay on his country.'

'That's good. I think he could be good for Tjulpan.'

'And,' said Frank, his face cracking into a grin, 'he's going through Law soon. Gonna come along with me.'

'That's great news,' said Esther, grinning at how pleased he was.

The community quietened as a dozen women walked into the centre of the bough shelter. Each carried a blanket or doona, which they spread out on the grass like a huge patchwork. When the blankets were positioned and smoothed they sat down in a circle and wrapped their arms round each other's necks, forming a tight ring. Heads together, they started to keen. As the sound rose louder and higher Esther felt the hairs prickle on the back of her neck.

'They're mourning the people who were massacred,' Frank whispered. 'And mourning Doreen too.'

The keening continued for about five minutes, then abruptly stopped. The women sat back and wiped their faces with the hems of their T-shirts.

Putting their heads together once more, they recommenced. Esther shot a querying glance at Frank.

'They're mourning the country,' he explained.

The keening stopped and the women folded their blankets. Gavin had once again been appointed as spokesman. The young man pushed through to the front and clapped his hands. 'It's almost time, everybody.'

They all turned to look at Mt Parker. The peak rose above the flat scrubby plain, clearly defined in the sharp light, set against a cerulean sky. Just like a dingo's nose, Esther thought, recalling how Tommy Possum had told them all the mountain's story. A wave of sadness washed over her.

Everyone was silent as they stared at Mt Parker. A handful of children screamed at each other as they fought over a football near the store and were sharply shushed.

Gavin's phone rang. He answered it and announced, 'Ten seconds.'

The silence was oppressive. Esther counted down in her mind. She saw others mouthing the numbers. Then a massive explosion rocked Mt Parker. Rocks torpedoed into the air. A child screamed. A dust cloud enveloped the peak. Esther strained forward to see. It seemed a long time before the dust cloud settled. When the air cleared Mt Parker was gone.

The women started keening again, their cries slicing the wounded landscape.

Esther groped for Kent's hand. He squeezed her fingers hard. Tears streamed down her face. She brushed them away, embarrassed, and her hand came away smeared with orange dust. She turned to speak to Kent and Frank, only to find that they, too, were surreptitiously wiping their eyes.

'Time to go, guys,' she said.

The pilot waited for the all clear from the mine site before he took off, banking sharply away from Mt Parker so the plane wouldn't hit the dust. Esther craned her neck to see. All that was left of Moolya was rubble. The peak had disappeared; the dingo's nose there no longer. On the ground tiny stick figures in hard hats ran round, waving to huge trucks with wheels the height of houses. Business as usual.

She sat back in her seat and turned to Kent. 'Home?' she asked.

'Home,' he answered.

Figures scampered over the landscape beneath them. The Dreaming dingo and his fugitive master unfurled from the rocks. The ghosts of Ruby's murdered family laughed and screamed with the women and babies in the birthing cave, all blending with the diggers and explosives as landscape past and present melded into one, and the memory of all who had lived and died there was imprinted in a single grain of sand.

ACKNOWLEDGEMENTS

I should like to thank Jim and Peter for providing comments on early drafts of this novel. Margaret – you were wonderful as always, thank you. Many thanks to Simon Fletcher for his sensitive editing, and to Corinne Souza at Picnic for all her support and encouragement.